# WILD MOUNTAINS, WILD PEOPLE

Seán Damer

Ringwood Publishing
Glasgow

Copyright Seán Damer © 2025

All rights reserved

The moral right of the author has been asserted

Issued in 2025

by

Ringwood Publishing

Flat 0/1 314 Meadowside Quay Walk, Glasgow

G11 6AY

www.ringwoodpublishing.com

e-mail: mail@ringwoodpublishing.com

ISBN: 978-1-917011-10-5

British Library Cataloguing-in-Publication Data

A catalogue record for this book is available from the

British Library

Printed and bound in the UK

by Lonsdale Direct Solutions

"Άγρια βουνά, άγριοι άνθρωποι."

["Wild mountains, wild people."]

(A proverb from Sfakia, Crete.)

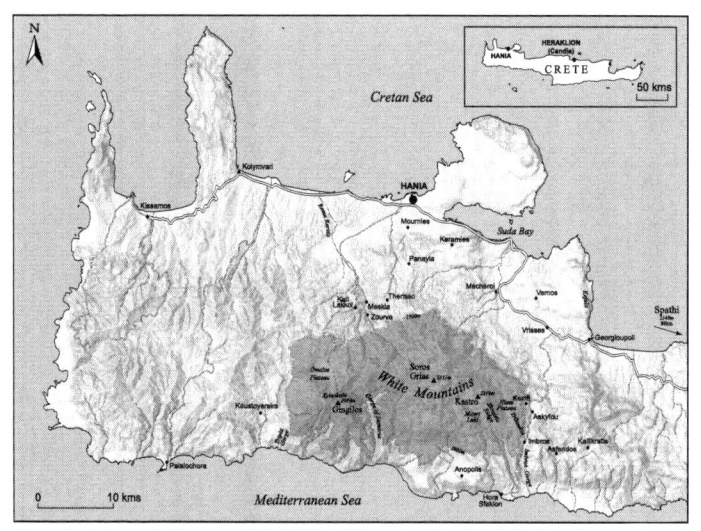

Map1. Map of Crete with White Mountains highlighted.

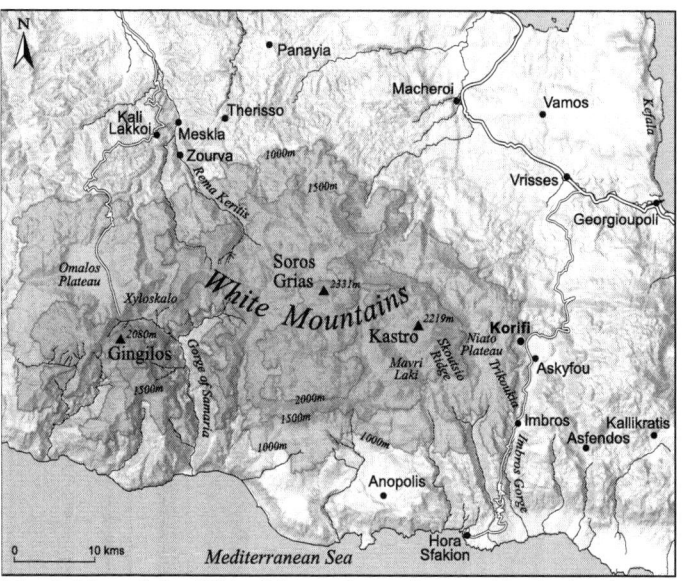

Map2. Map of the White Mountains as featured in the book.

## Dedication

To the memory of Sieglinde Manouras of Münster:
αιωνία η μνήμη της.

# Prologue

### Crete, March 1943

Sergeant John Gallagher stamped his feet in the wind-crusted snow, banged his hands together, wished he had brought gloves, and looked at his watch: five past two. Only twenty-five minutes to go, if everything went as planned.

On the Skoutsio ridge, a couple of hundred feet above Niato, John gazed down at the saucer-shaped plateau. Niato was rimmed by savage mountains, and in the winter of 1943, both the mountains and Niato were covered in deep snow. There was a full moon, and the plateau looked like a gigantic eerie stage set, the snow glowing in the ethereal light. It seemed still and silent and menacing. But the silence was an illusion. There was a constant slight susurration in the air as the slight breeze shifted snowflakes, so that the billiard-table like surface of the plateau appeared to be shimmering. Every now and then there was a *plop!* as a mini avalanche cascaded down the steep slopes. It was cold, and the glitter of the canopy of stars merely emphasized the freezing atmosphere. There was hardly a breath of wind in the air, which was just as well, for at four thousand feet, it was cold enough without a wind-chill factor.

John's local guide Kostas Sfakianakis muttered some Greek imprecation about the cold, moving his Sten-gun from one hand to the other. John envied his companion his traditional felted woollen cloak, while he himself shivered in his battledress, covered only by a home-made white camouflage cloak. His Tam O'Shanter with its distinctive black Commando hackle failed to cover his ears, which he rubbed vigorously. Down below on Niato, a group of his Andartes stood by the signal bonfires, a column of mules nearby. The occasional glow of a cigarette marked their position. He marvelled at the resilience of these partisans who, at the drop of a hat, would stop everything and head up the mountains in the middle of the night with their pack animals. Yorgos, the runner, had arrived in the village of Korifi a couple of nights previously with the news of the airdrop. He looked impossibly young to be charged with such important duties, but he was a legend amongst the British Liaison Officers who worked with the Cretan Resistance. Although he was small and slight, he covered impossible distances at great speed with unflagging reliability and good humour, and it did not seem to bother him that the Germans had put a price on his head, dead or alive. During his absence, some bastard had stolen Yorgos's family's few remaining sheep, but the teenager never once complained. John had made sure the family got a couple of gold sovereigns from the British fund.

Kostas nudged him and pointed up at the sky. John heard the drone of an approaching aircraft. He strained his eyes and suddenly, a Halifax swept right over their heads. Down on the plateau, a torch winked a signal in Morse code, and the plane repeated it with its wing-tip lights. There was a burst of activity, and the bonfires blazed out in their distinctive T-shape. The aircraft banked, circled, and approached the plateau low and straight, the dispatcher clearly silhouetted in the open door by the internal light. Clusters of parachutes appeared underneath the aircraft, mushroomed open, and floated down with containers suspended below them. The Halifax gunned its engines, climbed overhead, and disappeared, its wing-tip lights flashing a valedictory *dit-dit-dit-dah*: V for Victory.

A sudden gust of wind carried a parachute over John's head and dumped it with a thud in the snow a hundred yards higher up on the ridge. He and Kostas dashed towards it, their rubber commando soles squeaking in the snow. Just as they detached the container from the collapsed parachute, a burst of gunfire whistled past them. A bullet hit Kostas in the chest, and he collapsed, rolling a few yards down the ridge. John grabbed him by the collar, towed him into the cover of a large boulder, and dived down into the snow. He cocked his rifle and tried to spot where the fire was coming from. Kostas yelled, 'Run for your life!' in Greek and opened fire with his Sten-gun. John hesitated as he saw Kostas's blood staining the snow, but the Cretan yelled again, 'Go!'

For a moment, John was paralysed with indecision for it was against all his instincts to abandon his comrade, then he took a deep breath, grabbed the container and ran for it. Out of the corner of his eye, he spotted several German soldiers on cross-country skis higher up the ridge, firing. A burst hit Kostas again, and he flopped over, dead. As John slid down the far side of the ridge, a German soldier snow-ploughed to a halt, crossed his ski-sticks in front of him, rested his sniper's rifle on the 'X', aimed carefully, and fired. John yelled and toppled into space.

He came to and found himself buried in a snowdrift up to his thighs, the snow splattered crimson from blood leaking from a throbbing wound in his left shoulder. The container was beside him, but his rifle was missing. Dragging the container behind him, he struggled out of the snowdrift and set off downhill, sliding and slithering, feeling dizzy and nauseous because of his painful wound. As dawn broke, a blizzard was blowing, snowflakes were driving into his nose, mouth, and eyes, and he could barely see a couple of yards in front of him. He knew he had to find shelter before hypothermia set in. Blinking and peering around, he spotted a cave above him beside a tree with the entrance half blocked with snow. He scrambled up and crawled inside. Grunting with pain, he dumped the container and slid down the wall of the cave into a sitting position. He felt sick from the pain of his wound and tried to vomit but could only retch. Forcing himself to take deep breaths, he pulled off his tunic and pullover and examined the wound in his shoulder. A flesh wound, deep enough, but it hadn't touched the bone. The battlefield First Aid course had specified that you had to put pressure on a bleeding wound. But how was he going to get a field dressing over it? He had to stay focused. He held the dressing in place with his right hand and pulled the bandage ends free with his teeth. He jammed the dressing against the wall with his shoulder and tied it in place. It wasn't pretty, but it was better than nothing. He struggled back into his pullover and tunic as it was freezing in the cave, and he couldn't stop his teeth from chattering. Fortunately, he fell asleep for a short while.

When he woke, he opened the container which held ten aluminium tubes, about a centimetre in diameter and fifty centimetres long. He had to hide them as the Andartes would need them later. Using just his hands, he tried to dig a hole in the pebbled floor of the cave but fainted with the pain in his shoulder. Coming to, he tried again using his Commando fighting knife, with more success this time, although blood trickled down his arm onto his left hand. He jammed the tubes inside the hole, filled it with pebbles, and stamped it smooth. Sitting down again, he fumbled a map and notebook out of the map-pocket in his battledress trousers, and began scribbling with an indelible pencil, referring to the map every so often, making notes about his estimated position. He felt a cold fist clench his stomach as he thought of the death of Kostas, his guide and close comrade-in-arms, and he shuddered at his own close escape. As the day wore on, he slid in and out of consciousness, his shoulder throbbing. He ate a little chocolate and drank from his water-bottle. As he waited for nightfall, he checked his pistol.

After dark, he wriggled out of the cave and crept downhill,

pistol in hand. It had stopped snowing, the wind had abated, and the night was silent and still. Were the Germans still about? He checked the snow-covered bridlepath which led to the village in both directions – no tracks. Forcing himself to stay alert, he stumbled down the path to the outskirts of Korifi. Lying behind a drystone wall, he scanned the houses, his breath rasping. The village was sleeping, but the pungent smell of burning olive wood wafted through the night air, for in the winter, the villagers kept their stoves alight round the clock.

He rolled over the wall, gasped at the fierce stab of pain in his shoulder, staggered down a lane looking right, left and behind him, and reached the house at the end. There was no sign of movement. He lifted the latch and slid inside the house, pistol at the ready. The house was exactly as he had left it. He hobbled over to the kanabes, the wooden sleeping-bench, and put his pistol down on the table. In the dark, he counted his way to the third plank of the wooden panelling and pulled the upper edge. It sprung open revealing an alcove containing a tin box. Taking the map and notebook out of his map-pocket, he placed them inside the box, put it back in the alcove and clicked the plank shut.

He stood up and inhaled deeply, propping himself upright against the table for he was exhausted. He heard a footstep outside, grabbed his pistol with a shaking hand, spun round, aimed at the door, and collapsed at the feet of the two Andartes who charged in, weapons at the ready. His wound began to bleed heavily.

He swirled queasily in and out of consciousness before coming alert to the steady beat of an engine, and a prickling pain in his left shoulder. He was lying on a berth in a sick bay where a Royal Navy surgeon was stitching his wound. He looked about wildly.

'What the ... Where am I? I must ...'

'Easy does it, Sergeant,' the surgeon said. 'You're all

right. You mustn't do anything now except rest.'

'Where am I?'

'On one of our submarines, halfway to Alexandria. Before you know it, you'll be in a nice clean bed being looked after by a popsy. Now, you must rest. You've lost a lot of blood.' He put a dressing on John's wound.

'How, how did I get here?'

'Your Cretan chums carried you to the shore on the back of a mule. They knew there was a sub due. You're lucky to have friends like that.'

It must have been some of the Andartes in his band. He had a vague memory of a painful downhill journey in which he was lurching all over the place and being held upright by a couple of cursing Andartes, but nothing more specific than that. John sank back onto the pillow, exhaled deeply, and closed his eyes. The surgeon was right; he *was* lucky to have friends like that.

# Part 1

**Andy Gallagher: Glasgow 2010**

# Chapter 1

Professor Andy Gallagher was so absorbed in marking exam scripts that when his phone rang, he started.

'Telephone call, Professor,' his secretary said. 'I thought I wasn't to be …'

'It's your father.'

That was a surprise. His father Michael never phoned him at work. 'Oh. Okay. Put him through.'

'Hi Dad,' Andy said. 'Is everything alright?' He could hear his father's heavy breathing.

There was a pause, and then came his father's familiar deep rasping voice. 'I've just received a weird letter from Crete.'

'What kind of weird letter?.'

'A strange one, son.'

'What kind of strange?'

'From a woman who says she was my father's wife, and he only died a few weeks ago.'

'What? Grandpa John? The famous Commando? But he died in the War.'

'That's what we always thought. Missing in Action.'

Andy's grandmother Maeve used to tell him grand stories about his grandfather – the socialist activist and shop-steward, the footballer, the super-fit and fearless hillwalker, and wartime Commando. She had obviously doted on her partner and never stopped talking warmly about him. Andy sometimes wondered if his grandfather's legendary experiences in Crete had constituted the impetus for his own academic specialism in Minoan Studies. 'Who is this Cretan woman?'

'She says she was his wife.'

'It sounds like a scam, Dad. Or some kind of mistake.'

'I'm not so sure. I'd like you to take a look at the letter. Can we meet for a drink?'

Andy glanced at the pile of exam scripts on his desk. 'Aye. But I've got to finish some work first. Let's say five o'clock. The Lismore Bar? Right, see you there.'

Andy sat with a pint of IPA in the Lismore. He liked this pub and the way the owner had tried to recreate a Celtic ambience in it, for it was situated in Partick, the traditional neighbourhood of the Gaels in Glasgow. He also liked the fact that the fiddler depicted in the stained-glass window in the west wall was left-handed. How many people had noticed that? It reminded him of James Scott Skinner's reel '*The Left-Handed Fiddler,*' a tune the young generation of folkies didn't seem to know. The door opened, and Michael came in carrying a plastic shopping-bag and sat down opposite Andy.

'Hello, Dad,' Andy said. 'A pint of Guinness?.'

'Aye.'

Andy got up and went to the bar.

'Here you are, Auld Yin,' he said, placing the pint before his father. 'Did you have your dinner today?'

'Aye, I did. Gourmet mince and tatties. Which means I added some peas and Worcester Sauce.' He took an appreciative pull at his Guinness. 'I got this the other day in the post.' He took an envelope out of his plastic bag and gave it to Andy. It had a Greek stamp on it, and the handwritten address read:

*Mister Michael Gallagher*
*843 Govan Road*
*Glasgow*
*SCOTLAND.*

Andy stared at the address. 'But you haven't lived in Govan

Road for over twenty years.'

'More like thirty. But old Mrs Donnelly is still there, and she knew how to find me.'

Andy took the letter out of the envelope and opened it; it was undated. He read:

Dear Michael Gallagher,

I am Themia the wife of your father John Gallagher Sfakianakis. He did not die in the War, but he died a few weeks before. He ask me to tell you to come for the box he leaves with important papers. Come to Korifi village in Sfakia, Kriti, for the box I keep for you.

Themia Sfakianakis.

Andy's jaw dropped. 'Jesus Christ! What's going on here?'

'That's what I want to know. My father was posted Missing in Action in Crete in 1944, towards the end of the War. That's what they sent my mother at the time. She kept it until the day she died.'

He passed over a second faded envelope with MINISTRY OF WAR printed on the outside. Andy took out a telegram and read it; it was dated January 20th, 1945.

**REGRET TO INFORM YOU THAT YOUR HUSBAND 379433 SERGEANT JOHN GALLAGHER IS MISSING IN ACTION AS A RESULT OF LAND OPERATIONS IN CRETE ON NOVEMBER 19th, 1944. LETTER FOLLOWS.**

'I don't get it,' Andy said.

'Neither do I,' Michael said. 'There's something funny going on. If my father was killed during the War, what's he doing married to a Cretan woman, and, and abandoning my Ma … and me? And what does this woman mean when she says he died a few weeks 'before'? Before what?'

'It's what the Greeks say when they mean 'ago',' Andy said.

Michael burst into a fit of coughing and took an angry

gulp of his Guinness, close to tears. Andy put his hand on his shoulder.

'Take it easy, Dad.'

'Take it fucking easy? What kind of a man is it that abandons his lassie and a wean he's never even seen and marries a bloody foreign woman?'

Andy had never seen his father so upset. Women had emotions, but Glasgow working-class men did not, or if by some bizarre chance they did, they certainly didn't show them.

'He never came home on leave?'

'Never since he was posted overseas. His Commando battalion was sent to Egypt, and Ma got regular letters from there. That was when I was born. Then there was a gap of a year. Then she got a letter saying he was now back in Egypt after being on the run in Crete for a year after the big battle there. That was the summer of 1942. Then she got another letter saying he'd volunteered for something which he wasn't allowed to discuss. And for the rest of the War, all Ma got before the Missing-in-Action telegram were these postcard things saying he was okay. All the letters and postcards are in here.'

Michael gave Andy the plastic bag. Andy took out a packet of letters with an elastic band round them, a packet of postcards and a folder of photographs. 'This is all really weird,' he said. 'I don't know what to think. I'm as puzzled as you are. You're quite right – there's something very funny going on. But give me a few days and I'll see what sense I can make of it.'

'I knew you'd think of something. All these fancy university degrees have got to be good for something, eh?' Although he was trying to be light-hearted, Andy could see that he was still very confused and upset. Michael took another pull of his Guinness. 'So. How's it going back at the ranch?'

'Couldn't be worse,' Andy said. 'Alison is emphatic that she wants a divorce, and she's got it all planned down to the last detail. She wants to sell the house, divvy up the proceeds, and take custody of Eilidh. To tell you the truth, I feel quite shattered as it came right out of the blue. I had no clue she was thinking of ending our marriage, so I don't know whether I'm coming or going.'

'Looks like your bum is well and truly out of the window, son. But like I told you, Alison's a wee bit of a thrawn woman. How's Eilidh, by the way?'

'She's upset. She keeps yelling at me.'

'She's hurting, son. She blames herself for what happened.'

'That's daft. She had nothing to do with it. How do you know that anyway?'

Michael looked warily round the pub as if assessing if anyone could hear them. But there was only the usual teatime thrum.

'Eilidh comes and talks to me,' he said. 'I'm her granddad – she trusts me. And she's got a good head for a sixteen-year-old lassie. She's trying to work things out in her own way. She loves both of you and doesn't want to wind up as piggy-in-the-middle. And she's right, by the way.'

'That's never going to happen. At least not as far as I am concerned.'

'You know that. I know that. You make sure *she* knows that. You're her father and always will be. So just go with – what's it that the Young Team says again?'

''Go with the flow'.'

'Just go with her flow. Make sure that she knows you care about her, you want to spend time with her, and you're worried about how she's getting on at school. Know what I mean?'

'I do. For an auld yin, you're no daft.'

'I may be daft, son, but I'm not stupid.'
Andy laughed; Michael was anything but stupid.

## Chapter 2

The next morning, Andy was giving a lecture. It was one of his favourites, his polemical attack on Sir Arthur Evans' whole Minoan edifice. It got right up the noses of the archaeologists, but Andy firmly believed that archaeological noses were there to be got up. But suddenly, in the middle of the lecture, he froze. He stared into space, and for some reason heard Billie Holiday singing in the distance:

*You've changed*
*You're not the angel I once knew*
*No need to tell me that we're through It's all over now,*
*you've changed.*

In his frozen state, he was oblivious to the fact that the students were exchanging embarrassed and worried glances. So, he jumped when a girl stood up and said, 'Professor Gallagher. Are you all right?'

Andy came to with a start. 'Oh. Yes, yes. Sorry about that. Drifted off into a wee dwam. Now, where was I?'

'How did Evans know it was a palace?' the girl said. 'Yes, of course.'

After the lecture, when he returned to his office, Andy found a note from his secretary asking him to phone Professor Diane Fraser, his Head of School at the University. When he did so, she asked him to come and see her that afternoon.

Later, Andy sat opposite Diane, a brisk, efficient, no-nonsense woman of about sixty. 'Now, Andy' she said, 'I'm worried about you. This unfortunate business with Alison has taken it out of you emotionally, and quite frankly, it is showing. You've become increasingly vacant recently. So, I suggest you go and see Amy MacAllister in Counselling and Psychological Services. She's very good, and I think she could help you out of this crisis.'

That's it, Andy thought, this is the end. I'm being sent to a bloody shrink.

Amy the counsellor seemed to be very calm and attentive. Andy felt attentive, but not at all calm. They seemed to have been going round in circles for the last forty minutes.

'Well, your H.O.D. thinks you've become a little vacant recently because of personal issues, and this is affecting your work,' Amy said.

'Yes. That's what she thinks.'

'And what do you think?'

'I think I'm fine, I'm just the same as usual.'

'Diane thinks that you are suffering from an overload of stress because of your domestic problems. And she also thinks that this is affecting your work. How do you feel about that?'

'Diane is entitled to her own opinions. I happen not to share them.'

'But she is concerned for you.'

'I appreciate that. But she needn't be. I'm okay.'

About halfway through the session, Andy took a deep breath and continued. 'I would admit that I've been a bit preoccupied recently as my wife and I are going through a divorce proceeding.'

'Would you like to tell me a bit about that?' Amy said.

'Well, to be perfectly honest, it took me completely by surprise. I didn't see it coming. It was a bit of a shock. Still is, in fact.'

'What did 'it' look like?'

'Alison – that's my wife – suddenly said that I lived in an academic bubble back in antiquity two thousand years BC, and that I loved the Minoans and Linear A more than her.'

'And did you?'

'That's what I do, that's my job, that's what I research.'

'But do you think that your wife was correct when she said that you paid more attention to your research than to her?'

Andy stared at a framed print on the wall for several seconds. It was of a vase of freesias. Colourful but neutral, presumably to help induce a calm ambience. He felt anything but calm. He ripped a tissue from the box on the coffee-table between them and patted his eyes.

'It's true I spent a great deal of time on my research. But I don't think I neglected Alison. We do – we did – a lot of things together.'

'Like what?'

'Erm, cooking, going out for occasional meals. Going to the cinema and concerts. Going for a walk on Sundays. That kind of thing. The usual kind of things that couples do.'

'Maybe Alison wanted more than the usual?'

'Well, she never said so. We didn't really talk about our relationship much.'

'Oh? Why not?'

'I, erm, probably did spend more time thinking about my research than about my marriage. In fact, I don't believe I thought about my marriage much at all. I just took it for granted. As if being married was routine.'

'Really? Why do you say that?'

'We were married young. We both come from Catholic families where you were expected to marry and have children, and that was that. The marriage would look after itself.'

'How does that make you feel?'

'Bloody awful. It makes me feel very depressed to think that at age forty-four, after eighteen years of marriage, with a lovely teenage daughter, I don't know the first thing about relationships. I hadn't the slightest clue there was a problem with our marriage.' Involuntary tears ran down his cheeks.

He closed his eyes and patted them again with the tissue.

There was silence in the room for several seconds. Then Amy said, 'Eighteen years is a long time. You and Alison must have had something in common to keep you together for such an extended period.'

Andy thought for several seconds. 'Yes, we did. We liked each other. We respected each other. We talked to each other. We got on well. We never had any big arguments. We shared housework. We both liked cooking. It was a friendly relationship which just seemed to work effortlessly. We were very pleased when Eilidh came along, and we shared child-rearing duties. And we had quite a good sexual relationship, at least before Eilidh was born. Alison is a good-looking woman. And afterwards, as Eilidh was growing up, the sex didn't seem so important anymore.'

'It didn't seem so important. To whom?.'

'Oh. To me.'

'What about Alison?'

Andy paused again. 'I don't know.' He suddenly realised the implication of what he had just said. He hadn't a clue what his own wife felt about their sexual relationship. An acute spasm of guilt flashed through his body.

'We, erm, we never discussed that. The sex, I mean. I think we just took it all for granted.'

Amy leaned back. 'Okay. I'd like to take you back to the occasion when you found out that Alison was having an affair. What did you feel like at that point?'

'I felt sick to my stomach. And then I felt angry, I felt furious and I wanted to batter whoever the man was. I began to have all sorts of fantasies of beating him up. I even did some detective work and found out where he lived.' Andy managed a bitter laugh. 'And I found out he was a married man with two children of his own. That seemed to make my anger worse, and at one point I began to think about killing him. Aye. And then I began to feel angry towards Alison and wanted to hurt her. And then I began to feel guilty about that.'

'But you didn't do anything to either Alison or her lover?'

'No – but I wanted to and felt guilty about entertaining such violent emotions. They were quite frightening. How could I have felt like hurting my own wife, the mother of my daughter?'

'Emotions are neutral, Andy. They're neither good nor bad. They're simply feelings.'

'Emotions are neutral? Wait a minute, I can't get my head round that. What do you mean? I was entertaining murderous thoughts towards my own wife!'

'But you didn't act on them. You couldn't help your feelings, but you could help your action, your behaviour. And you chose not to act on your feelings, however violent they may have been.'

Silence. This is what they call a pregnant pause, Andy thought. 'This is very confusing.'

'Powerful emotions can be confusing. But you can't help feeling them. Now. We've come to the end of our time for today. Next week, same day, same time?'

'Fine,' Andy said, thinking this must be what touching the void felt like.

As he walked down the road, Andy felt very queasy. His body was trembling and lacking in energy, so when he reached his car, he turned on the heater and sat in the driver's seat for several minutes staring vacantly into space until the trembling stopped. He realised that as a result of the therapy, he was beginning to suspect that maybe he had spent so much time on his research because he didn't want to think about his marriage. Or maybe he didn't know how to. The thought made him feel made him feel guilty for it meant that he was deceiving himself – and Alison – for a long time.

# Chapter 3

In his study in the University, Andy stacked his grandfather's folder of letters chronologically and started his laptop. He opened the first letter, which was from John's pre-war girlfriend Maeve, and began to read.

64 Neptune Street
Govan.
July 17th, 1939.

Dear John,

 I've got a bun in the oven. This has been confirmed by my doctor. I was very surprised and frightened by the news. When I told my parents, my father went mental, called me a whore, and threw me out of the house. But my cousin Bridget helped me to find a room-and-kitchen back here in Govan. It's a good house and the neighbours are smashing, but I do feel a bit lonely. I'm still working at Shieldhall, but now we're packing rations for the Army. The Coop has a nursery here so the wean will be looked after when it is born, which will be in March next year. I hope this is what you want me to do, John, for this is <u>our</u> wean, and it needs a Daddy as well as a Mammy. Tell me what you think. Although Bridget looks in when she can, I feel lonely in the house all by myself. Is there any news of you getting home at all? I think of you every day and miss you a lot.

 All my love,
 Maeve XXX

What a letter to get out of the blue, Andy thought. I wonder what my Grandfather's reaction was. He found out in the next letter.

BFPO 103
Stirling. July 23rd, 1939.
My Dearest Maeve,

Thanks for your letter which arrived today. I was horrified to hear that you are pregnant, but I was blazing to hear that your parents threw you out when they heard the news. That was right out of order. I feel very guilty about your pregnancy, as I should have thought of French Letters when we went to Arran. You ask what you are to do. Maeve, you must keep the baby, our baby. I will of course marry you on my first leave if you will have me. Will you marry me, darling? Please say you will. I asked my Company Commander for Compassionate Leave to come home and marry you, but he said don't be ridiculous, there's a war going on.

Don't worry, darling, we'll be happy together. When the War is over I'll return to my trade. A joiner is never short of work in the Glasgow shipyards. The training here is tough, but I am well and in good spirits. I think of you all the time and can't wait to hold you in my arms again, my darling. Don't worry. We will be married on my first home leave.

'As fair as thou, my bonie lass, So deep in love am I;

And I will luve thee still, my Dear, Till a' the seas gang dry.'

Your loving John.
XXX

Then there was a gap in the correspondence, but a subsequent letter from Cairo contained a photograph, and a studio portrait of his grandfather as a Lance-Corporal, with a backdrop of two– dimensional pyramids and palm trees, stamped 'Cairo, February 1941' on the back. Andy realised he had the same square jaw and black curly hair as his grandfather. He typed the information into his laptop, then opened John's next letter.

ME BFPO 217
April 18th, 1941
My Dearest Maeve,

Thank you so much for the lovely photos of our wean. He looks like you! And I like the name Michael. I'm very pleased to hear that you are both doing well in Govan, but worried that I'm not there to look after you. I think of you every single day. It's still very hot here, but I'm in good health. All I worry about is you, my darling Maeve, and our wee baby boy Michael.

All my love to both of you.

'And fare thee weel, my only Luve! And fare thee well, a while!

And I will come again, my Luve, Tho' it were ten thousand mile!'

My company commander says it's actually about two thousand five hundred miles!!!

Your loving John.
XXX

Andy riffled through the next few letters, making notes on the sequence of dates on his computer. Nothing after late April 1941 until June 1942, and then one more, postmarked Cairo. Hmmm. He picked up the next packet. The contents were all standard format Army lettercards, each one carrying anodyne messages in John's handwriting about 'being well, and 'thinking of you.' They were all also post-marked Cairo and ran on a more-or-less monthly basis from September 1943 until October 1944, then nothing. Andy stared into space for a few moments, then closed the file, googled 'The National Archives' and opened the online catalogue. He couldn't find what he was looking for and realised he would have to go to the Archives in person.

A couple of days later, Andy found what he wanted in the Reading Room of the National Archives at Kew in London, filled out a couple of request forms and took them to the desk. When his requests were delivered, he took a sheaf of papers out of a folder and riffled through them. He found the sequence he wanted. It was a list – the 'Nominal Roll' – of British and Commonwealth soldiers and airmen evacuated from Crete by submarine and motor-launch in the summer of 1942. There had been several such evacuations that year. He ran his finger down the lists and stopped: Eureka! There was his grandfather's name. He then picked up a photograph from the folder. It showed a group of evacuees on the wharf in Bardia in Libya, wearing what looked like hospital pyjamas. He gasped: there was his grandfather John smack-bang in the middle of the photo! That meant he had been on the run on the island for a full year after the Battle of Crete.

Andy sat beside Michael in the Lismore pub, with the letters and cards on the table in three small piles, and a folder to one side.

'Right,' he said. 'This pile of letters is all from Egypt in 1940 and early 1941. That was when 11 Commando was sent to the Middle East. So, your father was based in Cairo in late 1940 and the first few months of 1941. We know he did the business with Grandma before he left, because you were born in April 1941.'

'That's right,' Michael said. 'Ma told me they had a weekend away just after he was called up, before he reported for basic training, in a Bed-and-Breakfast on Arran. They both came from the same neighbourhood in Govan, they'd been comrades in the same branch of the ILP for ages before the War, they were already winching, and nobody knew when the War was going to end. It must have seemed kinna natural to go to bed together in they days.'

'Aye. I suspect there was a mini embarkation-leave baby-boom all over Britain in those early years of the War. Anyway, there were a lot of disagreements about what to do with the Commandos in the Middle East. Some went to Syria, some went to Cyprus, and some went raiding in North Africa. But when the Germans invaded Crete in May 1941, a composite Commando of eight hundred men called Layforce was sent there.'

Andy took a gulp of his beer and continued. 'But it wasn't used for the raiding operations for which they were trained. As a result of the emergency in Crete, they were thrown into the battle as the rear-guard of the retreating British troops, along with some Aussies and Kiwis. But they didn't have any heavy weapons and were involved in pitched fighting from Day One. They helped delay the Germans long enough to let more than eighteen thousand British and Commonwealth troops be evacuated from the island, but they took heavy casualties.' Andy consulted his notes. 'In fact, six hundred of the original eight hundred Commandos landed in Crete were posted killed, wounded, missing or captured.'

'Jesus, that's a helluva doing.'

'It was. But in the confusion following the retreat, more than a thousand British, Australian and New Zealand soldiers refused to surrender and took to the hills. And John was one of them. Look what I found.'

Andy opened the folder and passed the photocopies of the Nominal Roll and the photo of the men in pyjamas at Bardia to his father. 'Look, there's John. He survived and was successfully evacuated after a year on the run.'

'Well, bugger me. This is unreal.'

'Aye.'

'What happened after that?'

'Well. The next letter is from Cairo shortly after the evacuation, where he's safe and well. But there are only two of these letters, and I wondered why.' Andy indicated the third pile. 'The rest are standard Army issue postcards, and they all contain similar bland messages. That puzzled me, because John's earlier letters are full of concern for Maeve and you. Then I remembered reading somewhere that SOE personnel …'

'SOE?'

'Special Operations Executive. A sort of secret army that Churchill established to set Europe ablaze,' Andy said. 'They were specially selected and trained men and women who were parachuted into Occupied Europe to help train the Resistance movements in guerrilla warfare and sabotage.'

'You mean …?'

'I mean I suspect that Grandad was recruited as an agent by SOE because he'd been on the run in the White Mountains for a year, he'd come to know the area well and had good contacts with the locals. I think he was sent back to train the Cretan Resistance. And as this work was secret and deadly dangerous, it could never be revealed where these agents were. So, before they were landed by submarine or parachute in these occupied countries, they all filled out a couple of dozen postcards with harmless, bland messages, and SOE sent them out to their families at the rate of one a month, or whatever.'

'Well, fuck me.'

'Look,' Andy said passing over a book about the history of S.O.E. with a Post-It sticking out. Michael put on his glasses and read a passage.

'Incredible. Well, you may be daft, son, but you're no stupid.' Both men laughed and drank some beer.

'The problem is that I can't prove this because I couldn't find a list of the men who were sent to the SOE guerrilla warfare school in Palestine in the National Archives. But I am pretty sure that's what happened to Grandad.'

'Okay, I can see that. But the problem is his postcards stop towards the end of 1944.

Then in early 1945 Ma gets the telegram saying he's Missing in Action. Which she and everyone else believed.' Michael waved the recent letter from Crete in the air, visibly upset. 'Then this arrives a few weeks ago saying that my father has been alive all these years. Why did he never write? Why did he never come home again to marry the mother of his wean and make an honest woman of her? Why did he stay in Crete? What the fuck happened to him?'

'I think the answer to all these questions must be in the box of papers that his widow mentions in the letter.'

'Then I've got to go to Crete to get it. Can you find me a flight?'

Andy stared at his father for a couple of seconds. 'I don't think you should go, Dad.'

'Why not, son?'

'I think this trip could be very stressful. And you don't speak the language.'

'So what? I'm only going to pick up a box.'

'I think it's going to be a lot more complicated than that. This woman, Themia, has a lot of explaining to do.'

'Well, she must speak English because her letter was in English.'

'Aye, but not very good English. And she may have got someone to write it for her.'

'So, what do you propose?'

'I could go to Crete and get that box for you. I think there's a direct flight from Glasgow to Hania once a week in the season. And remember, I've been travelling in Crete for over twenty years, and I know the place and the people very well now.' He could see the relief dawning in his father's eyes. 'I'll see if there's a flight during the university Easter vacation.'

'When's that, son?'

'In a couple of weeks. I can't go before then because I'm busy teaching.'

'Thanks, son, you're a dancer. But you mind yourself over there amongst them Cretans.'

## Chapter 4

A week later, Andy read an email summoning him to a meeting with his mentor, Professor Ramsay, a business economist. Andy loathed him as an impossibly unprincipled, ambitious careerist, a pompous prick who always wore a three-piece business suit. He dressed like a Volvo car salesman, Andy thought, but I wouldn't even buy a second-hand Mini from him. In his office, Ramsay said, 'Now Andy, we've known each other for long enough to avoid formalities. The purpose of this meeting is to review your research output over the last session and establish if you are meeting your own goals, as well as those of the School and the University. Agreed?'

'Agreed.'

'According to your own report, your output seems to have stalled recently. You originally reckoned you would produce three refereed articles, and finish your monograph on Eteo-Cretan, this session. But in fact, you have produced nothing in the last year. That's …'

'That's not true,' Andy said. 'I gave a paper to the Society of Antiquaries which was received enthusiastically, and which I will work up for publication in due course.'

'A conference paper is not a refereed article, Andy,' Ramsay said. 'It counts only as a conference paper.'

'The Chair of the conference was Sir Richard Bullivant, who said it was the most original and exciting paper he had heard in his whole career.'

'Remind me of the topic.'

'If you remember, last year I told you that I found a clay tablet outside Hania in Crete, in Apokoronas. In fact, a shepherd found it, took it home and forgot all about it. Then someone told him about me. I bought the tablet from him for one hundred Euros. Initially I thought the hieroglyphs were in Linear B. But then I realised that they weren't. I then thought they were in Linear A, but they weren't either, so I was really puzzled. But then, by deploying some ideas of Alan Turing, I began to realise that they were somewhere in between Linear A and B, and in fact constituted a new hybrid language which I have designated as Linear A.1. I have spent the last year trying to decipher it, so far without success, which is why I have made no progress with my other projects.' Ramsay was staring out of the window, bored.

'But I remain confident that I will eventually crack it,' Andy said. 'It just takes patience, a lot of patience.'

'But what is the product? Of what use is Linear A.1 to the community, to the businesses with which the university collaborates?' Ramsay said.

'It is of no use whatsoever to the business community,' Andy said. 'My product is knowledge. Knowledge about what was probably the earliest language in western civilisation. Knowledge in which the business community is not interested. Its only interest is in profit. And that is why it is a community in which I have no interest whatsoever. I will leave that to collaborators like yourself. And may I remind you that I generated a substantial research grant for this project from the Arts and Humanities Research Council entirely on my own initiative, but one from which the university benefits financially?'

Ramsay swivelled in his chair and looked Andy right in the eye, his face pinched white with anger. 'It's all very well for you to get on your moral high horse, Professor Gallagher, but the reality is that the university exists in the twenty-first century in a highly competitive academic market. We must justify all our posts, including yours, and subject them to a cost-benefit analysis. I don't think that Minoan language benefits a society which is in an economic crisis. In fact …'

'In fact, the Research Council would appear not to agree with you,' Andy said, trying to control his temper. 'I have been engaged in informal discussions with them about funding to establish a new Research Unit on Minoan Language and Culture within the School, one which would employ two new members of staff, a Cryptologist, and an early Greek Linguistics expert. They have encouraged me strongly to apply. If successful, this would make the University the world leader in research into Minoan language and Linear A.'

Ramsay choked with rage. 'Over my dead body,' he hissed.

Andy stared at him for several seconds, then in his best West Belfast accent, said, 'Sure now, that can be arranged.' He stood up. 'The top o' the mornin' to you, Professor Ramsay.'

Andy sat facing his daughter Eilidh in the University Café.

'I simply have to go to Crete, Eilidh,' he said. 'Grandpa Michael isn't in good health, and although he won't admit it, I don't think he's got long left. And he's shattered by this news about his father coming completely out of the blue. I've got to clear up this mystery so that he can end his days in peace. I'll go during the Easter vacation.'

Eilidh scowled. 'Thanks a lot, Dad – leaving me here with Mum and The Haircut.'

'The Haircut?.'

'Jason. Lover Boy.'

'I'll only be gone for a week. You can surely handle that. And it would be good if you could keep an eye on Grandpa Michael for me.'

Eilidh nodded reluctantly. 'All right.'

# Part 2

## John Gallagher: Scotland 1935-1940

## Chapter 5

Oh aye, I know all about fascism, you can be sure of that, for I imbibed socialism with my mother's milk, practically literally, after I was born on September 22$^{nd}$, 1920. My parents were both active members of the Glasgow ILP – the Independent Labour Party – and my naming ceremony was in the Socialist Sunday School where I was named after Red Clydeside leader John Maclean. Both of my parents had been active in the heyday of the Red Clyde. Patrick, my father, a shipyard riveter, was a friend of the militant shop-steward Harry McShane and was involved in the 40-Hours Strike in 1919, and 'Bloody Friday' in George Square. He never forgave Churchill for sending tanks and troops to Glasgow to crush the workers' movement.

Eileen, my Mum, worked in the food department of the Coop factory in Shieldhall. She had been one of Mary Barbour's 'army of women' in the 1915 Rent Strike in Govan, and our local organiser in Neptune Street. She too had been in George Square on Bloody Friday. Both of my parents were active in the National Unemployed Workers Movement (NUWM), my father in opposition to the detested Means Test, and my mother in opposition to rent increases. Heated meetings were going on all round Glasgow in the 1930s. Dad was heavily involved in representing fellow workers at the Labour Exchange, and he came to know the regulations about unemployment insurance better than the clerks. Mum was equally busy representing tenants against house factors trying to increase rents, arguing that the 1915 Rent Restriction Act stipulated that rents could be *de*creased if repairs were not done. It got to the stage where the factors grew to fear the very sight of Mum, because she was a deadly debater. Even before I left school, I watched with Mum as Dad set off from George Square on the 1932 Hunger March to London, preceded by a flute band – a memorable occasion for a wee boy. So even while I was serving my apprenticeship as a joiner in the Fairfield shipyard in Govan, I was learning about politics and the class struggle.

However, life was not totally about politics. Dad was a keen climber and hillwalker, and during the Great Depression in the 1930s when he was unemployed, he headed for the hills as often as he could, taking me with him from about the age of ten. So, I learned the elements of rock-climbing on The Whangie, the rocky outcrop half an hour north of Glasgow where Dad taught me how to climb, chimney and abseil. I also served my time in the hills, starting in Glencoe with the Devil's Staircase, moving on to Crowberry Ridge, and graduating on the Aonach Eagach ridge.

It was on the latter that I learned an important lesson in self-confidence. I was fifteen, and Dad was taking me along the ridge. As we passed Meall Dearg, the narrow ridge dropped in a series of pinnacles towards Stob Coire Leith, with a great deal of exposure on either side. We came to a sharp pinnacle with a terrifying dizzy drop below it blocking the way. Dad swung up onto it like a ballet dancer, seemed to switch feet and jumped down on the far side. I froze, as the drop below us was sheer. Dad spotted this.

'John. You see that ledge on the pinnacle in front of you, about knee height?.'

'Aye.'

'Well, it's as big as a door mat, and you can get both feet on it no bother. Get a good grip on the rock with your left hand, step up with your left foot onto the ledge, and swing your right foot up beside it. Then you do a couple of sideways steps on the ledge and step down. Easysapeasy.'

I took a deep breath and did as I was told, with my bum hanging over space and my heart in my mouth, and found the ledge was as big as Dad said. I did a couple of inelegant sideways shuffles and jumped down.

'Well done, son. If you can do that, you can do anything in the Scottish hills.'

I felt a sense of elation and, although I didn't know it at the time, this lesson in self-confidence was to prove important in my later soldiering days.

In 1933, Labour took over Glasgow Corporation for the first time under the inspired leadership of Paddy Dollan. My parents hoped the socialist millennium had arrived. Some hopes! Shortly afterwards, as a convinced socialist, I became active in fund-raising for the Republicans in the Spanish Civil War. In fact, I wanted to join the International Brigades – at age 16! – and told Dad. He said, 'That War's lost, son, due to the cowardice of British non-intervention. The real war with Fascism is coming soon enough.' Then the local Communist Party told me they didn't want ILP 'social fascists' like me anyway – whatever they were supposed to be. You should have seen their faces trying to explain away the subsequent German-Russian non-aggression pact. Eejits!

It was about this time that I first met Maeve MacManus, at an ILP housing meeting in Govan. A Tory Councillor was on his feet ranting on about the alleged anti-social behaviour of the tenants of the Moorepark housing scheme, a local slum-clearance scheme which had acquired the nickname of the 'Wine Alley'. He called them 'work-shy slum rats'.

Suddenly this teenage girl stood up. 'My family lives in that scheme,' she said, bristling with rage. 'And we're not work-shy slum-rats. My father's a fitter, and he's not working because there's a Depression in the shipyards. But maybe you haven't heard that up in your posh house in Mosspark, mister. And I work in the Coop food factory at Shieldhall, and my mother works doing laundry in the steamie for parasites like you. You've a pure cheek to talk about the work-shy given that you've never done a day's work in your bloody life and live off the profits of the half-dozen houses you own in Govan. So, take your snash and stuff it where the sun don't shine.'

Well, that was him told, and he sat down hurriedly to the jeers of the audience. I was well impressed by this feisty young woman, got talking to her at the end of the meeting, and learned that her family had originally come from Neptune Street, where we lived, and which was known locally as the 'Irish Channel.' We had that much in common. She was a bonnie lassie with flaming red hair, a buxom figure, pure dead bright, and cheerful. I was soon to learn that she was her own woman, spoke her mind, and didn't take any prisoners. I really fancied her, so screwed up my courage and asked her if she would like to go to the pictures with me – and to my delight, she said she'd love to. We did some serious winching in the back row of the cinema, in no time at all we were going steady, and then in 1939, when my apprenticeship was up, we became engaged informally. Shortly afterwards, War was declared.

## Chapter 6

In the late summer of 1939, I was called up and ordered to report to the Argyll & Sutherland Highlanders at Stirling Castle. But when I told Maeve, she really took the wind out of my sails.

'Look, John,' she said, 'we don't know for how long you'll be gone, and war is a dangerous thing. We've been going steady for quite a while now and we've talked about getting married. You know I want to marry you. I also want to have something to remember you by when you're gone. So, let's go away for a weekend, just you and me, and have something special to remember. What do you say?'

What could I say? This gorgeous girl was offering herself to me. 'Aye,' I said, trying to contain my excitement, 'I'm up for that.'

So, we went for a weekend on the Isle of Arran. We knew we were going to get married, we wanted to have a family, and we saw nothing wrong with going to bed together. Lots of people did that at the start of the War. But what went on in the bed and what went where was a mystery to both of us, for we had never gone beyond some heavy winching in the back row of the Lyceum Cinema in Govan Road. I asked Dad for some advice, but all he said was, 'Take the initiative, son, but take your time, be gentle, and let nature take its course.'

On our first night in the cottage in the village of Corrie on Arran, Maeve appeared in a nightgown which left little to the imagination, and I gasped, 'Jesus!' She grinned and said, 'No. Not Jesus. Maeve.' Her grin was bold but nervous, her apparent confidence wavering visibly as she stood before me. When I placed my hands on her shoulders, she gave an excited gasp, a sound of surrender and trust which undid me completely. Looking me straight in the eye, she slid off her nightie and stepped out of it. As I ran the tips of my fingers over her naked breasts, caressing her nipples, she gasped again, ripped off my pyjamas, and pulled me to her. Her fingernails digging into my bum was the most exciting feeling I had ever experienced, and her long, long kiss nearly melted me. The next thing was we were on the bed and our hands were everywhere, stroking, exploring, squeezing. Then, like Dad said, nature took its course. As the night wore on, nature took its course several times, in fact. We moved together with an urgency that blurred time, our excited laughter muffled by pillows as we discovered each other in new and clumsy ways. It was wonderful. And in the morning, we started all over again.

On our way back to Glasgow in the train, we discussed what we were going to do when the War was over, which we expected would be quite soon, as nothing seemed to be happening in France. We agreed the first thing we would do would be to get married. We then agreed we would keep our respective jobs, look for a room-and-kitchen house to rent in Govan, let nature take its course – as often as possible – and start a family. It all sounded idyllic. We were very optimistic young people.

Just after I finished my basic training with the Argylls, a notice came round asking for volunteers for 'hazardous duties', and that seemed far more exciting than square-bashing. So, I volunteered, and was sent to north to Achnacarry Castle with some other soldiers for what I learned was the Commando course.

To our surprise, this course started the moment we got off the train at Spean Bridge. Several NCOs surrounded us, shouting and bawling, and we were doubled off all the way to Achnacarry – eight miles. We passed several graves on the way with legends such as: *Shot by Mistake, Didn't Keep His Head Down,* and the like. It wasn't encouraging. I wondered what I'd let myself in for. I soon learned. For a kick-off, our accommodation was in tents in the grounds of the castle, and if you know anything about the weather in the Scottish Highlands, you'd soon realise that it wasn't luxurious. In fact, what with the rain, river-crossings, bogs, boat work and beach assaults, we were soaking wet and cold for practically all of the six weeks of the course.

We were subjected to relentless pressure designed to bring us to a peak of physical and mental fitness. The name of the game was endurance, so we did endless speed marches over the hills. We were trained to a high level of proficiency in small arms – the .38 revolver, the .303 Lee Enfield rifle and bayonet, Sten and Thompson sub-machine guns, the Bren light machine-gun, and a variety of German weapons. We were taught sabotage and demolition, small boat use, beach landings, rock and cliff-climbing and abseiling, street-fighting and house clearance, silent killing with the Commando dagger, fieldcraft, and map-reading. We did the 'Tarzan course', involving the 'death-slide' on a fixed rope across a river with explosives going off below us. We learned all about brutal unarmed combat, and I always remember one of the Physical Training Instructors saying, 'You may think this isn't cricket. Well, the Germans don't play cricket!'

Sometimes the training was dangerous. When we were practising beach landings, for example, a Bren-gunner on the shore was firing live bursts close to the side of us.

Fortunately, it was a very accurate weapon. But on one occasion, as we were jumping out of the boat, one of the men, a big heavy ungainly Scots Guardsman stumbled and knocked another soldier staggering right into the line of fire. He was killed instantly. Still and all, I came to enjoy it. I was reasonably fit at the start of the course and fighting fit at the end of it. I liked being stretched and developing a sense of self-confidence and self-reliance and learning how to develop adaptability and use my own initiative. I passed the course with flying colours, was awarded my Fairbairn-Sykes Commando dagger, promoted to Lance-Corporal, and posted to No. 11 (Scottish) Commando battalion. In early 1941, we were told we were being sent to Egypt.

**Part 3**

**John Gallagher: Egypt 1941 & Crete 1941-42**

## Chapter 7

Egypt was stinking hot and full of flies. Middle East Headquarters didn't seem to know what to do with us Commandos, and there were quite a few senior staff officers who didn't want to know us at all. We were bored stiff. Then, I received a letter from Maeve out of the blue.

64 Neptune Street Govan.
March 7th, 1941.
Dear John,

I'm still working at Shieldhall, but we're packing rations for the Army now. The Coop has a nursery here so the baby will be looked after when it is born, which will be any day now. Is there any chance of you getting home at all? I'm frightened, I think of you every day and miss you a lot.

All my love,
Maeve.
XXX

Worried sick, I went to my troop commander and asked for compassionate leave – but no chance. I wrote back to Maeve immediately.

ME BFPO 103
April 18th, 1941.
Maeve Darling,

I asked my Troop Commander for Compassionate Leave to come home for the birth of the wean, and to marry you, but he said don't be ridiculous, there's a war going on. So, I'm afraid I can't be with you for the birth, but you're a strong lassie and I'm sure it will go well. We'll also have to wait a wee while before we can get married. Don't worry, darling, we'll be happy together. When the War is over, I'll return to my trade. A joiner is never short of work in the Glasgow shipyards.

Nobody knows what's going to happen to our battalion but there are rumours of a move soon. It is very hot here where I am and there are flies everywhere. But I'm well and in good spirits. I think of you all the time and cannot wait to hold you in my arms again. Don't worry, darling. We will be married on my first home leave.

Your loving John.
XXX

The next thing I knew was another letter from Maeve telling me that I now had a baby son. I hastened to reply as it was plain that we were about to be deployed although nobody knew where yet.

ME BFPO 103
April 29th, 1941
My Dearest Maeve,

Thanks for the lovely photo of our baby son. He looks like you! And I like the name Michael.

It is still very hot but I'm in good health. As it looks like we are going into action soon, all I worry about is you, my darling, and our wee baby boy Michael. All my love to both of you. In haste,

Your loving John. XXX

Not long afterwards, on May 28th, we were embarked on a landing ship, and as we sailed, we were briefed. Unknown to us, the Germans had launched a large-scale airborne invasion of Crete, and although they had apparently taken enormous casualties on the first day, they had overwhelmed the British and Commonwealth forces which were now in retreat to the south of the island for evacuation by the Navy. We were to be landed to harass the German lines of communication so that the evacuation could proceed smoothly. But we were embarked with such haste that we had no heavy weapons – no Vickers machine-guns and no mortars – and indeed, no radios or transport. By this time, I was a Bren-gunner, and I was grateful that we still had a few of them in our troop.

We were disembarked at a small fishing village called Hora Sfakion on the south coast of Crete. We were then ordered to march north at speed to participate in the rearguard of the retreating British and Commonwealth troops. There was a lot of discontented muttering about this, for we were supposed to be specialist hit-and-run raiders, and we lacked heavy weapons. I thought it was a pure liberty, myself. But we slogged our way steeply uphill to a village called Imbros where the terrain levelled out. What we encountered there was chaos.

There was a whole rabble of undisciplined Australian troops in the village tavernas getting legless on the local wine, with no officers to be seen. Hordes of dispirited and exhausted soldiers shambled past towards Hora Sfakion, with a frequent cry of, 'Aircraft! Aircraft! Take cover! Take cover!' A line of abandoned Army lorries blocked the road outside the village so cursing soldiers had to detour round them and a section of the roadway which had been blown up. The road itself was littered with abandoned equipment – packs, boxes of ammunition, piles of stores, water bottles, mess-tins, a complete field kitchen, and an open suitcase out of which spilled an officer's mess dress. Then I heard steadily marching feet, and a company of Maori troops swung past in good order, shouting cheerful greetings. Nobody seemed to have a clue what was going on. It was a shambles.

We descended onto a dirt road going north from Imbros and soon reached a village called Askyfou, on a large plateau rimmed by mountains, held by an Australian battalion against a possible airborne attack. Our troop commander ordered my section to a position at the entrance to the village, on a mountainside overlooking the approach road. My loader, Private Kenny Mackenzie, and I found an old fortified post on the top of the mountain overlooking the approach road. It must have had something to do with the fighting against the Turks in the nineteenth century. We had both a good field of fire, and a good view of the retreating army – except that it was now more of a rout than a retreat. Kenny was a Hebridean crofter whom I had met during basic training in the Argyll and Sutherland Highlanders at the beginning of the War, and we became close mates as my talkative Glaswegian personality was complemented by Kenny's thoughtful nature. We had volunteered together for the Commando course at Achnacarry Castle.

After an hour holding up the advance of a platoon of German mountain troops, we found to our dismay that we were cut off as in the chaos, the rest of the British rearguard in Askyfou had retreated hastily without warning us. As we were about to be outflanked, we took off south-west into the heartland of the White Mountains at full speed.

## Chapter 8

We crossed a shattered lunar landscape, weapons at the ready. It was boiling hot as we crested a ridge, and below us was a village set in a picturesque, cultivated plateau. We took cover behind a dyke, and I scanned the village with the pair of Zeiss binoculars I had taken from the body of a German officer I had killed. There was no sign of the enemy, although the odd villager could be seen working the land. I gestured Kenny forward. As we approached the village through the fields, an old man was hoeing a potato plot. He saw us, dropped the hoe, grabbed an ancient rifle, and pointed it at us.

He said something in Greek, which was obviously, 'Who are you?'

'Anglos,' I said. It was no time to be arguing about the differences between Scotland and England. The old man lowered his rifle, smiled broadly, and shook each of our hands.

We couldn't understand what he was saying in Greek, but it was obviously a friendly welcome. He gestured, 'Come with me.' He led us to a nearby house and sat us down at a table in the courtyard in the shade of a luxurious vine. A young teenage boy was sharpening a knife; he looked up and smiled.

'Stelios,' the old man said, pointing at the boy, who grinned cheerfully. The old man tapped his chest and said, 'Thanassis.'

There was a carafe of Tsichoudia, the potent Cretan raki, half a dozen glasses, and a bowl of walnuts on the table. The old man poured three glasses, which we clinked.

'Se yeia,' Thanassis said. 'Slainte,' we replied.

The old man pointed to our uniforms and then gestured up at the mountains. 'Polloi Angloi.'

'I think he means there's lots of our lads up there,' I said. 'Themia,' Thanassis shouted.

A young woman about eighteen, dressed all in black, came out of the house, drying her hands on her apron. She had a black scarf wrapped round her head, which she untied with deliberate care, her fingers lingering over the knot before shaking loose her dark curls. Her gaze held mine, questioning and unafraid. She had the crazy light-blue eyes which I was to learn were distinctive of Crete, flecks of gold at the rim of the iris, and full and finely-sculpted lips. She shook my hand firmly, then Kenny's. She wore a wedding ring on her right hand, like all Cretan married women. I noticed that she had a very erect carriage and moved with great dignity. 'Kalos orisate,' she said.

'I think that means 'welcome',' I said. 'Cheers, missus.'

The old man rattled something off in Greek, indicating the table. The young woman inclined her head in graceful assent, and said, 'Amesos, Papa,' and went back into the house.

'She's gorgeous and no mistake,' Kenny said, leaning forward to watch her departing.

'Behave yourself,' I muttered. 'She's a married woman, and Thanassis is her father.'

A little later, we finished a meal of omelettes, fried potatoes, Feta cheese, bread, and wine, and belched happily. What astonishing hospitality to two complete strangers.

Thanassis refilled our glasses from a jug of wine. I raised my glass to the old man, Themia and Stelios, and said, 'Thank you. Thank you very much.' Themia, her father and the boy smiled happily, and we all clinked glasses yet again. Just then, Thanassis did a double take, scowled and muttered something uncomplimentary under his breath. I turned my head to see what he was looking at. A man, obviously a villager, had stopped on the road and was looking directly at us. When he saw us looking back at him, he moved hurriedly on.

Thanassis and Themia exchanged a knowing look – the stranger was plainly no friend.

He then took a gulp of wine and launched into an excited speech in Greek, but we couldn't understand a word. 'I think he's saying something abusive about the Germans,' I said, as I had picked out the word 'Yermanoi' in the old man's tirade.

As Themia cleared the table, I pointed at her wedding ring. 'Where's your husband, Themia?'

The young woman stood up straight, squared her shoulders and said something solemn in Greek; a tear trickled down her cheek. She put the dishes in a tray and walked into the kitchen with great dignity. The old man gestured 'wait,' and went into the house. He came back out with a framed studio photograph of a young Greek soldier in uniform, with a black ribbon across one corner. He made another short, impassioned speech in which the word 'Italoi' featured several times, while his hand made a diving motion. There was no mistaking his meaning.

'Themia husband's dead,' I said to Kenny. 'He was killed, probably fighting the Italians.' We exchanged sympathetic glances with Thanassis, and I patted the old man's shoulder; he merely lifted his hands up in a resigned shrug.

In the evening, Themia tried to explain something to us. From her gestures, she thought it unwise to stay in the village. So, carrying a pile of handwoven Cretan rugs, she led us to a circular threshing-ground outside the village, which we learned was called Korifi. She gave each of us a couple of blankets, and then gave me a bottle of Tsichoudia and two glasses.

'Kali nichta,' Themia said with a smile.

'Good night,' we said. As Themia left, we spread out the blankets, and I poured a drink.

'These people are amazing,' Kenny said.

'Aye, they are,' I said. 'Their generosity is magic.'

'I don't know what this gargle is, but it's good stuff.'

'It's raki. I got some off the Greek soldiers in Cairo. They distil it from the skin of the grapes they've trampled to make wine.'

'It's strong stuff.'

'Aye, it is that. Best not to drink too much of it. Well, mate, we better turn in. You never know what the morning will bring.'

We lay down and covered ourselves with the blankets. I stared up at the vast canopy of stars for a few moments, sighed contentedly, and drifted off to sleep.

I woke with a jolt as Themia burst onto the threshing-ground just as dawn was breaking and yanked the blankets off me. She hissed something in urgent Greek, and I caught the word 'Yermanoi.'

'On your feet, Kenny, Gerry's here,' I snapped, jumping to my feet and grabbing my Bren-gun as Themia bundled up the blankets. She pointed to a path rising steeply up the mountainside and gestured – hurry! – before she sprinted back into the village. As we tore up the path, we could hear the roar of trucks approaching the village. This was where the Achnacarry training kicked in. We streaked up that mountain and didn't stop until we reached the crest of a ridge and found a small chapel. Taking cover behind a wall and looking down, we saw German soldiers piling out of the trucks, shouting and bawling, kicking doors in and dragging people outside. The teenage boy Stelios ran for it and just as he was about to disappear into the olive groves, was shot down. The soldiers lined up the men and the boys, selected half-a-dozen at random, including Thanassis, bundled them up against a wall, and shot them. Themia ran screaming towards her dead father and was clubbed to the ground with a brutal rifle butt. I felt my gorge rise. Bastards! Fucking bastards! Kenny cocked his rifle, adjusted his sights, and took aim.

'Stop. Don't be daft,' I snapped. 'What? Why?'

'We're outnumbered and outgunned. If we open fire, we're both dead.'

Down below, the Germans lined up a second batch of men, shot them, and then climbed back into their trucks and drove away. Themia staggered to her feet, blood streaming down her face, and collapsed on top of the body of her father, screaming her grief.

'Oh my God,' I gasped. 'They're shooting them because they helped us. Let's get out of here, we can't go back down there.'

The screaming of the women followed us as we tore down the other side of the ridge.

But how did the Germans know we were in the village? I wondered if the man who had stopped outside Thanassis's house had anything to do with it. I couldn't stop crying. The women's screaming seemed to penetrate all the chambers of my trembling body. Tears dripped off my chin and soaked my shirt collar. I'd get these bastards if it was the last thing I did. I stopped and threw up. Kenny, shaking and white as a sheet, patted my back and said, 'Are you all right, mate?' As we continued, the screaming faded to be replaced by Kenny's non-stop muttering in Gaelic. I didn't know what he was saying but it was obvious he was swearing in spades.

## Chapter 9

For the rest of 1941, we travelled in ever-increasing circles in the White Mountains. It was unsafe to stay in one spot, and unfair to depend on any one set of villagers for sustenance. We had eye-witnessed the reprisals taken by the Germans in Korifi to Cretan villagers who helped us. So, we trekked from the villages of eastern Sfakia to western Selino, and as far north as Meskla and Therisso, encountering dozens of Allied soldiers on the run – British, Australian, New Zealanders, Greek Cypriots and even a few Palestinians. Most of the men were Other Ranks, but we encountered the odd officer – an Australian sapper officer, and two clueless upper-class English officers with cut-glass accents from some posh county regiment, who insisted on issuing streams of meaningless orders until I told them to fuck off.

During our travels, we hardly ever encountered any Germans who seemed unwilling to venture into the high mountains, and the Cretan villagers went out of their way to look after our men on the run. They fed us, they clothed us, they hid us in caves and cellars, and they kept us posted about the whereabouts of the Germans. And I began to learn Greek by memorising the words for food and drink and directions. I made phonetic notes of these words in the local dialect, as well as of the names of the units in the German garrison patrolling the roads and sketched the igloo-shaped drystone construction of the mitata, the upland sheilings where the sheep were milked, in a notebook I carried. We also attempted to beg, borrow, or steal a small fishing boat to escape to the 8th Army in North Africa, with no luck. There were endless rumours of an evacuation, but these rumours never came to anything, and we became increasingly despondent. However, the end of the year brought a surprise. As we descended towards a remote mountain village on the evening of Hogmanay, we heard it before we saw it.

'Listen, mate,' I said to Kenny. Drifting up from below was the raucous but unmistakeable sound of men belting out *Waltzing Matilda*. Entering the village, we found a taverna full of a dozen or so tipsy British, Australian and New Zealand soldiers celebrating the New Year. The owner, wearing a Black Watch Glengarry at an impossible angle, poured glasses of Tsichoudia, while his wife, sporting an Australian slouch hat, dispensed tumblers of wine.

'Grab a seat, Jock,' an Australian soldier yelled, 'and join the fun,' passing over a jug of wine.

'Cheers, mate,' I said, sitting down and pouring a couple of tumblers of wine as the Aussie explained that there were no Germans for miles around. These were some of the dozens of British and Commonwealth troops who had ignored the order to surrender after the Battle of Crete and taken to the hills. Like us, they had been on the run for weeks, being cared for by the Cretan mountain villagers. The Diggers finished their song with the ghost of the swagman, to thunderous applause. They were promptly followed by the Kiwis singing 'The Trooper's Farewell.' I nudged Kenny and told him we were on next along with a couple of boys from the Black Watch. What were we going to sing? No problem.

'Ah belang tae Glesga, dear auld Glesga toon.' Happy New Year!

The winter of 1941/1942 was brutal. It was no joke surviving in the freezing, snowbound White Mountains as our boots were disintegrating and our battledress threadbare. A lot of the men were ill and in poor spirits, because there was little food apart from horta, the edible wild greens which tasted a bit like spinach, and beans, bloody beans. There was also a hard bread called bobota which was made from corn or maize or something and took a helluva lot of chewing. Both Kenny and I had lost more than a stone. The villagers weren't doing much better. Our host, the elderly Proedros, or Provost, of the village of Meskla, explained the situation.

'When the Makaronades invaded Greece,' he said, 'all ….'

'What are the Makaronades?' Kenny said.

'It's what they call the Eyeties,' I said. 'It means something like the 'Macaroni-Bashers'.' I nodded to the Proedros to continue.

'In 1940, all the men between eighteen and fifty were called up into the 5$^{th}$ Cretan Division to fight the Makaronades in Epirus in north-west Greece,' he said. 'We drove them back into Albania. But we were forced to surrender when the Germans swept in behind our boys and then disarmed them. The Germans made sure that our men weren't provided with any transport to get back to Crete. Consequently, the harvest hasn't been fully brought in, and some of your lads have been helping the women and the old men to bring in wheat and corn, and grapes for the wine. So, they're very welcome! But there's still a shortage of food as the Germans requisition everything – vegetables, fruit, sheep, and goats. There's a lot of hunger about.'

But while there wasn't much food about, there was always plenty of bevvy – wine and raki. Some of the men on the run were permanently semi-pissed! I really couldn't credit how generous the villagers were. They would share their last bit of food with us, even if it meant going short themselves. And they knew what would happen to them if they continued sharing their provisions, for the Germans went mental with reprisals in any village where the locals had been helping the fugitives. I made notes of mass executions in several villages in this area alone. As I said to Kenny, 'We must get these bastards when the war is over, and string them up.'

We were also sick of hearing stories about evacuation.

Every now and then an officer from Middle East Headquarters in Cairo popped up in Crete from a submarine to assess the situation, but nothing ever came of it. There were constant rumours of submarines coming to pick us up, but I'd believe that when I saw one. In the meantime, Kenny and I based ourselves in a cave, for we didn't want to hole up in a village, although we were more than welcome, for fear of more German reprisals. It was a miserable winter.

Spring eventually came, and our spirits were raised by the sun and warm weather. By early May, we had made our way back eastwards in the White Mountains based on yet another story about an evacuation from the south coast. We were holed up in a remote, uninhabited mitato high above the mountain village of Korifi to which a local shepherd had guided us. There was a spring nearby. This was the village where we had first witnessed the massacre of local men, and I remembered the summary execution of our host, Thanassis, with horror. I also remembered his daughter, the friendly young widow Themia.

As we rested in the sun, I said, 'Do you know what I fancy?.'

'What?' Kenny said.

'A fish supper with plenty of vinegar, and mushy peas.'

Kenny laughed. 'I fancy a big dish of crowdie, with a plate of oatcakes.'

'What's crowdie?'

'It's a cream cheese we make in the Hebrides. It's delicious.' He suddenly started and pointed downwards. 'Oh-ho. Someone's coming.'

We could hear the hollow rattle of sliding stone, so we grabbed our weapons and assumed firing positions. I focused my binoculars. A figure carrying a basket was making its way uphill. As it rounded a boulder, I laughed out loud – it was Themia. She was carrying not only the basket but also had a sakouli, the local handwoven shepherd's knapsack, on her back. Oh Jesus, what am I going to say about the execution of her father? My Greek was simply not good enough.

As Themia approached, she smiled. 'Yeia sas, pedia.'

I knew what that meant: Hello, boys. She put the basket down and as I helped her off with the sakouli, her warm woman's body odour – a heady mixture of skin, fresh dough, and a hint of cologne – engulfed me. Themia took food out of the basket – bread, Graviera cheese, hard-boiled eggs, and a cold roast chicken. Then she took a bottle of wine and a small bottle of Tsichoudia out of her knapsack and passed them over. Just as we were about to fall upon the grub, Themia reached into her bodice, and I caught a glimpse down her blouse before I could turn my head away. But she just hid a smile as she extracted a folded sheet of paper and handed it over. I opened the note. It read:

*BE ON THE BEACH AT THE FOOT OF THE TRIPITI GORGE THE DAY AFTER TOMORROW MAY 12th AFTER DARK BUT BEFORE 2400.*
 *JC*
 *Lt., R.N.*

'Is that the gorge below Koustoyerako?' Kenny said.

'That's the one. Ya beauty. It must mean we're going to be evacuated at bloody last.'

Kenny couldn't contain his excitement. 'Yes-yes-yes! About bloody time!' I turned to Themia and thanked her profusely. 'Parakalo,' she said – don't mention it. We fell on the food as if there was no tomorrow. I poured Themia some wine in a tin mug. She took a few sips and handed it back. Then she stood up – she had to be back in Korifi before curfew. I took her hand in both of mine, gently, and tried to think what to say. 'Your Papa. I'm sorry for your loss.'

'Ti na kanoume?' Themia said. Her sad look conveyed her meaning: there's nothing we can do about it. As she slung her *sakouli* on her back, she said, 'Kalo taxidi.' Bon voyage. She smiled at us and set off down the mountain with an athletic stride. Forget Betty Grable! As she approached a big boulder, I thought, will she, won't she? Themia stopped, turned, smiled, and waved. We waved back.

'She fancies you, you lucky bastard,' Kenny said. 'She is absolutely gorgeous.'

'Chance would be a fine thing.' But I experienced a sudden acute pang of guilt as I remembered Maeve waiting for me back in Glasgow.

As we crept down onto the small shingle beach that night, we could discern the shapes of a couple of dozen men, and hear whispered conversations in British, Australian and New Zealand accents. I glanced at my watch: 2330. Someone flashed 'Sugar-Baker' in Morse – *dit-dit-dit/dah-dit-dit-dit* – out to sea. A shape materialised out of the dark. It was a submarine, which approached the shore and stopped, its engine ticking over quietly in neutral. There was a splash, and a rubber dinghy appeared rowed by a couple of sailors, towing a floating line. Someone jumped out and a voice with the unmistakable authority of a naval officer said, 'Right, you Pongos. Strip off all your clothes and boots and leave your weapons on the beach. On the double!'

An Australian voice said, 'Strewth! Why do we have to do that, mate?' The English officer's voice said, 'Because we don't want any of your lice on our lovely clean sub, that's why. And the weapons are for the Cretan guerrillas. Now get a bloody move on. Swimmers: help the non-swimmers out along the floating line.'

We all stripped off and swam out to the submarine. We were hauled on board and directed below, where a cheerful sailor gave each man a blanket, a mug of hot cocoa containing a tot of rum, and a couple of doorstop sandwiches. As we munched away, Kenny and I couldn't stop grinning at each other like idiots – made it at last! A sudden vibration and a tilt of the sub showed that we were heading out to sea. I stuck a triumphant thumb up to Kenny.

**Part 4**

**John Gallagher: Egypt 1942**

## Chapter 10

In the barracks in Alexandria, I waited for the Captain from the Intelligence Corps to finish consulting his file. 'You were on the run for a year after the Battle of Crete, Corporal?'

'Aye sir,' I said. 'One year, two weeks and one day.'

'Splendid, splendid,' the Captain said. 'Very well done. The first thing to say is that you have been promoted to substantive Corporal with effect from the day you were evacuated from Crete.'

'Thank you, sir,' I said, thinking the extra money would be welcomed by Maeve back home.

'The second thing is that you have officially been Mentioned in Dispatches for your initiative in evading capture, and this will show on your service record. Congratulations!' I murmured my appreciation.

'Now,' the Captain continued, 'I see from the questionnaire you completed that you learned Greek while on the run.'

'Aye, sir.'

'How good is it? Is it fluent?'

'No sir, I couldn't say that. But I can get by well enough on a day-to-day basis. I wrote down a lot of key words, but I don't understand the grammar very well. But I could work out a wee bit of it.'

'How did you do that?'

'Well, sir, I remembered how Latin declined from school. And Greek seemed to work in the same sorta way.'

'You did Latin at school? In Glasgow?' the Captain said, failing to hide the surprise in his voice.

'Oh aye, sir.' Did the English prick think we were illiterate in Glasgow? 'And then what did you do?'

'I served my time as an apprentice joiner in the Fairfield

shipyard in Govan.'

'I see,' the Captain said, sliding a map of western Crete across the table. 'Now.

Could you describe your route from the day you took off?'

I traced my route on the map from Askyfou up to Korifi, then on to the plateaux of Tavri and Niato, over the White Mountains via the mitata at Pirou and Katsiveli to Therisso, up to Zourva, and south-west to Livada and Koustoyerako in Selino.

'I spent a lot of time with the shepherds, sir. And one time with a bandit.'

'A bandit? Really?'

'Aye, sir. Sheep-stealing in these mountains is like the national sport, and it's as common as dirt. But this sheep-thief had killed one of the guys who came after him, so that meant a vendetta. He …'

'A vendetta?'

'Aye, sir. Vendettas are the runner-up national sport in Crete. It means a permanent blood feud, and the island is littered with them. So, this guy was on the run for the rest of his life. He knew every inch of the White Mountains, the secret paths and hidden springs, and he moved only at night. He never put a foot wrong, and he never made a sound. I swear that man could smell danger.'

'Smell danger? What do you mean?'

'There was this one time, sir. We were on a remote high path in the middle of the night on our way to a spring, and the bandit stopped suddenly. He gestured ahead – Germans – and we turned round and crept up the mountain into cover. At dawn, we saw a German patrol heading downhill. They had been lying in an ambush position on the path all night long. How that man sensed they were there is beyond me. But he saved our bacon.'

'Remarkable.'

'It was sir. So, me and Kenny teamed up with the bandit for a wee while as we were all in the same boat, meaning on the run. I wouldn't say we were friends exactly, but we learned a lot from that man. And we moved from village to village.'

'How well do you know these villages?'

'Och, pretty well, sir. But I didn't like to spend time in any one of them, to protect the villagers, for the Germans took terrible reprisals in the villages which helped our lads on the run. And there were dozens of men up there – British, Aussies and Kiwis.'

'You must have made some friends amongst the Cretan villagers up there?.'

'Oh aye, sir. I've a lot of Cretan mates in these mountains.'

'And what was their attitude to you? And to the Germans?'

'The Cretans went out of their way to help us, sir. They couldn't do enough for us. They hate the Germans like poison because of their massacres, on the one hand, and the fact that they requisition all their sheep and goats and crops, on the other. The villagers are on our side and nae messing. If they were organised, they could cause the Germans a lot of trouble.'

The Captain leaned back, revolving his pencil between his fingers, and looked me right in the eye. 'That's exactly right. I won't beat about the bush, Corporal. You could be very useful to us. We're looking for volunteer NCOs who know the mountain terrain in Crete to be trained in guerrilla warfare and sent back to instruct the local partisans pending an Allied invasion of Crete. This is strictly on a voluntary basis. How would you feel about that?'

I leaned back and stared round the office. All I could think of was Maeve, and our baby son, Michael, whom I had never seen. I knew I loved Maeve and missed her dreadfully. And I knew that if I volunteered, I would be operating under the German Occupation of Crete, which was merciless, and I might not live to tell the tale. But I also knew that the Cretan villagers risked their lives daily in looking after the British soldiers on the run, and many had already given their lives. The silence went on for a long time.

'Well, Corporal, what do you think?'

The truth was I didn't know what to think. I forced myself to take a couple of deep breaths, focused my gaze on the officer, and said, "Aye. I'd be up for that, sir.'

'Jolly good show. Now. Before you go. This last letter you've written to your fiancée. You've included far too much detail about the Battle of Crete, your year on the run, and your evacuation. This would constitute very valuable information to an enemy agent. And many of the Gyppos *are* enemy agents. So, I'm afraid this letter cannot be sent, and I must destroy it. D'you follow?'

'Aye, sir.'

'You're quite the writer, Corporal. Where did you learn to write like that?.'

'At school in Glasgow, sir.'

'In Glasgow? 'No Mean City'? Razor gangs and all that? And yet you still learned how to write the English language?'

'Aye, sir. We did. In Glasgow, home of the razor gangs, where we studied Lamb and Addison and Steele, and wrote English compositions, at school. I even write letters home for some of the lads.'

'Really? Well, well. By all means write another letter to your fiancée, but avoid any details of our location, training or operations. Understood?'

'Aye, sir.'

'One final question. You wrote **S.W.A.L.K.** on the envelope. What on earth does that mean?'

I laughed. 'It means 'Sealed With a Loving Kiss,' sir. It's a joke, a kinna code the boys use to send wee personal messages to their womenfolk back home. There are others like **I.T.A.L.Y.** and **H.O.L.L.A.N.D.** They mean 'I Truly Always Love You,' and 'Hope Our Love Lasts and Never Dies.' And then there's **B.U.R.M.A.** and **E.G.Y.P.T.**'

'And what do they mean?'

I looked round the office and swallowed. 'Em, 'Be Undressed Ready My Angel', and, eh, 'Eager to Grab Your Pretty Tits.' Sir.'

The officer laughed. 'I see. Well, just remember, no more operational details in letters to your fiancée, or they will be censored. Carry on, Corporal.'

I saluted, about turned, and marched off. Bloody censorship, I thought. Quite the writer'? 'No mean city?' Patronising gett. Still fuming, I went straight to the NAAFI and bought a large notebook with hard covers. If I can't send official letters to Maeve without censorship, I'll damn well keep a journal and give it to her when I return home. Tickety-boo!

**Part 5**

**Andy Gallagher:  Crete April 2010**

## Chapter 11

Driving east from Hania on the Cretan national highway in his hired Panda 4 × 4 car, Andy spotted a road sign reading: SFAKIA, indicating a turning to the south. He remembered the Greek *mantinada,* the rhyming couplet:

Αν έχεις Σφακιανό φίλο, Κράτα ένα κομμάτι ξύλο.

'If you think you've got a friend from Sfakia/You'd better be carrying a wooden club!' – for the men from Sfakia were legendary warriors. Korifi was not far off the main road south to Hora Sfakion. As Andy turned south into the dramatic White Mountains, the sunlight was dazzling. It seemed to have a metallic shining quality which emphasised the rugged contours of the mountains and rendered them even more impenetrable.

The well-made road ascended in a series of spectacular Z-bends, but the old unmetalled road was still visible in places. That was the route of the retreating British and Commonwealth troops after the Battle of Crete in 1941. No wonder they were knackered, Andy thought. There was no shade and no water. Every now and then, a dirt road angled off up into the mountains, leading to the high-altitude mitata, or sheilings, of the shepherds.
    They were stone, igloo-shaped structures built with horizontal slabs of the local limestone.
    Andy often wondered how the shepherds constructed the domed roofs.

He soon reached the top of the pass to Korifi, parked the car at the side of the road beside an iconostasis, and got out. He closed the door and looked down. The view was spectacular.

Below him was a large green plateau more than a kilometre in diameter, rimmed by dramatic mountains, and filled with a colourful patchwork of cultivated fields and vineyards. In the middle, a picturesque ruined fort sat on the summit of a rocky hill. The fort was one of a line of such fortifications which the Turks had built as signal stations within eyesight of each other, all the way from the south coast of Crete to the north coast, after the 'Great Rebellion' of 1866. If the warlike Sfakiani rose in rebellion yet again, their Turkish rulers could signal the alarm by bonfire or semaphore or trumpet.

Andy drove slowly down the road which hugged the perimeter of the plateau, past a church and a road sign which said **KORIFI** in both Greek and English. It was riddled with bullet-holes – the local boys having some target practice with their toys. As he drove into the village, he saw a modern-looking taverna and Pension called 'Barba Manoussos.' He knew 'Barba' was the affectionate, familiar Greek for 'uncle,' or 'old man.' He pulled over and parked in the shade of a large mulberry tree. A sign indicated that the establishment had Wi-Fi.

There didn't seem to be anyone about, so Andy wandered out onto the plateau, passing an aloni, the communal circular threshing ground, and came to vineyards containing the villagers' vines – bordered by numerous chestnut and pine trees bathed in sunlight. The fields were dotted with open circular drystone reservoirs fully twenty feet deep, to collect winter snow-melt for the purposes of irrigation. A lot of hard manual work must have gone into their construction. The fields were carpeted with the wildflowers of spring, worked by numerous bees, and the air was full of their scent and that of herbs. The whole area was alive with small birds, and Andy spotted warblers, goldfinches, wheatears, and nuthatches. The plateau was surrounded by mountains, providing a breath-taking setting. It's screaming out to be filmed, Andy thought. It's impossibly beautiful.

He returned to the taverna and went inside. A footstep crunched behind him. Andy turned round to see a tall, elderly, barrel-chested man wearing a black sariki headband, a black shirt and breeches, stivania – knee-length black boots, and carrying a stout shepherd's crook. He had pure white hair, a jutting Ajax-cut white beard, a fiercely hooked nose, and glittering eyes. He twisted his extended thumb and forefinger in the Greek interrogative.

'Good morning,' Andy said in Greek. 'I'm looking for a room.'

'Of course,' said the tall Cretan. 'For how long?'

'Three or four days.'

'Come,' the Cretan said. He went to a desk, hung his crook from a nail, and took down a keyring with two keys on it. 'This way.' As they headed for the external stairs, Andy glimpsed a woman, her head and face hidden by a black scarf, working in the kitchen.

The Cretan unlocked a door and showed Andy a clean and comfortable room with a double bed, an ensuite toilet and shower, and a balcony looking out over the plateau.

'How much is it?' Andy said. 'Forty Euros a night.'

'Fine. I'll take it. Three nights, maybe four.'

'Entaxi.' Okay.

They went back downstairs, and Andy handed the Cretan his passport. 'Are you Barba Manoussos?'

'I am.'

'I am Andreas,' Andy said. Barba Manoussos studied Andy's passport and looked up sharply.

'Andreas Gallak-herr?' he said in Greek. 'From Scotland?.'

'Yes. That's right.'

Manoussos beckoned Andy over to a wall where there were several framed black-and-white photographs from the Second World War. Manoussos pointed to a photograph.

'Kapetan Yiannis Gallak-herr,' he said. 'From Scotland.'

The photograph showed his grandfather John in the middle of a group of heavily armed Andartes. Andy leaned forward and stared at the photo, absolutely flabbergasted. 'My God,' he said. 'Wait a minute.'

He went out to the car, took a plastic folder containing the studio photograph of his grandfather in Army uniform out of his laptop case, and compared it with the photo on the wall. There could be no doubt – it was one and the same man. Andy showed Manoussos the British Army photograph. 'He was my grandfather,' he said in Greek.

Manoussos examined the photograph, looked at the photo on the wall, then studied Andy's face, then exclaimed in Greek, 'Good Lord! You look just like him.' The elderly man enveloped Andy in a powerful bear-hug, kissed him on both cheeks, and said, 'Welcome to Korifi, Andrea. Your grandfather was a mighty warrior. My father Kostas fought beside him during the War. Come. Come with me. You have a car?'

Manoussos got into the car and directed Andy to the village cemetery, a few hundred yards up the road. He parked the car and followed the elderly man inside. The cemetery was full of white tombstones, many bearing photographs of the deceased person. That's a nice custom, Andy thought. He wandered about aimlessly as Manoussos sat on a tombstone, watched, and said nothing. Suddenly, right in front of Andy was a tombstone with the Greek legend:

YIANNIS SFAKIANAKIS 1920 – 2010
*HERO OF THE RESISTANCE 1941 – 1945*

The tombstone bore a photograph of a man with a luxuriant moustache, wearing the traditional black crocheted sariki, or headband, and a black shirt. But it was unmistakeably his Grandad, John. In front of the tombstone was a vase of fresh flowers. Andy gasped, wondering why his grandfather had a Greek surname. His head whirled with astonishment at the numerous questions which now demanded answers. Hoping there might be some in his grandfather's box, he took several photographs with his mobile phone realising it was true; he bore a distinct resemblance to his grandfather.

They drove back to the taverna, where Manoussos had a word with the woman in the kitchen. She glanced at Andy as he sat down and nodded. The old man came out, put a carafe of Tsichoudia, a couple of glasses and a bowl of walnuts on the table, and sat down opposite Andy. He poured two glasses. 'To the memory of Kapetan Yiannis.' They clinked glasses. 'Se yeia!'

'Se yeia!' Andy replied.

Manoussos rolled several walnuts together in his hand, crushed them open, and passed a few to Andy. I wouldn't like these hands round my neck, Andy thought. Two elderly men, obviously brothers, strolled into the taverna; they too were dressed in the traditional costume of mountain men. Manoussos introduced them as Yorgos and Stratis Ammoudarakis. When he explained that Andy was the grandson of Kapetan Yiannis, the brothers slapped him on the shoulder, and soon, a serious Tsichoudia-drinking session was under way. The three men told him stories about his grandfather's wartime exploits, but Andy only got about sixty per cent of them, for although he spoke good Greek, he wasn't acquainted with the ferocious Sfakiani dialect.

The woman appeared with a tray and laid out food at an adjoining table. There was singlino, the local smoked pork, chips, horta, Graviera cheese, yoghurt, bread, a Greek salad, and a large carafe of red wine.

'Ready,' the woman said in Greek.

Manoussos gestured to the men to move, and they all sat down to the food. He moved the dish of singlino in front of Andy. 'Help yourself,' he said as he poured tumblers of wine.

The woman sat down opposite Andy. 'This is Andreas from Scotland,' Manoussos said to her, 'the grandson of Kapetan Yiannis.' To Andy he said, 'My daughter, Maria.'

As Andy turned to look at her, she removed the black scarf from her face to reveal a stunning woman in her thirties, with the distinctive Cerulean blue eyes of Crete, and an unruly mop of black curls. She leaned back, looked Andy directly in the eye, smiled, and shook his hand firmly. 'Welcome to Korifi, Andrea,' she said in English. 'I am pleased to meet you. Your grandfather was a very famous man in this area during the War.'

Andy couldn't keep his eyes off Maria. She was wearing a wedding-ring on her right hand. 'Thank you, thank you,' he stuttered.

They all clinked glasses. While the men took a good swig of wine, Maria took only a sip. She smiled and said in English, 'Do you like the wine? It is our own, we make it.'

'Oh yes, yes,' Andy said.

A little later, the men were cheerfully tipsy, and the table was covered with the wreckage of the meal. Manoussos poured more wine as Maria cleared the table. To Andy's horror, Manoussos suddenly produced a pistol from his waistband, followed by Stratis and Yorgos. Frightened, Andy ducked, but the men aimed off to one side over the empty plateau and blasted off a round or two. In the background, Maria watched with a pained look on her face.

'Here, have a go,' Manoussos said, passing his pistol to Andy, who took it gingerly, watched like a hawk by the village men. In for a penny, in for a pound. He aimed out over the plateau and fired. *Bang!* 'First time,' he said. The men clapped him on the shoulder, exclaiming, 'Bravo, Andrea!'

There was a brief scowl of distaste for all this boys-and-their-toys display on Maria's face. But there was more to it than that. Her face showed real pain. She turned on her heel abruptly and vanished into the kitchen. Stratis and Yorgos got up and left the taverna for their siesta. Manoussos turned to Andy and said, 'So, Andrea. What brings you to Korifi?'

Andy handed the old man the letter from Themia and translated it into Greek.

'My father, Michael, John's son, is too unwell to come to Crete,' he said. 'I have come instead to collect this box of papers and take it home to him.'

'I see,' Manoussos said.

Maria re-appeared. 'Themia was my father's cousin,' she

said. 'She died only a few weeks ago.'

'Oh, my goodness. Oh dear, I had no idea. I'm very sorry to hear that.'

'Thank you. To tell you the truth, I don't think she wanted to live any more after her husband died.'

'I see. Now I get the connection. But wait a minute, if Themia was your aunt, you must have known my grandfather, John – Yiannis, that is.'

'Yes, of course. I knew him very well. Although we weren't blood relations, he was my aunt's husband, after all.'

'I see. What, what was he like? What kind of a man was he?'

Maria didn't hesitate. 'He was a lovely man, a very fine man. He was kind and friendly, he had a terrific sense of humour, he was a hard-working shepherd,

and was very well respected both in this village, and Sfakia at large. He had great filotimo.'

Andy nodded. Filotimo was a difficult concept to translate into English but had profound meaning in Greek. It encapsulated notions of dignity, self-worth, pride in family and community, and behaving well. Perhaps the nearest you could get to it in English was to say that a man who had filotimo was an honourable man.

'Yes,' Manoussos said. 'Kapetan Yiannis was a true pallikari. He was one of us.'

This was another of these difficult Greek words. Essentially, a pallikari was a courageous, daring, and manly young warrior, one who never feared danger, and loved wine, women and song. It looks like my grandad was something else, Andy thought.

'I see,' he said. 'Do you have his box?'

Maria glanced at her father, who nodded. Manoussos stood up and said, 'I will see you later, Andrea.'

Maria vanished into the kitchen. She reappeared a moment later carrying a large black tin box, walking with the distinctive, dignified, erect carriage of Cretan women.

'What's in it?' Andy said.

'I don't know,' Maria said.

Andy took it and put it on the table. It was padlocked. 'Do you have the key?'

'No. We don't know where the key is. We couldn't find it amongst my aunt's things.'

'Not to worry,' Andy said. 'We'll open it back in Scotland.'

'Aren't you going to open it here?' Maria said. 'No. It's for my father, so he should open it.'

Maria nodded agreement. She sat down and studied Andy for a moment. 'You speak very good Greek, Andreas.'

'I'm a Professor of Classics at the University of Glasgow and I've travelled extensively in Crete.'

'You're a classicist?'

'Yes.'

'Oh no, not another one,' Maria said, with a mischievous grin. 'Not another one?'

'Greece is full of English classicists who on the one hand, tell us about our ancient history, and on the other, tell us we aren't capable custodians of it.'

'That's not fair, Maria.'

'Oh, is that so? I was once at a party in the British Archaeological School in Athens, and an eighteen-year-old English undergraduate who couldn't speak a word of Greek told me that the Elgin Marbles would never be returned because we couldn't look after them. The marbles which were stolen from the Parthenon by a fellow countryman of yours.'

'I happen to believe that the Elgin Marbles should be returned to Athens and have said so in public in Britain.'

'How very generous of you.' Maria said, leaning back in her chair. 'Maria, that's not ...'

'Let's face it, the whole role of Britain relative to Greece since the founding of the Greek state has been one of manipulation and betrayal – particularly during and after the Second World War.'

'That really is a bit over the top.'

'You think so? I suppose you also think that the British liberated Greece at the end of 1944 and saved it from communism? Let me tell you something. Greece was liberated by ELAS and other resistance groups before the British Army even arrived.'

'Maria, I know. I agree with you. I don't see the point of …'

'The point is that we Greeks have every reason not to trust the British. And that is even more true of Crete during the War.'

'But not my grandfather, apparently?'

'He was different,' Maria snapped. 'He was one of us.' She stood up, turned on her heel, and strode back into the kitchen.

Later, Andy rang his father. When Michael answered, Andy said, 'Hello Dad, it's me.'

'Hi son. How's it going?'

'Well, I'm in the village of Korifi and I've got your father's box. It's padlocked so I'll bring it home for you to open. But what I've learned already is amazing. It seems that your father was some kind of guerrilla commander up here in the mountains during the War. He was called Kapetan Yiannis – Captain John – and appears to have been quite famous locally, a bit of a hero, in fact. I'm hoping the full story is in the box.'

## Chapter 12

A sudden loud peal of Greek Orthodox Church bells in an irregular rhythm woke Andy. He came to with a start and listened, initially disoriented, then grinned as he recognised what had woken him. He swung his legs out of bed, pulled the curtains, stepped out onto the balcony, and looked out over the plateau which was bathed in morning sunlight. There was a clatter of plates and the murmur of conversation from the taverna below him. He dressed and went down the stairs to the taverna where Maria greeted him and served him with a breakfast of freshly-squeezed orange juice, toast, fried eggs, and feta cheese.

When he finished and Maria had cleared up, Andy spread his map out on the table and beckoned Manoussos over.

'Can you show me where my grandfather operated during the War?' Andy said.

Manoussos sat down, and Maria listened in the background.

Manoussos pointed at the map. 'We are here. The runners for the British officers would come over this way, from Asi Gonia down to Korifi, and our people would look after them.'

'Was there a German garrison in Korifi?'

'No. There was one nearby, in Askyfou. But only a platoon. They were watched day and night, so the Andartes always knew what they were up to. The runners would continue over this way, up to Niato, and out to the west where your grandfather had his band. The Germans went there at their peril, for our people always knew when they were coming, and which route they were taking.'

'So, the next leg from here was up the bridlepath to

Niato?'

'Get in my agrotikon and I'll show you.' Manoussos got up, went over to his pickup truck, and opened the door.

'Are you going up to the Madares?' Maria said, referring to the high-altitude summer grazing grounds of the sheep and goats.

'Yes,' Andy said.

'These are very dangerous mountains, you know. Very. Be careful.'

Andy didn't like the condescending tone of her voice, and retorted, 'If my grandfather could survive up there, I can. And we also have dangerous mountains in Scotland, you know.'

A little later, Manoussos stopped his pickup on the Niato plateau, and he and Andy got out. The old man pointed up at the peak towering over them.

'Kastro,' he said. The Fortress, Andy translated in his head – aptly named.

'The runners would climb up over the shoulder of Kastro,' Manoussos said, 'and carry on west towards the Omalos plateau.'

They would be heading into a trackless stony wilderness, Andy thought. You'd need to know what you were doing in there; it wasn't for the faint-hearted.

A few days later, Andy parked his Fiat Panda in the shade of a tree on the Niato plateau. He wore walking boots and a sun hat, had binoculars slung round his neck and a day bag on his back. He opened his telescopic walking poles and set off across the plateau towards Kastro. The ascent was steep, the terrain was the usual shattered grey limestone, but there did not appear to be any difficult obstacles. The route was clear: a zigzag up to the ridge and then straight up to the summit.

An hour later, Andy reached the summit, to find a trig point, a small concrete pillar used for surveying. Heaving a sigh of relief, he took off his day bag and took a swig from his water bottle. He scanned all three hundred and sixty degrees around him with his binoculars. Away to the west lay the stony wilderness of the White Mountains, punctuated by dramatic and forbidding peaks. In the distance, he could see the north coast of Crete glittering in the hard metallic light. The silence at the top of the mountain was uncanny. There wasn't the clink of a sheep's bell, the chirrup of a bird, or the sigh of a breeze. Tipota. Nothing. Just a leaden and oppressive silence. Andy sat down with his back to the trig point, facing west, and took a packet of sandwiches out of his day bag. Using his compass, he oriented his map and looked west to an imposing peak.

'Grias Soros,' he murmured.

He took out a sandwich and ate while admiring the view. These mountains are wild, he thought, real badlands. You'd need a good head in there.

As Andy came off the slope of Kastro onto the Niato plateau, a large, savage dog streaked towards him, barking furiously. Andy gulped and reversed one of his walking poles like a sword, the dog lunged at him, and he fell over backwards, snapping the pole. There was a yell and a piercing whistle in the distance, and the dog ran away. Andy saw Yorgos and Stratis outside a mitato at the edge of the plateau, milking sheep. They waved him over.

'Andrea,' Yorgos shouted, 'Come on over.'

Andy walked over. Yorgos explained that the dog was there to guard against sheep-thieves. The sheep-pen was constructed of a continuous drystone wall shaped like a bottle and was full of sheep. Inside, a young boy drove a couple of sheep at a time towards the neck of the bottle, where Yorgos and Stratis stood. They bent over, seized the sheep between their thighs, heads pointing behind them, and milked their udders into a large copper cauldron set in a saucer-shaped hole in a flat rock on the ground.

Yorgos gestured to Andy to have a go. He put his day bag, binoculars and walking poles aside, and approached tentatively. He grabbed a sheep by its oily wool, managed to get it between his thighs, and grabbed its teats, but the animal bucked like mad and bolted, sending Andy flying. Yorgos, Stratis and the boy fell about laughing as the embarrassed Andy picked himself up, gasping with pain.

'You're far too clean,' Stratis said, 'you're wearing clean clothes, so you don't smell right, and the sheep is frightened. Look.' He gestured towards his old Greek Army combat trousers greasy with the oil from the sheep's wool and impregnated with their scent.

'Ah, I see,' Andy said.

Stratis gave him an old pair of combat trousers and Andy tugged them on over his lightweight walking trousers. He rubbed his hands on the combat trousers until they were greasy, grabbed a sheep and tried again. Although the sheep fought his grip, he managed to get a little milk out of it, and grinned triumphantly as the shepherds congratulated him.

Yorgos filled a tin mug from the foaming milk in the basin and offered it to him. Andy drank the fresh sheep's milk; to his surprise, he enjoyed it. If Eilidh could see me now, he thought, her father the looney professor pretending he was a shepherd!

They all went into the mitato, Stratis carrying the cauldron of milk. He introduced the boy as Mitsos, their twelve-year-old nephew, who was learning the shepherd's trade. There wouldn't be many twelve-year-olds in Scotland doing such work, Andy thought. As the boy lit a fire of twigs in a hole in the outside wall, Stratis placed the cauldron on a stand above the fire. Andy looked around. There were three sleeping bunks made of drystone rocks, with mattresses of dried thyme bushes and hand-woven rugs. Several books lay on one of the beds, including the *Erotokritos,* the 17th century Cretan courtly epic, and the *Thessaloniki Programme*, the

Syriza Party manifesto. So Stratis and Yorgos are Lefties, Andy thought – good to know. A handmade shelf contained a radio, a couple of camping-gas lamps, and boxes of pills and syringes for the sheep. Two shotguns hung from pegs driven into the wall, where there was also a calendar and a couple of icons of the Panayeia, the Virgin Mary and Child. Food, plates, and cutlery were stacked on the table, which was a cedar tree split in half lengthwise. Cosy and neat, Andy thought, a home from home.

Yorgos laid out a couple of strips of kitchen roll on the table, and put bread, Graviera cheese, cold boiled mutton, apples, and a jug of wine on them. 'Sit, sit,' he said to Andy, pouring him a tumbler of wine as Stratis continued to stir the milk, which was now simmering. Yorgos poured himself some wine, and they clinked glasses. He pulled a Cretan winged knife from his belt and cut himself a chunk of mutton.

'My father told me many stories about your grandfather,' Yorgos said. 'He fought with him during the War. They killed many Germans. The Germans didn't know the mountains like us, so it was easy for us to ambush them.'

'Of course,' Andy said.

Mitsos took over the stirring, and Stratis sat down to eat. Andy looked in the cauldron: the milk was beginning to solidify. Yorgos pulled a rifle out from under a rug on the bed. It had been well-cared-for.

'Your grandfather arranged a parachute drop of arms for us,' Yorgos said, 'in the winter when this plateau was covered with snow. That way, the rifles wouldn't get damaged. Come.'

They went outside. Yorgos pointed to a white rock about three hundred metres away. 'The white boulder. Do you see it?'

'Yes.'

Yorgos worked the rifle-bolt, aimed, and fired, all in one

fluid movement. A chip of rock flew off the boulder. Andy gasped. 'Wow!'

Yorgos handed Andy the rifle. It was the first time in Andy's life that he had ever handled one. He cocked it clumsily, brought it to his shoulder, aimed, fired, and was surprised at the strength of the recoil. He missed the boulder by a couple of metres. Stratis appeared, took the rifle, aimed, and fired. Another chip of rock flew off the boulder.

'Bravo,' Andy said.

Yorgos grinned. 'You're not used to it,' he said. 'We are.'

'I can see that,' Andy said. He picked up his day bag, slung it on his back, and picked up his walking poles. Stratis gestured, *wait,* went into the mitato, and came out again with a shepherd's crook made from Zelkova wood, which he gave to Andy.

'A gift,' he said.

Andy was gobsmacked. 'Thank you. Thank you very much.'

'Parakalo,' Stratis said.

Andy took off his day bag, collapsed his walking poles, put them in a side pocket and slung the bag back on his back again. He flourished the crook, grinned, and said in New Testament Greek, ' Εγώ είμαι ο πημήν ο καλός και γιγνώσκω τα εμά καί γιγνώσκομαι υπό των εμών.' I am the good shepherd; I know my sheep and they know me.

Yorgos and Stratis roared with laughter. 'Bravo, Andrea!' Yorgos said.

'Go well,' Stratis added.

Manoussos looked up from his newspaper as Andy stepped into the taverna. 'Welcome to Andreas,' he said. 'Ah-ha. You've got a good shepherd's crook.

Where did you get that?'

'It was a present from Stratis,' Andy said. 'You've been up to Niato?'

'Yes. And to the summit of Kastro.'

Manoussos gave Andy a long look. 'Kastro? The summit? Really?.'

'Really.' Andy could see that the old man didn't believe him.

'What did you find up there?'

Andy didn't know the Greek for 'trig point,' so he sketched the shape with his hands. 'A thing like this made of concrete.'

'Mia piramida.'

'Mia piramida. Exactly.'

Manoussos got to his feet and slapped Andy on the back. 'Bravo, Andrea! I built that piramida. I built every piramida in the White Mountains. I got the contract from the Army. Come, let's eat.'

As Manoussos, Maria and Andy finished their meal, she said in English, 'My father tells me that you now have a shepherd's crook.'

'Yes,' Andy said. 'Stratis gave it to me. What's the local word for a crook?.'

'Ee katsouna. Do you want to learn some words and phrases in Sfakiani?.'

'Yes. Yes, I would like that very much.'

'I will teach you some tomorrow afternoon. Here at five o'clock. Entaxi?.'

'Entaxi.' Okay.

'I'm going to teach Andreas some Sfakiani,' Maria said to her father in Greek. 'Good idea,' Manoussos said.

Maria got up and smiled at Andy. This time her smile had some warmth in it. 'You speak very good English, Maria,' Andy said.

'I'm an English teacher. I studied English at the University of Athens. And I did a placement in London, in Chelsea.'

'My condolences.'

Maria laughed as she collected the dirty dishes and took

them into the kitchen.

Manoussos stared into space for some time, twirling his komboloi, his worry-beads, round and round his fingers.

'Things have changed a lot in my lifetime, Andrea,' he said. 'In the olden days, if a woman was widowed, that was that. She was a widow for the rest of her life. Always dressed in black. Yes.' He twirled his worry-beads again, click-clack. 'But times have changed. I don't think that it's necessary for a woman to be a widow for the rest of her life these days, especially a young woman. I think she should be allowed to remarry and find happiness again. Yes.' Manoussos twirled his worry-beads again. 'What do you think?'

'Oh yes,' Andy said. 'Yes. Absolutely.'

Manoussos got to his feet and headed off for his siesta. What on earth is the old bugger up to? Andy thought. Then he suddenly realised to his surprise that he hadn't thought about Alison once since arriving in Korifi. And with a flash of guilt, he wondered if Eilidh would like it in Korifi, for the girl was no mean hillwalker.

## Chapter 13

A couple of days later, Andy loped down the mountain on the bridlepath to the village, using his shepherd's crook for balance. As he passed above the cemetery, he paused to admire the view. Suddenly, he heard a chilling keening from below. In the cemetery, Maria was putting fresh flowers in a vase beside a tombstone, her shoulders convulsed with her weeping, her whole body rocking backwards and forwards in terrible grief, crying out incomprehensible words. Andy's face clenched with sympathy for Maria – the poor woman. But who could the dead person be? An unexpected tear trickled down Andy's cheek as he tiptoed away, not wanting to disturb Maria's desolation.

In the evening, Andy asked Manoussos for whom Maria was grieving.

'Her husband,' the old man said. His baleful look convinced Andy not to ask any more questions.

Andy wrapped a towel round the tin box and fitted it into his suitcase, stuffing clothes round it before shutting the lid and locking it. He turned his laptop off and put it in its case. Then he carried both down the stair and put them in the boot of his car, watched by Manoussos and Maria. Andy shut the boot, stepped up to Manoussos and held out his hand.

'Thank you, Barba,' Andy said. 'Thank you for everything.'

'Don't mention it,' Manoussos said. 'Safe home to your own country.' He shook Andy's hand.

'I will be back,' Andy said.

'You will be welcome,' Manoussos said.

Andy turned to Maria. 'Thank you too, Maria.' He extended his hand, which Maria shook.

'Safe journey,' she said.

Andy took her hand in both of his, very gently. 'I am sorry for your loss. My condolences.' He wanted to say something more comforting, but he didn't know what to say. Maria blinked and smiled sadly.

'Thank you, Andrea,' she said. 'Thank you.'

Andy got in his car, started it, and drove off with a couple of toots on the horn, and a wave from the window. Manoussos and Maria waved back.

Andy stopped his car at a vantage point, got out, and admired the dramatic view of the White Mountains. He sighed deeply. This place suited him very well. It was so beautiful.

And peaceful. And he was going back to trouble and strife in Glasgow. He'd much rather have stayed here.

**Part 6**

**John Gallagher: Palestine & Crete, 1942**

## Chapter 14

Kenny Mackenzie had also volunteered for the Guerrilla Warfare course, so he and I were sent to Palestine by train together, in August 1942. There we were in the Holy Land! The Guerrilla Warfare School was in an old monastery on Mount Carmel with great views of the Bay of Haifa – all very biblical. The trainees were being schooled to go back into Occupied Europe and train the Resistance movements. I was expecting to be sent back to Crete as I'd been getting special Greek lessons. There was quite a mix of NCOs and officers. The latter were posh characters we called 'Ruperts,' who all seemed to have been university lecturers in Archaeology or Classics before the War. I didn't think these Ruperts would have lasted a week with the Argylls! But there was a Kiwi Sergeant called Perkins in our Greek group who was very impressive. He wasn't very talkative but seemed fearless and indestructible. I was surprised he wasn't an officer, in fact.

The training was a more focused version of the Commando course. We spent a lot of time learning how to blow up trains and bridges. We also did a lot of demanding night navigation and exercises. Although I had learned how to shoot from the hip with a pistol at Achnacarry, we spent more time here on what was called point-shooting, which meant firing by instinct rather than by aimed shots. We also got lectures on the politics of the different Resistance movements. My group, which was aimed at Greece, got a lecture from one of these Ruperts with a double-barrelled name and a posh English accent. He seemed to have a bee in his bonnet about the Greek Andartes all being Communists with a sinister postwar agenda. When I said I hadn't seen much evidence of that in a year on the run in Crete, he glared at me and said, 'Don't be so bloody naive, Corporal. You're not on the Red Clyde now preaching to the converted.' I realised it would be smart to keep my mouth shut, as that officer was obviously a mental Tory and a bampot with it.

We also did a lot more unarmed combat training, but the rule was: no kicking, no biting, no gouging. In one of these sessions, a Rupert jabbed me in the eyes with two fingers when the Instructor wasn't looking. I remembered my dad's saying ...

*If at first you don't succeed,
In with the boot and in with the heid –*

So I gave him a Glasgow kiss and kneed him in the balls. That sorted him out.

There was one small group which intrigued me. They were German and Austrian Jews, and they really were tough guys, for they knew they were sliced bread if they get caught by Gerry. Although they kept themselves to themselves, I retained a distinct impression that they had a hidden agenda.

Anyway, I finished the course successfully, and was then sent on a parachute course at a place called Ramat Dan. I also passed this course and was promoted to Sergeant. I was pleased about that, for it meant more money in the kitty to send to Maeve. I hadn't been told officially yet where I was going to be sent, but odds on it would be back to Crete. In the meantime, I was attached to an officer called Major Ford, who knew his stuff. While it was all very exciting in Palestine, I still worried about Maeve every day. There was no saying when the War would end, so I hadn't a clue when I would see her again and hold her in my arms. That's all I wanted – to be with Maeve and our wean Michael.

## Chapter 15

Inside the Liberator bomber on the way to Crete, it was freezing, even although Major Ford and I were wearing padded Sidcot flying suits. So, we wrapped ourselves in as many blankets as we could find. The Major dozed off immediately and I marvelled at how he could sleep through the roar of the engines. Beside him was the container carrying the three metal canisters with our wireless, weapons, and personal kit. I must have nodded off myself, for the next thing I knew, the Royal New Zealand Air Force dispatcher was shaking me and telling me we were twenty minutes from the Dropping Zone.

Major Ford and I put on our solid rubber helmets. The dispatcher hooked our static lines onto the strong-point and tugged them to demonstrate that they were attached. The aircraft tilted and swung in a large circle. Unwieldy in all my equipment, I hung onto a strut. The dispatcher spoke into his intercom, turned to me and held up five fingers. Bending down, he opened the circular hatch-cover in the floor of the plane. A blast of cold air whipped in, and there was a strong whine from the slipstream round the hatch. The roar of the engines was deafening. I shivered despite myself.

The snow-covered White Mountains sailed past below, lit up with an eerie glow from the full moon. With some difficulty, I sat down with my legs hanging out of the hatch, the slipstream whining and tugging at my trousers. Mountain tops rose up on either side of the plane – we must be flying into a valley. The Liberator's exhausts made a series of sharp reports as the engines were throttled down. I caught a glimpse of a T-shape formed by nine bonfires, and was thankful that we had arrived at the correct DZ. I just hoped that it was Andartes rather than Germans waiting down below. The red light went on. I braced myself. Ten seconds to go. Red on, green on – go!

A moment later, I was dangling in space, whipped away in a sitting position and buffeted by the slipstream. There was a jerk, a tug in my armpits, and a *plop!* as the canopy opened, and the training took over. Looking up, I checked that my parachute was open, and wriggled into position, feet vertically below me, even although I was still swinging violently. The major floated down behind me, followed by the chute with our container. The Liberator was banking and climbing over the mountains, the four blue flames from its exhausts clearly visible.

The pendulum motion ceased, and I looked down. The stillness was total. The bonfires blazed down below, surrounded by a group of tiny men. The reflected moonlight was so intense that it seemed as if the snow was glowing. Suddenly, I whooshed into deep powder snow, my parachute canopy collapsing silently over me. Staggering to my feet, I spat snow out of my mouth and shook myself. Good, a perfect safe landing. I whacked the release button of my harness with the heel of my hand, and as I started to roll up my chute looked around. Major Ford was doing the same fifty yards away, the parachute with the container landing just beyond him, and the bonfires were guttering out. There was the rapid crunch of boots on snow, and I was seized in a hairy embrace as a group of Andartes rushed up to welcome us.

I was surprised but delighted to find that one of the reception party was Themia, now wearing Greek Army trousers and carrying a British Army Lee-Enfield .303 rifle. She greeted me like a long-lost friend and kissed me on both cheeks. But I was fair taken aback when she asked me if she could have my silk parachute – to make underclothes, she explained.

As we went down to Korifi, Themia explained that following the executions in the village, she wanted revenge. 'The Germans murdered my father and my brother,' she said, 'so all I wanted was to kill as many of these bastards as possible.' So did two of the other village women whose men had been killed. They went to the Kapetan of the local ELAS band and asked to join. He had just laughed and said that women couldn't become Andartes, that was men's work. So Themia said if you don't give us rifles and train us, we will take our men's shotguns and go down the mountain and kill the first Germans we see. The Kapetan didn't like that, she explained, for he knew the result would be further reprisals in Korifi. But we were adamant. So eventually he accepted us into his band, and we started training.

Simple as that. I was well impressed with Themia's and the other village women's determination.

When we reached the village in the middle of the night, an impromptu welcoming party was organized. I was pleased that we were able to contribute with some bars of chocolate and a bottle of whisky. Later, amidst a volley of ribald jokes in Sfakiani which I didn't get, Themia took me to her house, showed me into the bedroom, smiled goodnight, and shut the door.

In the morning, there was a bit of an argument amongst the Andartes, with Themia being emphatic about something. I couldn't follow it for they were all speaking in dialect loudly and quickly. The upshot of it was that while I was in Korifi, I was going to lodge with Themia, for she had a spare room – the room of her late father. I can't say I was displeased.

## Chapter 16

My job was to train the Andartes in all the usual aspects of guerrilla soldiering: small arms, fire-and-movement, ambush drills, sabotage and demolition, moving at night, and so on. In some senses, it wasn't that difficult for the men – and quite a lot of the women too – were natural warriors. They were already fighting the Turks, and before that the Venetians, for hundreds of years before the Germans arrived. And the men were hunters. They were naturals at fieldcraft, excellent shots, and very fit. But in military terms, they lacked any fire discipline, so I had a hard job controlling them.

It was funny but I managed to get on quite well with my spoken Greek. I had learned the basics of the grammar on the course at the Guerrilla Warfare School, and I had brought a Greek dictionary with me. I soon learned a lot of the local dialect, and the boys gave me a nickname: Kapetan Yiannis, which means Captain John. But I wasn't sure if they were taking the mickey. The women fighters were easily as tough as the men, but a lot better looking – like Themia. Despite that, all I could think about was Maeve and our wean Michael and wonder when on earth I was going to get home to see them. I wondered if wee Michael was talking yet. If he was, I hoped he was saying Celtic forra Cup!

There was talk of an invasion of Crete to force the Germans to surrender but I thought that would be a near impossible job, because there was a huge garrison, and they were well-armed with heavy weapons and armoured cars. It was difficult for us to keep the lid on the Andartes as they were spoiling for a fight.

My guide was Kostas Sfakianakis, a shepherd from Korifi.

He was physically and mentally tough, and phenomenally fit. One evening, he invited me to a krasáki, a cooked meal with lashings of wine, with the local Andartes ELAS band. I was keen to go as it would give me a chance to meet and assess these left-wing partisans.

We climbed up deep into the forest above Korifi, and I smelled it before I saw anything, a rich smell of stewing meat. We entered a clearing deep in the forest, where a sweating cook worked over a cauldron suspended from a tripod over a fire. Twenty or so heavily armed Andartes sat around makeshift tables drinking wine, their conversation carried on at a roar. It looked like a medieval feast, something out of Robin Hood and his Merrie Men.

We sat at a table full of fresh bread, jugs of wine, dishes of yoghurt, and a large bowl of salad with olives and a soft white cheese called Misithra. Themia and a couple of other young female Andartisses were in the company. She smiled her welcome. Kostas introduced me to Kapetan Manolis, the leader of the band. He was a middle-aged but imposing man wearing a black sariki tasselled headband, a magnificently embroidered waistcoat with numerous loops and straps, several Greek military medals, stivania jackboots up to his knees, and a black cummerbund in which were stuffed a winged Cretan knife, and a Luger pistol.

Manolis poured large glasses of wine and offered me a loaf of bread – real wheaten bread as opposed to Bobota. The toast was: To Victory. I could drink to that!

The cook put a large steaming bowl of lamb stew and a large dish of rice on the table.

The Andartes got tore in, ripping the meat off the bones with their teeth, scraping the remains off with their knives, cracking the bones and sucking out the marrow, dunking their bread in the gravy, and drinking great gulps of wine. I did the same. When in Crete …

After the meal, Manolis told us about the campaign in the

snow of Epirus in the winter of 1940/1941 against the despised Italian invaders, the Makaronades, the 'macaroni-bashers.' He had been a Sergeant-Major.

'When we were fighting in the snow in defence of the motherland,' he said to me, 'the King, Glucksberg, ran away. We stayed to resist the German and Italian invaders, and we now fight to liberate our country. But we will also resist the return of the King until an election is taken amongst the Greek people to decide his future. And I can tell you now that the Greek people do not want the return of Glucksberg.'

I had already realised that the Greek King was very unpopular in Crete, but didn't know why. 'Why don't you want the King back?' I asked.

Manolis snorted. 'Because he sided with the dictator General Metaxas, and dissolved parliament, which was illegal. And …'

'... and he also dissolved the trade unions, imprisoned labour leaders, and made strikes illegal,' Themia chimed in. 'He supported the dictatorship.'

'Dissolved the trade unions and imprisoned labour leaders?' I said. 'That's ready heavy.'

'And he persecuted the KKE.,' Themia added. 'He sent hundreds of Communists into exile on islands in the Aegean.'

I knew that the KKE was the Greek Communist Party, but that was about it. I knew nothing about its persecution and internal exile. It sounded like the King and Metaxas were nasty pieces of work. Well, so much for His Greek Majesty! Given my socialist background, I could sympathise with that feeling. It was becoming obvious to me that these ELAS Andartes were good comrades, and I was pleased to be in their company. They seemed to be natural democrats. The night ended with the men singing the ELAS anthem, 'O Antartis Tou ELAS.' As the sonorous cadence rolled through the forest, I translated the words in my head:

*With my rifle at the shoulder,*

*In cities, plains and villages, I clear the road for freedom,
I lay her bay-leaves, and she passes.*

I knew that bay-leaves were symbols of honour and glory, and reflected that such men could never be defeated. To my surprise, Manolis asked me if I could contribute a song. 'Yes,' I said, 'I can.' I sang the British Army's satiric song:

*Hitler has only got one ball.
Rommel has two but very small.
Himmler has something similar.
But poor old Goebbels has no balls at all.*

The Andartes loved it and were quick to learn the words! The Andartes lacked any sense of fire control. This was particularly true of the Bren-gunners who, instead of firing controlled bursts of three or four rounds, tended to hang onto the trigger and empty the magazine in one long burst. It took me a long time to get the Andartes to realize that they were wasting ammunition.

The Andartes were also volatile in ambush drills, and prone to fire far too early before the simulated enemy had reached the designated killing ground. I also found that when training with hand-grenades, they were likely to throw the grenade without sighting the target, and duck down immediately without seeing where it landed. I had to haul them back on their feet to watch where it landed before ducking for cover. The fact of the matter was that these young men were scared.

On one occasion, a young Andarte, perhaps fifteen years old, threw the pin at the target and dropped the grenade at my feet. Quick as a flash, I flipped the grenade over the drystone dyke and hurled the Andarte to the ground just as it exploded a yard away on the other side of the wall. I realized that the boy was left-handed, and made him repeat the drill, this time successfully.

Themia and the other young women in the local band were in no respects inferior to the men, who were impetuous to a degree. Indeed, the women listened much more carefully and learned more quickly. When they did fire-and-movement exercises, Themia internalized the principles of an interlocking fire-group and an assault-group very rapidly. I found the young widow in my company quite a lot as she sought me out to ask intelligent questions. I soon realised that there was more than intelligence to her company – she fancied me. While she was gorgeous, I had to remember I was spoken for back in Glasgow, so I tried to keep Themia at a distance because I felt guilty about the fact that I fancied her too. But this wasn't so easy in the close confines of a guerrilla band.

## Chapter 17

A week or so later, Major Ford went off to a meeting with another SOE officer in the village of Askyfou. As my band had just completed a weapons training exercise successfully, I gave everyone a couple of days off. I decided to explore Korifi which I had been unable to do so far as I was too busy. I strolled out onto the plateau, passing an aloni, the circular threshing ground, and remembered that was where Kenny and I had slept the night before the massacre. The air was fresh and fragrant, and the sunlight shimmered. I came to vineyards containing the villagers' vines – some had already been trimmed. There was a mosaic of cultivated fields of potatoes, wheat, barley, and beans, bordered by numerous chestnut, pine and plane trees bathed in spring sunlight. The plateau was dotted with open circular drystone reservoirs fully twenty feet deep, to collect winter snowmelt for the purposes of irrigation. A lot of hard manual work must have gone into their construction. The fields were carpeted with the wildflowers of spring, numerous bees were working them, and the air was full of their scent and that of herbs – particularly thyme and oregano. The plateau was surrounded by mountains, providing a breath-taking and impossibly bonny setting.

Then my eye was caught by something at the side of the dirt road to Askyfou. I bent down and saw a miniature Orthodox chapel built of pebbles, on a flat rock. It must have been built by a shepherd to pass the lonely hours. I studied it closely. It was totally of drystone construction, with no mortar or mud. That's magic, I thought. Where's your Meccano now?

The next day, after checking that there were no Germans

about, I decided to climb the peak of Kastro, the mountain which towered over the village. The ascent was steep, the terrain was the usual shattered, grey limestone, but there didn't appear to be any difficult obstacles. The route was clear: a zigzag up to the ridge and then straight up to the summit. The only problem was that the rock was so shattered that you kept sliding back.

An hour later, I reached the summit, and heaving a sigh of relief, took a swig from my water bottle. I looked round through three hundred and sixty degrees with my binoculars.

Away to the west lay the stony wilderness of the White Mountains, punctuated by dramatic and forbidding peaks. In the distance, I could see the north coast of Crete glittering in the hard metallic light. The silence at the top of the mountain was uncanny. There wasn't the clink of a sheep's bell, the chirrup of a bird, or the sigh of a breeze. Nothing. Just a leaden and oppressive silence. Using my compass, I oriented my map and looked west to an imposing peak – Grias Soros. These mountains were savage, real badlands. No wonder the Germans didn't like to come up here. It was a guerrilla's paradise, and the shepherds knew every inch of this wilderness.

As I approached the village, I saw a man coming towards me on the path. He was dressed differently from the villagers, wearing a collar-and-tie, a respectable jacket, and neatly pressed trousers. He was the man who had paused outside Thanassis' house on our original encounter. He stopped and said, 'Ah, you must be Kapetan Yiannis. Welcome.' We shook hands. It wasn't a warm shake.

'I'm Dimitris Mavridakis,' he said in good English. 'I'm pleased you're here to train our men to fight the Germans.'

'Thank you,' I said. 'You speak very good English, sir. Are you from Korifi?.'

'No, I'm from Kallikratis. But I live in Hania. I'm a schoolteacher in the high school. Well, nice to meet you. I must catch the bus for Hania. Bye-bye.'

'Cheerio.' I watched him depart. He hadn't smiled once during our brief conversation. There was something about him I didn't like, but I couldn't quite put my finger on it.

Back in the house, I asked Themia about him. She scowled, swore in Greek, and said, 'Monarchikos einai.' Ah, Mavridakis was a monarchist. That was unusual, for there were precious few monarchists in western Crete. She told me that he also worked for the British in Hania. That suggested that he must be some kind of SOE agent. Hmm.

## Chapter 18

One day, the Andartes' training became a reality. A shepherd boy tore into the village at dawn to warn us that a German platoon was approaching through the mountains to the east. I quickly divided my Andartes into two sections, leading the assault section myself, with Themia in charge of the fire-section.

'Themia,' I said. 'I'll take my section into cover behind that small hill. You wait until the Germans are halfway across the plateau, then open fire, and I'll attack immediately. While I'm doing that, sprint with your section below the skyline to the other end of the plateau and cut the Germans off as they retreat. You'll have the double advantage of height and cover.'

'Entaxi,' she said.

To my horror, Themia's men opened fire the moment the first German soldiers entered the plateau, and they took cover. I had no option but to launch an instant attack, while Themia and her group sprinted round the contour to cut the Germans off. Fortunately, after a brief firefight, the Germans retreated east at speed, leaving one dead soldier behind, with one of the Andartes wounded.

I was furious. That could have been a disaster, as the Andartes were facing highly trained German infantrymen. My Andartes might have been impossibly brave, but they were also impossibly reckless. My instant attack had saved their bacon on this occasion. Themia's group had captured a Corporal, whom they led down to the village in triumph. The German NCO was terrified as several of the Andartes brandished their knives, making it plain what they would like to do with him. I insisted he remained unharmed. I tried to interrogate him, but we didn't have a language in common. Major Ford was due in the village that night, so I waited for his decision. He said a Royal Navy boat was due on the south coast soon and would take the prisoner to Alexandria for the Intelligence people to deal with.

Once the excitement had died down, I took Themia aside and gave her a lecture. I explained that firing prematurely was a potentially deadly mistake. In future, fire control orders had to be rigid if the Andartes were to win the firefight. If she was in charge of a section, she had to take charge – even though they were all men. She had to impose her will on them. She got it and was suitably contrite.

When the German Corporal had been evacuated successfully, Major Ford and I had a meeting. He told me that my orders were to continue to train the Andartes, on the one hand, but keep them from going off at half-cock, on the other, until a strategic decision about an invasion of Crete was made. But if the truth be told, this job was well-nigh impossible.

Crete was now swarming with armed bands of guerrillas, some led by the Kapetanioi, some based on local clans, and some led by individual British SOE NCOs like me. With typical impetuous Cretan courage, they all wanted to have a go at the enemy, but this would only have resulted in fearful reprisals as the Germans and Italians now had massive garrisons on the island. There was in fact one enemy soldier to every five civilians. But the villagers kept their ears to the ground and told us that with the Allied victory at El Alamein, and the Red Army's dogged defence of Stalingrad, the Germans knew that the writing was plainly on the wall. All they wanted to do now was go home.

It was plain to me that the biggest Resistance organisation in Crete was ELAS, which was made up of left-of-centre comrades. Its leaders were practically all retired Greek Army officers, many with combat experience in the Balkan

Wars, and it was well-disciplined and well-led. But except for Major Ford, our SOE officers on the ground insisted that it was a Communist-front organisation which we were to avoid arming. They also treated its leaders with contempt. This was nonsense. It was plain daft as not only were the Greek officers senior to the SOE officers, but also there was no other organisation to compete with it. I didn't get it.

Major Ford had at last arranged an airdrop in January onto the high-level plateau of Niato above Korifi. I was put in charge of organizing the reception party as the Major had been called to an SOE summit meeting in Lotus-Land, which is what we called the Amari Valley. By now, I was making every effort to improve my Greek, for none of the Andartes in my band spoke English, which made my job of instructing difficult. Themia was keen to learn English, and she was as sharp as a tack, so from time to time, we tried mutual lessons. The problem was I had to try hard not to stare at her eyes as she spoke, for the golden pinpoints in the blue iris seemed to glow. Oh, and those full lips …

One evening, I came back to the house to find Themia weeping bitterly. At first I thought she was crying for her dead husband, but there was more to it than that. Through her sobs she went into a tirade that was so fast I couldn't follow it. So, I took her hands and said, 'Siga, siga' – slowly, slowly. Themia did slow down and repeated the word 'hira' frequently. This was a word I didn't know so I went next door for my dictionary. The word meant 'widow'. Eventually I pieced together what Themia was saying. She said that following the death of her husband in action, she would be a widow for the rest of her life, for up here in the mountains of Sfakia widows never remarried – and she was only nineteen. So, she would never have a child. And after the war was over, she would have to wear black for the rest of her life. She wouldn't be allowed to dance, sing, or wear jewellery. She would be the target of persistent malicious gossip and mockery. And if she even looked at another man, let alone talk or joke with them, the men in her own family would kill her for the sin of 'ntropi' – for bringing sexual shame to the good name of the family.

I could scarcely believe such medieval nonsense, but Themia was plainly terrified at the prospect of her bleak future and started shrieking her desperation all over again. It was heart-breaking to hear and to watch. I got up and hugged her close. I could feel the heat of her skin through her faded Greek Army shirt. After a minute or two there was silence, and I realised that she had fallen asleep in my arms. I picked her up, laid her gently on her bed, removed her boots, covered her with a blanket and went quietly to my room next door.

## Chapter 19

The next day, following the Major's instructions, I set about organising the reception party for the airdrop. This wasn't difficult as I was overwhelmed with volunteers from Korifi. There was little work in the village in the winter for the shepherds had taken their flocks, or what was left of them, down to their lowland pastures. I picked a dozen or so men with mules and donkeys, while a ring of shepherd boys formed a perimeter in the mountains surrounding the village to keep an eye out for the Germans, who didn't seem too keen to venture out into the snow-covered mountains. Or so we thought. I knew this airdrop would contain arms, ammunition, explosives, rations, and hopefully personal mail for the Major and myself – and maybe even a bottle or two of whisky. When we set off uphill on that still January night, we were in an optimistic mood.

We were caught in a German ambush as neat as ninepins. A section of Gerry troops in white camouflage had skied up into the mountains without being seen. They must have come the long way round from the west and bypassed our sentries. While the villagers with their heavily laden mules managed to get away, Kostas and I were caught out in the open on a ridge above the Niato plateau dealing with a rogue parachute and its container. Kostas was killed outright, and I was wounded. I remember wondering how on earth Gerry had got wind of the airdrop, but as a blizzard blew up, I concentrated on getting into cover before I died of hypothermia. I was lucky enough to find a cave and was able to stay conscious for long enough to bury the aluminium tubes, as it was vital that Gerry didn't get them. But I don't remember much after that until I came to in a submarine being patched up by a naval surgeon.

I spent some time in hospital in Cairo, and fortunately my wound healed well. I was debriefed by an Intelligence officer who was as baffled as I was by the German knowledge of the airdrop. 'Looks like an inside job at your end, Sergeant,' he said. This was something I found hard to believe, for knowing the Cretans' predisposition for gossip, I kept all operational information to myself on a strict need-to-know basis. I racked my brains trying to think where the origins of the leak might be. In the meantime, I was given leave. But I didn't want to visit the fleshpots of Cairo, I wanted to be back in Korifi with my Andartes.

My only consolation was a packet of cheerful letters from Maeve containing snaps of Michael, now three. He was a handsome wee boy who had inherited his mother's good looks.

Another thing which motivated me to get back on active service as soon as possible was the behaviour of some of the Cretan SOE officers on leave in Cairo. They were a bunch of upper-class hooligans whose drunken parties were notorious. We were known as Force 133, and it is hardly surprising that many senior Regular Army officers in Middle East Headquarters would have liked to disband us entirely. It's not surprising that I was more than happy to be ordered to prepare for being landed back in Crete by sea in the early summer of 1943.

I was landed at Tripiti on the south coast of Crete by a Royal Navy Fairmile motor launch along with a few other Force 133 British officers and NCOs, and several Cretan Andartes who had attended the guerrilla warfare school. After a couple of days of hard marching, I was reunited with Major Ford in Korifi, and we were both pleased to see each other. I was also more than pleased to see Themia again, and judging by the enthusiastic way she hugged and kissed me, the feeling was mutual.

# Part 7

**Andy Gallagher: Glasgow & Crete, 2010**

## Chapter 20

Michael examined the padlock on the tin box. It was a small but strong brass affair. 'Screwdriver?'

Andy produced a large screwdriver. Michael inserted it in the hasp of the padlock and gave it a quick wrench. The padlock flew open. He lifted the lid. The first thing he saw was a handwritten letter addressed to: *Michael Gallagher.* Michael opened the envelope, took out the letter and started reading. He came to the end of the letter, handed it over and hurried into the toilet, but not before Andy had glimpsed the tears in his father's eyes. Andy read the letter.

Korifi Sfakion.
13th February 2010.
Dear Michael,

I know you will be surprised to receive this letter if you ever do receive it. But I felt the need to write to the son I never knew, after all these silent years, because I feel my own end is near. For all of my life, I have felt guilty about abandoning your mother and you. But as you will see, there were good reasons why I could not return home and marry her at the end of the War. Maeve is a good woman, and maybe we should never have slept with each other before getting married. But we did. We were in love, we were engaged, we were comrades in the Independent Labour Party, there was a war on, and nobody knew what would happen.

Anyway, I spent most of the War in Crete and kept a journal which is in the big notebook with the stiff covers. After the Battle of Crete, I escaped but was parachuted back onto the island to train the Resistance. The details are in my journal. For reasons which are also explained in the journal,

I did something which made it impossible for me to return to Scotland. So, I had to arrange that I was posted Missing in Action. I went to the village of Korifi, married Themia, a local woman, an Andartissa and a war widow, adopted a Cretan identity, and ever since I have been protected by the villagers.

I have been very happy here amongst these wonderful people. As I say, I always felt guilty about your mother and you, but had to live with that. It wasn't easy. I don't even know if Maeve is still alive. If she is, please ask her to forgive me. I thought about writing to her directly many times after the War, but felt it was better that she believed I was dead rather than opening new wounds, knowing that I was still alive but unable to come home. I've decided to write now because I haven't got long to live and wanted you to know the truth.

So that is my story, son. If this reaches you, I hope you will read my journal. The whole story is there, and it is one which should be told. SOE in Crete was not all it was made out to be. There was a lot of very dirty work at the crossroads. I hope you are well and happy in your life, and perhaps you will now be able to understand why I did what I did and forgive me. I hope you will, because I am truly sorry that I had to abandon both you and your mother. Mea Culpa, mea culpa, mea maxima culpa. I never once forgot either of you over all these years, and that is the truth.

Your father,
John.

Andy whistled his astonishment at this incredible story. The toilet flushed, Michael came back into the sitting-room wiping his eyes with a handkerchief and sat down.

'Are you okay, Dad?' Andy said.

'Aye. No. It's all just a bit of a shock.' Michael reached into the box again and took out a worn leather wallet. Inside was a Greek identity card in the name of Yiannis Sfakianakis but containing his father's photo. There were also some 50- and 20-Euro banknotes and, in a zipped compartment, a few coins. These he passed to Andy who examined them. They were gold sovereigns from the reign of Queen Victoria.

'You're in luck,' Andy said. 'They're worth a few quid.'

'Fair enough.'

The next item in the box was a tattered Wehrmacht 1:50,000 scale map of the White Mountains. Then there was a medal, with an oak leaf on the blue, white and red ribbon.

Andy googled it. It was the Military Medal, and the oak leaf was the symbol of a Mention-in-Dispatches. 'Look, it's got my father's name on the rim: Sergeant John Gallagher,' Michael said.

He then lifted a black Sykes-Fairbairn fighting knife and gasped his appreciation. 'That's some chib.'

'It's a Commando dagger,' Andy said.

The next item in the box was a thick handwritten manuscript. It had *Everyday Life in Korifi* on the cover.

'Wow!' Andy said. 'It looks like your dad wrote a book as well as his journal.'

Michael then took out a thick British NAAFI notebook with hard covers. It contained his father's handwritten journal, complete with dates. Michael passed the notebook to Andy.

'Here, you read this and tell me what's in it.'

'But don't you want to …?'

'No. I've had enough for one day. Better you read it. You know all about the War in Crete, and you can tell me what he … erm, my father … says. Okay?'

'Okay,' Andy said. 'Okay, Dad. No problem.' He realised his father couldn't face any more shocks at the moment.

Later, Andy riffled through his grandfather's journal. He saw that it was in two sections. The first was labelled *The War in Crete: 1941-1945*, and the second was *Civil War in Crete:*

*1946–1949.* Andy realised that the journal constituted a unique, first-hand, English-language account of a stormy period in Cretan history. He started reading.

## Chapter 21

In the kitchen, Andy poured some hot milk into Alison's coffee. He thought that hot milk in coffee was a disgusting French habit which he deplored. He added a splash of cold milk to his own and sat down. Eilidh sipped a smoothie.

Alison glared at him. 'What are your plans for the summer?' she said. 'I'm spending the summer in Crete doing research,' Andy said.

'Well, Jason and I have booked to go on holiday to Ibiza. If you're going to Crete, you can take Eilidh with you. I don't see why I should always be the one who looks after her.'

'I resent the implication of that remark. I'm her father and I look after her too.'

'Who took her to swimming lessons and drama classes?'

'Who took her hill-walking? Who ...?'

'Stop it, you two,' Eilidh said, scowling. 'Why don't you ask me what *I* want instead of arguing amongst yourselves?'

Andy felt a pang of guilt at his daughter's outburst. 'What do you want?' he sighed.

'I don't want to go to Ibiza, and I don't want to go to Crete. I want to stay here, get a summer job as a waitress, and spend some time with my friends.'

'Oh no you don't, young lady,' Alison said. 'You're not staying here all summer on your own having riotous parties and drinking cider and smoking dope.'

'Yes. I don't think it's a good idea for you to be here on your own, Eilidh,' Andy said. 'I think you'd like Crete. It's cool. You're interested in running and hill-walking and the outdoors. And I'll be working in the White Mountains in Crete, and you can't get more outdoors than that.'

'Where will you be working?.'

'In the village of Korifi.'

'Has it got like any clubs or discos?'

'No, it hasn't. Eilidh, it's a village high-up in the mountains. The men are mainly shepherds, and both men and women work as cheese-makers from the sheep's and goats' milk. These villages don't have discos and clubs.'

'I'd be bored out of my skull then. Has it even got Wi-Fi?.'

'Yes, it does. So, you can listen to music or use your laptop.'

Eilidh scowled. 'I don't fancy doing that all summer. What are you doing up there anyway?'

'In his journal, my grandfather says he hid something important in the area during the War, and I want to find it.'

Eilidh's face showed a flicker of interest. 'What is it?'

'I don't know,' Andy said. 'That's why I want to find it, whatever it is.'

'And where is it hidden?'

'In a cave somewhere near Korifi.'

'So, you're looking for you-don't-know-what in you-don't-know-where?.'

'Effectively, yes.'

'Unreal, Dad. Unreal.'

Alison snorted. She was about to say something when Andy decided he had to move fast or Eilidh would wind up in Ibiza for the summer. 'I'll tell you what,' he said. 'I'll do a deal with you. I'll work in the village from Monday to Friday, and then I'll take you down the town of Hania for the weekends. Hania is coming down with clubs and discos and bars where the local teenagers hang out. And there are frequent gigs by bands. Deal?'

'Deal. But no boring old archaeological sites, okay?.'

'No. I promise.'

Eilidh nodded reluctant assent. 'Okay then.'

Andy heaved an internal sigh of relief as he said, 'That's settled, then. I'll book you on the first available flight after the end of school term.'

## Chapter 22

Andy pulled up outside the taverna in Korifi and parked. As he got out of his car, Manoussos strode towards him, embraced him warmly, and shook his hand. 'Welcome, Andrea.

Welcome back to Korifi. It's good to see you again.'

'It's good to find you,' Andy said, using the standard Greek reply to a welcome.

Maria appeared, drying her hands on her apron. She extended her hand, smiled, and said, 'Welcome, Andrea.'

Goodness me, Andy thought, she smiled!

'Will you stay long in our village?' Manoussos said.

'Yes. Yes, I would like to. I would like to stay for the summer. I want to explore where my grandfather operated during the War. And walk in the mountains.'

Andy watched as Manoussos and Maria had a sotto voce discussion; he said something to her. She objected forcefully. Manoussos repeated what he had said. Andy could see this was a direct order and looked away in embarrassment.

'My father says you will stay with us, for as long as you wish,' Maria said. 'Thank you. Thank you very much.'

'Come,' Manoussos said to Andy. 'I will take you to your house.'

'My house?'

'Yes, your house.'

They drove slowly through the village. Andy saw men playing backgammon outside a kafeneion. A woman came out of the bakery carrying a round metal pan with a tea towel over the top. A priest wearing a stovepipe hat ambled past and waved to Manoussos. A shepherd with his crook braced over his shoulders behind his neck drove a flock of sheep along the road, their bells tinkling, past a man leading a mule laden with bags of fertiliser.

Manoussos indicated a dirt road climbing up a slope. 'Up here.'

Andy drove up the road which led to a house on its own on a hillock. It was a traditional one-story village house with a courtyard shaded by a mature vine. The view out over the plateau was spectacular, and the house would catch both the morning and afternoon sun. Manoussos unlocked the door and ushered Andy into a simply furnished but comfortable sitting room with a modern wood-burning stove, a large sofa, a couple of easy chairs, a desk and office chair, bookshelves full of books, a clock on the wall, an Internet router, a TV, and hand-woven rugs on the floor. Manoussos opened the shutters and sunlight flooded into the room.

'This was your grandfather's and Themia's house,' Manoussos said. 'She left it to Maria. But stay here for as long as you want.'

Andy was staggered by the generosity of the offer. 'Thank you.'

'Bring your things in from the car and unpack, and I'll see you later,' Manoussos said.

Andy put some books on the bookshelves. They were all about the Battle of Crete and the subsequent Occupation and Resistance. He examined the books already on the shelves and found a number in Greek on the very same subject. He then put his laptop on the desk, plugged it in, opened it and then checked that his iPhone was connected to the Wi-Fi.

Andy went into the kitchen. It was simple but modern with what looked like IKEA kitchen units, an electric cooker, a microwave, a fridge-freezer, and a washing machine.

Andy looked in a few of the drawers; they contained all the crockery, pots and pans, cutlery and utensils you could dream of. He then went into the bedroom and looked around: a double bed, a chest of drawers, a wardrobe, a couple of chairs, and colourful hand-woven rugs on the floor. He pressed the double bed – nice and firm. A framed photograph sat on the chest of drawers. He picked it up. It was a wedding photograph of Maria and a handsome young man, both with radiant smiles. Andy frowned. Why was he being allowed to stay in the young couple's house?

There was the roar of an expertly double-declutched motorcycle from outside. Andy went to the door just in time to see Maria dismount from a large motorbike and hang her helmet on the handlebars. She took a basket out of the top-box.

'Wow! That's some machine,' Andy said.

'It was my husband's,' Maria said. 'He taught me to drive it.' She glanced at the house and scowled.

'Come in, come in.'

Maria came in, put the basket on the table and said, 'Some things for you.' She took out Graviera and Misithra cheese, bread, paximadia – the double-baked Cretan rusks, a bowl of yoghurt, a jar of honey, village sausages, a 5-litre plastic container of red wine and a bottle of Tsichoudia and put them on the table.

'My goodness!' Andy said. 'Thank you very much.' He hummed and hawed for a moment. 'Maria.'

'Yes?'

'Maria. This is your house. The wedding photograph in the bedroom. Your husband. What, erm, how …?'

'He's dead.' She went into the bedroom, came out with the photograph under her arm, grabbed the basket and muttered, 'Come to the taverna in the morning for your breakfast.' She swept out of the front door, visibly upset, started the motorbike and drove away.

The next morning, Andy woke and swung his legs out of bed thinking how funny it was to be sleeping under only one sheet after the weather in Glasgow. And how different the tranquillity of the village was from the hustle and bustle of the city.

After a shower, he walked down the main street of Korifi carrying his map of the White Mountains in a plastic map-case. As he passed the kafeneion, Yorgos and Stratis waved their recognition.

'Kali mera, Andrea,' they called. 'Kali mera,' Andy replied.

As Andy approached the taverna, the sounds of a heated row inside in Greek spilled out into the street. He recognised the voices of Manoussos and Maria. He paused to listen, feeling embarrassed.

'The grandson of Kapetan Yiannis is always welcome in my house. And he's a good lad,' Manoussos said.

'That's not the point, Dad,' Maria said. 'He may be a good lad, but he's naïve. He doesn't understand the history of the village, or what happened here during the War, or the fact that Kapetan Yiannis had enemies, like the Mavridakis clan. And we don't know what's in Yiannis's journal. It may be dynamite. If he goes poking around in his grandfather's past, skeletons will come dancing out of cupboards, you mark my words.'

'I don't think so. All these family troubles happened some sixty and more years ago. Andreas's grandfather and my father fought together during the War, so he stays for as long as he wants, and that's final.'

Outside, Andy frowned. He knew the phrase "family troubles" in Greek was a euphemism for vendettas. And who on earth were the Mavridakis clan? There was a clatter of dishes and Maria swept out of the taverna, scowling. She stopped dead when she saw Andy in the courtyard. Andy was embarrassed to be caught eavesdropping. He resolved the tension by saying, 'Kali mera, Maria.'

'Kali mera,' she replied.

A few days later, Andy had settled in. He had his dozen or so books on the Battle of Crete and subsequent Occupation and Resistance laid out on a bookshelf, along with a couple of framed photographs of Eilidh. He had bought some flowers from a travelling van, and they were in a vase on the table. He was just sitting down with John's journal when he heard the motorbike approaching. Oh dear, he thought, here I am in Maria's house, and she's not happy about it. The machine stopped outside, and there was a knock at the open door. He turned to see Maria with a basket of eggs.

'Yeia sou, Andrea,' she said. 'I have some eggs for you. We have too many.'

'Thank you,' Andy said. 'Come in, come in.'

Maria put the basket on the table, and said, 'More research?.'

'Oh yes.'

'What is it precisely that you are researching?'

'Sit, sit,' Andy said. 'Well. There's a bit of a mystery in my family. Just before the War, my grandfather John – known to you as Kapetan Yiannis – had a girlfriend back in Glasgow, who was his fiancée. When he knew he was going abroad, he and his girlfriend went to bed together. A little later, she found she was pregnant.'

'Ah. It happens.'

'It does. The girlfriend was thrown out of the family home by her parents because of the shame she had brought on them, but she was lucky enough to find another house. The girlfriend, who was called Maeve …'

'Maeve?'

'Yes. It's not English, it's Irish, and it means 'queen of the fairies'. Anyway, Maeve wrote to John telling him about the pregnancy and the baby, and he wrote back to say he would marry her on his first home leave. That was the clear understanding between them. The baby was born – a boy. That was my father.'

'This is the first time I heard that Kapetan Yiannis had a

wife and child in Scotland.

My aunt Themia would never have married him if she had known that.'

'They weren't married, Maria. Maeve was his fiancée at the time, not his wife.

Anyway, Maeve received several letters from John from Cairo, but they stopped abruptly in May 1941.'

'Presumably because he was involved in the Battle of Crete.'

'Precisely. But somehow or another, John got left behind following the British surrender and was on the run in the mountains for a whole year.'

'Yes, I know. It was when he met my grandfather Kostas.'

'Yes, that's right. And we know he was landed back in Crete a second time, and I'm just about to read his journal which I hope will explain how and when and why. I think I know why he came back but I want the proof. But apparently John – Kapetan Yiannis – then did something which made it impossible to return to Scotland, and I am hoping that I will also learn why from the journal.'

'Oh. I see.' She looked around and picked up a photograph of Andy and Eilidh laughing together. 'Your daughter?'

'Yes. Eilidh.'

"Eilidh?' I have never heard that name before.'

"It's Gaelic, the old language of Scotland and Ireland. In Greek it would be 'Eleni'.'

Maria picked up another photo, of Eilidh in school uniform. 'She's lovely. How old is she?'

'Sixteen. Seventeen this summer.'

'She has your eyes. Honest eyes. And your wife? No photographs?'

'No photographs. We're in the process of getting divorced.' Suddenly, it all came flooding back. To his intense embarrassment, Andy felt hot tears coming to his eyes. He grabbed a tissue and blew his nose. Maria put her hand on his shoulder.

'I'm sorry.'

'Thank you.'

'What happened?' Maria said. 'But if you don't want to discuss it, it doesn't matter.'

'No, it's okay. I had really become too obsessed with my academic research, and Alison – my wife – became bored. She took a lover, and it appears I was the only person in Glasgow not to know.' Andy snorted. 'She said I loved Crete more than her, and if I wanted a woman, I should find a Minoan one. She wants a divorce. End of story.'

'It sounds like you weren't paying her enough attention.'

'Exactly.'

'Bad mistake. Women need to know that they are loved.'

'That's exactly what my father said,' Andy said. He glanced at Maria. She was studying him with that focused, penetrating Cretan gaze which seemed to search for your very soul. The silence seemed to last a very long time.

'Maria.'

'Yes?'

'Were you loved?'

Tears welled into Maria's eyes. She stood up. 'Yes. Yes, I was. Very much.'

As she left, she said, 'I'll give you your first lesson in Sfakiani tomorrow,' over her shoulder.

## Chapter 23

Andy tried hard not to stare at Maria's eyes as she spoke, for they seemed to glow. Oh, and those full lips were made for kissing.

'One of the key characteristics of the Sfakiani dialect is the transposition of the letters lamda and ro,' she said. 'This happens before the vowels a, o, and u. I'll give you two examples. As you know, the Greek for welcome is kalos orisate, often shortened to kalos. In Sfakia, we say: karos. My second example is the Greek word for sea: thalassa. Up here we say: tharassa.'

'Ah-ha!' Andy exclaimed. 'What?'

'Now I remember. There was a nineteenth century Cambridge classicist called Robert Pashley, who wrote a two-volume book called *Travels in Crete*. He noted the transposition you mention.'

'That's interesting. Do you have Pashley's books?'

'I do, back in Glasgow, in a facsimile edition. I'll photocopy the relevant section when I go home and send it to you.'

'That would be good; thank you. Now, another key characteristic is our pronunciation of the letter kappa. We say something like 'che'.'

'Yes, like 'Che' Guevara. That one baffled me because I couldn't work out was being said. Your father does it all the time.'

'My father speaks only Sfakiani, and he also knows a lot of the old songs and ballads in Sfakiani about the fights with the Turks in the nineteenth century.'

'I must record some of these. My area of research expertise is in the Minoan and Eteo-Cretan languages, and

I am interested to see if there is any linguistic connection.'

'Well, Sfakiani is directly descended from the ancient Dorian.'

'I hate to disillusion you, but that simply isn't true. I know people in Sfakia like to claim that, but it's a myth. Sfakiani is descended from the Athenian koiné, like ninety-eight per cent of Modern Greek.'

'Panayeia mou! I didn't know you were an expert in these old Cretan languages.'

'Well, Maria. I may be naïve about the culture of Sfakia, but I do know a lot about ancient dialects in Crete and have published extensively in this area.'

Maria blushed. Andy immediately felt like a heel for point-scoring with this young woman, who was only trying to help him. She sat back in her chair and studied Andy for a couple of moments. 'No, it's true, I haven't asked you much about your research,' she said. 'I'm sorry. Please tell me about your work.'

Andy told her all about his post as a Classics Professor in the University, and his research into the Minoan and Eteo-Cretan languages and Linear A. This somehow or another led him into explaining his separation and impending divorce from Alison, and his consequent partial separation from Eilidh. 'I feel as if I've lost something important.

Something intimate.'

'That is so sad. But I think it is vital to have an emotional life in a relationship, one which doesn't revolve around work.'

'I couldn't agree more. The problem was I learned that too late.'

'What a pity. What about Eilidh? When will you see her?'

'In a few weeks. She finishes school for the summer holidays, and she's flying straight out here to be with me.'

Maria smiled. When she smiles, which is seldom, Andy

thought, she is unbearably beautiful. 'Good. I'm looking forward to meeting the beautiful daughter of the famous professor.' It was Andy's turn to blush. 'Next time I'll tell you about some of our local words and phrases.'

'Kara,' Andy replied. Maria laughed out loud at Andy's idiomatic pronunciation of the Sfakiani. 'Bravo, Andrea.'

## Chapter 24

Andy, Manoussos and Maria sat round a table in the taverna.

'In his journal, my grandfather says that he buried something in a cave south of Niato after the airdrop when he was wounded,' Andy said.

'A cave?' Maria exclaimed. 'There are caves all over the White Mountains.' She and Andy and Manoussos stared at the map on the table.

'There's a small cave with an underground lake on the ridge going up to Kastro,' Manoussos said.

Andy couldn't help himself, and quoted, 'Ακόμη ένα πηγάδι σέ μιά σπηλιά.' Yet another well in a cave.

Maria laughed out loud. 'Bravo, Andrea. Yorgos Seferis.'

Manoussos looked puzzled, and Maria explained, 'It's from a poem by Seferis, Papa.'

'Oh,' Manoussos said, plainly not interested in Greece's Nobel Prize-winning poet.

'There's another cave – more like a vertical hole – on the way over to Grias Soros. It's called 'Ee Mavri Tripa'.'

The Black Hole, Andy translated.

'The Andartes threw dead Germans down there, and traitors they executed,' Manoussos said.

'But your grandfather wasn't in either of these caves,' Maria observed.

'How do you know that?' Andy said.

'Come on, it's obvious. In the first place, he was waiting for the parachute-drop on the Skoutsio ridge south-east of Kastro, and the cave with the water is on the north-east ridge leading up to the summit of Kastro. And in the second place, if he had fallen into The Black Hole, he would never have got out.'

'How can you be so sure?' Andy said.

'Because I've been there. It's a deep vertical hole.' Hmm, Andy thought. Not just a pretty face.

Manoussos pulled the map over to him and made a circle with his finger. 'It's got to be somewhere in here, between Skoutsio and Kefala,' he said. 'We know that Kapetan Yiannis was on this ridge because the next morning the Andartes found the body of Kostas, my father, here. The Andartes knew your grandfather was wounded because there was a trail of blood in the snow on the ridge. But apparently it ended abruptly and although they searched the area the next day, they found nothing. It was the following night when they found your grandfather in his house in the village, wounded, and took him to the coast to meet the submarine. So, the cave has got be in this area here. Does the journal say anything more?'

'No,' Andy said. 'It doesn't.'

'Well,' Maria said. 'You are going to have to search this area very thoroughly and see if you can find a cave.'

'Right, I'll start tomorrow.'

Andy parked the Panda beside Stratis and Yorgos' mitato. There was no sign of the brothers, but their savage dog circled at a distance guarding the building and growling, so Andy kept his katsouna ready as he started climbing. He reached the point on the Skoutsio ridge where he thought his grandfather had been hit, sat on a boulder, and oriented his map. The area below him to the south into which John must have staggered went steeply downhill. Andy scanned it carefully with his binoculars but could see no sign of a cave. He tried to think himself into his grandfather's shoes. It was early summer now, but when John was wounded, it was mid-winter, and the landscape would have looked very different. The mountains would have been covered with deep snow, so John could not have gone far.

Because of his wound, he would have been in a state of

shock and would automatically look for shelter. Andy took a bearing on the top of the hill called Kefala to the south, not far away, and decided to search the area in strips of one hundred metres wide for an hour at a time.

The ground in front of him was the usual limestone, covered with oregano, thyme, sage, rosemary and malotira bushes, and wildflowers. It was difficult terrain even for an experienced, fit and sure-footed mountain-walker like Andy, so how a wounded man had traversed it when it was covered with snow was quite another matter. But then maybe the snow was compacted and supported John's weight, Andy thought. Even so, the risks of hypothermia for a wounded man were high. He set off downhill, scanning his first strip.

For the next few days, Andy combed the area, but there was no sign of a cave. Where the Hell was it?

At the end of the week, Andy sat in his courtyard looking out over the plateau, a glass of ouzo with ice to hand. It was six o'clock in the evening, hot, and completely still. The only sound was the clinking of sheep and goats' bells on the mountainside, the quiet persistent resonance creating a curiously hypnotic atmosphere. He loved this time of the evening. The mountains seemed to approach slowly so that you could see almost every rock and bush, then they faded backwards again, and suddenly, it was dusk. Something to do with long light-waves, he thought, vaguely remembering physics lessons at school.

Andy felt very well indeed. He was completely relaxed, slept well, and all the walking in the mountains made him fit and healthy. The problems with Alison seemed very far away now, and not so important. The tranquil pace of village life was a welcome relief from the pressures of the academic life, now that the university had been turned into more of a competitive business than a centre for learning and research, Andy thought, with a flash of malice. He enjoyed the company of Manoussos and Maria and was pleased that the young widow seemed a little more relaxed with him. But he still felt distressed by her palpable grief. He wanted to know more about the death of her husband. He dozed off in the heat.

Alison lent over him in the operating theatre, shaking her head in the negative. 'There's nothing more to be done,' she said. 'So, we're withdrawing life support.'

'No, no, no,' Andy cried, struggling to get up off the operating table. 'You can't …'

He awoke with a jolt, spilling some of his ouzo. Jesus, I could do without dreams like that! Suddenly, he started. Eilidh was due in a few days.

Andy stood in the Arrivals hall of Hania Airport. After a few minutes, Eilidh appeared towing a large suitcase. Seeing her father, she dropped the suitcase, rushed over, and gave him an enthusiastic hug. Andy picked up the suitcase and said, 'I've booked us into a hotel in Hania for the night. I want you to see the town, and the drive up to the village, in the full light of day.'

'Cool.'

## Chapter 25

Andy took Eilidh through the maze of backstreets and alleys in the Old Town of Hania down to the harbour. Eilidh gasped when she saw it. ''Sake, man. That's awesome.'

'It's Venetian,' Andy said. 'Crete was part of the Venetian Empire from the thirteenth to the seventeenth centuries, and Hania was a major port. They built and repaired their galleys here.'

'So that lighthouse is Venetian?'

'No,' Andy said. 'But the original lighthouse was. It was built at the end of the sixteenth century and was one of the oldest lighthouses in the world. But it fell into disrepair and was rebuilt in the nineteenth century.'

'Cool. Can we go and look at it?'

'We'll come back another day so that you walk out to it. And go shopping. But I'd like to get on the road up to the village now.'

As they drove up towards Korifi, Andy pointed to a fertile plateau. 'This plateau is called Krappi,' Andy said.

'Because it's full of crap?' Eilidh said with a giggle.

Andy laughed. 'No. And that narrow entrance there is the old kalderimi up to Korifi and the other mountain villages in Sfakia.'

'What's a kalderimi?'

'The best translation would be a bridlepath. That's because the main traffic in pastoral society is salt up, cheese and yoghurt down, all on mules. The salt's necessary to make the cheese, so there are several places on the south coast where you can still see the saltpans.'

'That's interesting. So they brought the salt up on the mules?'

'Yes. These kalderimi can be works of art. They're made of cobblestones paved together horizontally by hand, and some are ancient, centuries old. I know one that is built on Byzantine and Roman originals and has retaining walls twenty to thirty feet deep in places.'

'Amazing. And they're still standing?'

'Aye. The word itself is Turkish, but the Cretans say that they copied it from the Greek kalos dromos, meaning a good road, and turned it into the Turkish kalderimi, which then came back to Greece under the Ottomans as a two-way loan word. But I think that's a bit of Cretan old wives' tales.'

As they climbed up through the mountains, Andy stopped the car and gestured downwards. Eilidh gaped at the view.

'Wow!' she said. 'That is awesome.'

'That gorge below us is called Katré, and the old kalderimi into Sfakia runs along it. That was the only way in and out in the olden days. This road didn't even exist until well after the Second World War. During the 'Great Rebellion' of 1866, the Sfakiani ambushed the Turkish Army in there, and they say the blood ran all the way down onto the Krappi plateau.'

'They sound a bit like Scottish Highlanders ambushing Redcoats.'

'That's right. There are marked similarities, historically speaking. Pure dead Rob Roy. Like clan vendettas, ferocious hospitality, sheep-stealing, and a touchy sense of honour. I've written a paper about it.'

When they reached the top of the pass into Korifi, Andy stopped the car and said, 'Jump out and have a look at this.'

Eilidh gasped at the view. 'That is awesome.'

'Aye, it is. Korifi has got to be one of the most beautiful villages in Crete.'

'What are these field colours?'

'The yellow ones are wheat, and the green ones are either vineyards or potatoes.'

'And what's this thing?' Eilidh said, pointing at a roadside metal structure.

'It's an iconostasis. Literally, the 'place of the icon.' It usually marks a spot where someone was killed in a car accident. And sometimes where the Germans executed someone during the Second World War.'

They drove on down into the village and Andy pulled up outside Manoussos' taverna. The old man came out to see who it was.

'My daughter, Eilidh,' Andy said. 'This is my friend, Manoussos Sfakianakis.'

'How do you do,' Eilidh said, sticking out her hand. To her surprise, Manoussos shook her hand, then kissed her on both cheeks.

'Welcome,' he said. 'Welcome to Korifi, Eilidh.'

Maria appeared. 'Ah-ha,' she said. 'This must be Eilidh.' She too kissed the girl on both cheeks and then turned to Andy. 'Omorfo koritsi.' Beautiful girl. It was true, Andy thought. Eilidh had her mother's athletic figure, heart-shaped face, and long blonde hair.

'Sit, sit,' Manoussos said.

'I will bring you something to eat,' Maria said. 'Come and help me,' she said to Eilidh.

As Manoussos poured two glasses of Tsichoudia, they could hear laughter coming from the kitchen. The old man smiled and said, 'Eilidh can keep Maria company. That's good. She needs company. Se yeia!'

## Chapter 26

Andy heaved a sigh of relief when Eilidh said she really liked the house in Korifi. He showed her round the village and the plateau but noticed that she seemed to enjoy spending time in the taverna talking to Maria. One evening she came home carrying a big round tray covered with a dish towel, and said in an excited tone, 'Look what I made.' She put the tray on the kitchen table and removed the towel.

'Wow!' Andy said. 'What have we here?'

'It's a spanakopita. Maria showed me how to make it. It's got spring onions, spinach, parsley, dill, eggs, feta cheese, and filo pastry. And Maria added a little grated nutmeg.'

'You're a clever girl! We'll have that for our tea, and I'll make a Greek Salad to go with it.'

'Cool,' Eilidh said, with a proud smile.

On the Friday evening, he and Eilidh drove down to Hania where he had rented an Airbnb flat. He showed the girl the waterfront bars in the harbour which were full of local teenagers and left her to it. In the morning, Eilidh told him she had been chatted up by local boys keen to practice their English. 'They're cool,' she said, 'and I've been invited to a party tonight.'

'Well, just be careful,' Andy said, 'and watch the bevvy.'

'It's okay, Dad, I can take care of myself. They can't be any worse than the boys in the West End of Glasgow.'

I certainly hope not, Andy thought.

On the way back up to Korifi on the Sunday afternoon, Andy heard all about the party. 'The boys here don't drink as much as the boys in Glasgow, but they're twice as sexist,' Eilidh said. 'They've got some funny old-fashioned ideas about women. They were really astonished to learn that I played in the girls' football team at school. But they're into bands, which is cool. They played some Greek bands, but I thought their music was like weird, like sort of oriental.'

'Yes, traditional Greek music is very different from ours,' Andy said. 'That's because it's in a different mode, or scale. And to complicate matters, Cretan music is quite distinct. Here, there's a tradition of singing what are called mantinadas, which are rhyming couplets.'

'Do you know any?'

'Yes. Here's one.' Andy sang a couplet:

*'Ta Kritika ta chomata opou kai an ta skapseis Aima palikarion tha vreis, kokala tha ksethapseis.'*

'What does that mean?' Andy translated:

*'Wherever you happen to dig in Cretan soil,*
*You will find the blood of warriors; you will dig up bones.'*

'That's like a bit gruesome,' Eilidh said.

'Well, it's a warrior society in Crete,' Andy said. 'They've been fighting invaders for centuries – Venetians, Turks, Germans. Their music and literature and culture reflect that.'

'Wow. It all sounds a bit complicated.'

After a couple of weeks, Andy was pleasantly surprised to learn that Eilidh no longer wanted to go down to Hania every weekend. She was spending an increasing amount of time with Maria, and the two women seemed to get on like a house on fire, despite the age difference. Eilidh was even beginning to speak some Greek. That's all good, he thought. Cool, even. But he himself felt despondent, for despite all his efforts, he had failed to locate his grandfather's cave. And the quest was impeding his research on Linear A, which annoyed him. He grew increasingly irritated.

# Part 8

## John Gallagher: Crete, 1944

## Chapter 27

Major Ford was off to a meeting in central Crete, and I was in charge here until he returned. It looked like Gerry was retreating to a base round Hania and our job was to keep an eye on them and attack them as and when ordered by Middle East Headquarters. The situation here was complicated by the fact that there were now two Resistance groups in Crete. One was called EOK, which stood for the National Organisation of Crete. And the other was ELAS. This stood for the Greek People's Liberation Army.

The EOK mob was run by the British SOE officers and wasn't much more than a bodyguard outfit for them. They protected the SOE wireless stations, supported the Greek King, and did bugger-all fighting. ELAS was a left-wing outfit, and its politics were quite like the ILP – but maybe even more to the left. There were quite a few Communists in the leadership, so the SOE officers thought it was a Commie organisation, but it was more complicated than that. Most of the ELAS officers were Venizelist liberals and in Crete that meant they were against the Greek King. There was nothing remotely like it in Scotland. But they were good comrades, well-organised but very short of weapons and ammo. I really didn't understand why we didn't arm and equip them for even one of the anti-communist SOE officers, a guy called Paddy, admitted they were the biggest and best-organised Resistance organisation in Crete.

Major Ford had just returned and the two of us were to be attached to the ELAS Division in western Crete. This was good news for it meant we were going to be working with comrades! And the Major was a very experienced and competent officer with considerable irregular warfare experience, unlike most of the other SOE officers in Crete who were upper-class cowboys playing at soldiers.

Major Ford and I travelled over the mountains looking for ELAS headquarters in western Crete. It took us some time exploring the foothills of the White Mountains before we found ELAS. They called these foothills the 'Rizes' – the roots – of the big mountains. They were incredibly beautiful – a patchwork of woods, olive groves, orchards, vineyards, and wheat fields – all on dizzily steep hills. We were directed to the Keramies area south of Hania town, where we found the HQ of ELAS's 14th Brigade near the village of Panayia. It wasn't anything like a full-sized Regular Brigade, but ELAS liked to pretend it was a Regular Army! The gaffer sent me on an inspection tour of the area, escorted by one of the ELAS Andartes.

What I found out was astonishing. EAM, the political wing of ELAS, had organised literacy classes, a People's Court, food rationing, a police force, a hospital, and a political theatre in this region. It was unbelievable, it was a mini-socialist society in the making! Most of the ELAS officers were either reserve, retired, or invalided-out Greek Army officers, and their training programme for the Andartes showed a high degree of professionalism, but they were woefully short of arms, ammunition, and clothing. They were also short of food, and the Andartes survived on wild greens and beans, no kidding. They seldom saw butcher-meat.

These officers said that Aleko, the code name for the young British SOE officer in charge of western Crete, was bitterly opposed to them, and went out of his way to ensure that they were not supplied. That officer was the one who poked my eyes during the unarmed combat session at the guerrilla warfare school in Palestine! I think we should have armed and trained these people immediately. They were excellent guerrilla material.

I attended a trial in the People's Court of the village of Therisso of a man who was accused of hoarding. I noticed right away he was a fat bastard which is uncommon in the villages. An old dear accused this man of trying to sell her a tin of olive oil at a hopelessly rigged price.

She wanted to know how he had spare oil when everyone else had handed theirs into the communal store for rationing. The judge, who was the village Provost, said they would inspect his storeroom right now. Everyone trooped off to the storeroom, including me. The Judge made Fatso open it and it was full of food – olive oil, a sack of rice, and tinned food. The villagers started yelling and bawling to shoot the hoarder right there.

The Judge turned to me and said, 'Kapetan Yianni, as our honoured guest and ally, perhaps you would like to pronounce sentence on the hoarder?'

This took me completely by surprise, and as it was plain that quite a few of the villagers wanted him shot, I did some quick thinking and said, 'I suggest that all the stores of the accused be confiscated immediately and distributed to the villagers on the basis of need.'

There was a roar of agreement, and the Judge said the sentence of the Court was that *all* the contents of the storeroom would be confiscated and removed to the communal village store for immediate redistribution. Any further hoarding on the part of the accused would result in his execution. I felt quite pleased with myself – this wouldn't happen in the Glasgow Sheriff Court. Talk about a Solomon come to judgement!

## Chapter 28

Although the village of Therisso was not far from the town of Hania as the crow flies, it was protected by steep mountains, and the road from the north coast ran through a narrow gorge. Consequently, it was very hard to mount a surprise raid on the village. But the villagers' intelligence service in Hania had informed them that the German Sonderführer Schubert had sworn to eliminate the strong local ELAS band led by Kapetan Haretakis. Schubert was a very nasty piece of work who commanded a specialist counter-guerrilla unit which was feared and loathed for the atrocities it committed: beatings, torture, rape, murder, pillaging and arson. This unit contained Cretan jailbirds as well as some German volunteers, and although they wore German uniform, these had no distinguishing unit badges. However, so far Schubert's threat had proved empty as the shepherd-boys in the surrounding hills could always give ample warning of an approaching German column.

I was talking with Haretakis when one of these boys ran up to say that three strangers were walking into the village on the road from the north. So Haretakis and his men hid. I watched the three strangers approach and they were plainly Cretan. They said they were from Kapetan Bandouvas's band which had been rolled up in central Crete and wanted to join Haretakis's band to keep fighting the Germans. I tipped Haretakis the wink and his men seized the strangers. They were all carrying German I.D. and were from Schubert's unit.

The local Andartes had their knives out, and these traitors were going to meet a sticky end. But I knew it would be foolish to interfere. These Cretans are hard, hard men.

By September of 1944, Gerry had pulled back in force to a perimeter round Hania. He knows that for them, the War is nearly over, and all they want to do is go home. Me too! It seems ages since I held Maeve in my arms. Well, come to think of it, it *has* been ages. And I still haven't seen my wee boy. This long separation is absolute murder, and is very hard to take, especially as I haven't a clue when I'll get back to Glasgow. And to tell you the truth, I'm worried that Maeve might find another man in my absence.

We were just to the south of Gerry in the Panayia area, but we have been ordered not to attack them as they would take reprisals on the civilian population in Hania town. And they have artillery and armoured cars. So, the problem is keeping the Andartes under control because they want to get stuck into the Germans. I keep them busy with training exercises.

I've been training the boys in ambush drills. The Germans come out of their perimeter and do a patrol towards us as regular as clockwork every morning at dawn. Major Ford's idea was for me to study their routine, and ambush them one morning. Yesterday morning, we went out before dawn and laid an ambush. My men were well camouflaged and perfectly still. As Gerry approached, a mountain hare ran into the killing ground, and the Andartes blazed away and blew the bunny to bits! What can you do with men like that? The only reason we got away scot-free was that the Germans retreated rapidly when they heard the gunfire. Although I still sympathised with the radical ideology of EAM/ELAS, I gave the Andartes a right row back in the village. Their recklessness was lethal. But I kept my political sympathies to myself because I didn't want any problems with the SOE officers.

In autumn 1944, Major Ford sent me to Selino to find out what the situation was between EOK and ELAS. He specifically wanted to know if the latter had received any systematic training by SOE, or arms, ammunition, clothes and supplies in the recent airdrops in the area. I met the Major called Aleko there and said simply that I was a Platoon Weapons Instructor and had been sent to assess local training needs. Aleko told me that the Kiwi Staff Sergeant Perkins had been doing a great job with the Andartes from the Koustoyerako area. He was the Kiwi I had met at the Guerrilla Warfare School. Aleko then asked me to visit the local ELAS band, assess their military capabilities and political intentions, and report back to him. He was asking me to spy on them, in short. His attitude to ELAS was completely mental. He kept raving on about 'Communists' and how we had to control the ELAS Andartes so that they were powerless when the War came to an end. I said I would but returned immediately to Keramies and reported to Major Ford. He said it was all of a pattern in western Crete, that SOE was working to ensure that ELAS had no military capability when the War ended. I realised that he was right. SOE was trying to neutralise Cretan ELAS militarily. This was outrageous given that the Andartes of ELAS were doing all the fighting. But for the life of me, I couldn't see what to do about such a blatant betrayal.

## Chapter 29

I decided it was time to stage a real ambush and try and knock out one of the German Hanomag half-tracked armoured cars. It would be an opportunity to see if the Andartes were now disciplined enough to let the vehicles come close to them before opening fire. I chose a section of the road where there was a sharp bend with deep ditches on either side. I stationed my men in the ditches and ordered one of them to sprint across the road the instant the Hanomag appeared round the bend. My idea was that the driver and commander would be looking at that man and not behind them. And I would have positioned myself in cover above the road so that I could attack it with grenades.

We got into position early knowing the Germans would be punctual, and sure enough the Hanomag appeared on the dot of six-thirty. As it rounded the bend at a slow speed, my Andarte, an elderly man, jumped to his feet and bounded out onto the road. But to my horror, he stood in the middle of the road and began firing his rifle at the armoured car, which immediately opened fire on him with its machine-gun. The Andarte went down, and the car continued towards him, obviously going to run him over. I scrambled down onto the road, sprinted up beside the slow-moving Hanomag, lobbed a grenade in through the driver's open hatch, and slammed it shut. The grenade exploded and the car slewed sideways into the ditch.

As the crew bailed out, the Andartes finished them off.

I ran up to the Andarte who had been hit in the chest but was still alive – just. There was no point in telling him he was a bloody fool. We made a makeshift stretcher, carried him into Panayia, and the Andarte doctor operated on him immediately. It transpired that the German bullet had not hit any vital organs, and he would live. While I was pleased that he survived, it was yet another example of the Andartes' reckless behaviour under fire, and I made sure his comrades knew it.

## Chapter 30

I wrote my Report to the Major towards the end of October 1944. In it, I said that in my opinion, local ELAS was a well-disciplined and well-led guerrilla force whose officers were more than effective leaders. What the Andartes needed was much more battle training, but this was extremely difficult because of the acute shortage of small-arms ammunition. I also said I was worried about both the diet and the clothing of these men. There was very little food in the Keramies area, and although the British Military Mission in Crete received supplies of rations, it all went to its supporters. Even though the local ELAS and EOK units were supposed to be brigaded together, no food ever reached the former's position here at Panayia. Consequently, the Andartes survived on horta and beans. Also, the clothes and boots of these Andartes were in tatters and this was no joke with winter coming. I didn't know if Cairo was depriving them of supplies deliberately, but it was an absolute liberty to treat so many men and women who were fighting the Germans so badly. Major Ford said he was going to arrange an airdrop of supplies for ELAS on the Omalos plateau. When I asked him how he was going to do this, the Major grinned and said, 'I have friends in low places!' He was as wide as the Clyde, the Major!

The airdrop was arranged for a week ago, and I went up to the Omalos with three of my Andartes to collect the containers and make sure none were stolen – which happens all too frequently. The Omalos plateau lies at 1350 metres in the centre of the White Mountains and is about a mile in diameter. It is rimmed by mountains and is quite spectacular. It was also the base for the Andartes fighting the Turks throughout the nineteenth century. The Germans had built an airstrip there which was used by spotter planes, but otherwise it was deserted as it was a prohibited zone. Our drop went like clockwork, and we soon gathered all the containers. But when we went to the nearby Lakkoi, an EOK village, they refused to lend us any mules to supply 'the Communists.' I waited until nightfall, stole a truck, loaded it and drove it to Panayia. The containers contained battledress, boots, and tins of bully-beef, all of which were received with great excitement. We celebrated with bully beef hash and village wine!

Major Ford then ordered me to mine or blow all the roads leading out of the German perimeter round Hania so their armoured vehicles couldn't get into the foothills. We always did this at night, and we were often close enough to the German sentries to hear their conversations.

Major Ford then drafted his teport on ELAS in western Crete for Colonel Dunbar, the Commanding Officer of SOE in Crete and he gave it to me for my comments. It was a very good report, incorporated my own observations, and didn't pull any punches. He certainly stuck his neck out. He gave the ELAS Order of Battle and short biographies of its senior officers. He reckoned there were 600 men in the 14th Brigade organised in three well-led battalions. He described the first-rate military hospital it maintained, one which treated Andartes, Cretan civilians and enemy soldiers without fear or favour. He pointed out that ELAS maintained good relationships with the locals and there was no looting. He said the political wing, EAM, was very good at negotiating and reconciling differences with EOK. His actual words were:

'It should be recorded that incidents between the EOK and EAM in CRETE have been remarkably rare. Order has been preserved; several ugly situations have been saved by calmness and good will on both sides; it is doubtful if any murder on purely political grounds has yet occurred.

I consider that ELAS can be relied upon for full cooperation operationally, but it will attempt to retain its political freedom, as being the army of a political party. It is considered that 85% of EAM in CRETE are left-wing democrats. But it is the personality rather than the programme of EAM which is of importance. I was most impressed by its self-imposed discipline and its inculcation of a social sense amongst its members. It is often said that EAM retains and controls its membership on mainland Greece by terrorism. For West Crete this is simply not true.

It is my considered opinion that ELAS in western Crete is a well-organised, well-disciplined, and well-led guerrilla force, with an aggressive spirit, good morale, and great potential for harassing and disrupting the German garrison in the Hania area. Sergeant Gallagher, whose efforts in training the Andartes have been exemplary, shares this opinion but regrets that the shortage of small-arms ammunition hinders effective battle-training as well as both offensive and defensive operations. That ELAS has been starved of both ammunition and food by SOE thus far is a scandal. It is therefore my strong recommendation that we arm and equip this force forthwith.'

The Major hit the nail right on the head. The point was: would Colonel Dunbar listen to a report which told him what he didn't want to hear?

## Chapter 31

By the end of September 1944, the entire German garrison of Crete was now inside a heavily fortified perimeter round the Hania area. The main Resistance unit facing the Germans was ELAS's 14th Brigade, based in the Keramies area, with its forward battalion round the village of Panayia, but it was still desperately short of small arms ammunition. The SOE officer in charge of the area, the man codenamed Aleko, had arranged that an EOK unit was to brigaded with ELAS, as it would look bad if EOK did not participate in fighting the enemy. But, shortly afterwards, the EOK unit withdrew and watched the fighting from the village of Madaró. I began to wonder if SOE had deliberately set ELAS up to be liquidated by the Germans. Major Ford ordered me to take up a position just south of Panayia and both observe and advise ELAS if fighting broke out. I had my own runner.

Then in October, there was an ugly incident. The ELAS commander in Panayia came to me with the suspicion that one of his Andartes was a spy for EOK. He was a Mavridakis from Kallikratis. I remembered that name. That was the name of the man whom Themia said was a monarchist, and who had introduced himself to me. I wondered if they were related. The Andartes set a clever trap involving false information about an impending ELAS raid, and the guy walked right into it. He was to be tried that night, and the commander asked me to be present to ensure fair play. It was a drumhead court-martial, but a fair one.

When the spy knew he was found out, he confessed he had been reporting on ELAS dispositions to EOK for onward transmission to SOE. He had been bribed with several gold sovereigns. The verdict was guilty. Several Andartes took him away, fingering their knives.

A little later, there was the most awful screaming. It seemed to go on for a long time, then eventually subsided into agonised groaning. The Andartes came back, wiping their bloody knives clean. I slipped away and found the traitor. His naked body had been sliced to ribbons, there was a gaping red hole in his groin, and he was dripping blood, but he was still alive, writhing and groaning in agony. He saw me and croaked, 'Pirovólise me.' Shoot me.

Sick to my stomach as this appalling sight, I took out my pistol, put the muzzle to his temple, and shot him. The shot sounded very loud in the night air. His body convulsed once, then was still. I put the toe of my boot under his body, gave an almighty heave, and toppled it into a ravine. There were several scraping noises and then a dull thud – what a way to end the life of a human being. My body suddenly started trembling and I felt nauseous. I sat down abruptly on a boulder and tried deep breathing. After a couple of minutes, the shivering stopped, but I still felt shaky. I walked slowly back into the village, fighting the nausea, and downed a large glass of Tsichoudia. The Andarte commander asked me if I had shot him, and when I said I had, he shrugged and said, 'Waste of a bullet.'

## Part 9

**Andy Gallagher: Crete, 2010**

## Chapter 32

It was a very hot day. Andy went to the fridge and poured himself a cold drink. Eilidh was down in one of the kafeneia in the village with some of the local teenagers, talking about bands. The local kids were keen to practice the English they were all learning at school.

Andy was pleased about this for he had noticed that the normally ebullient girl had become unusually quiet when she learned that he and Alison were going to split up. She had been very upset by the whole affair, but she seemed to be returning to her normal cheerful extroverted mode, and only the other day he had heard her and some of the local teenagers arguing amicably about which was Beyoncé's greatest song. And it was plain that some of the boys fancied her. That's all good, Andy thought.

He decided to go for a swim to cool down. Maria had told him about a small, secluded cove on the south coast where the villagers went, so he collected his trunks, a towel, a Walt Longmire novel, his suntan cream, a sunhat, and a bottle of cold water, shoved them in a bag, put on his sunglasses and drove off. He stopped briefly at the kafeneion to tell Eilidh where he was going.

As he bumped down the dirt road towards the cove, Andy saw Maria's motorbike parked at the top of a steep path and pulled in behind it. At the foot of the path was a small shingle beach with a bath-towel and a straw bag laid out on it; there was no sign of Maria. He felt slightly embarrassed as he did not want to encroach on her privacy, so he laid out his own towel at some distance from hers. He plastered his face, chest, stomach, arms and legs with suntan cream, and as much of his back as he could reach, put on his hat, lay down and started reading.

A figure came into view swimming round the headland, and he recognised Maria, who seemed to be carrying something. She swam in close to the beach and stood up. She had a spear-gun in her hand with a large sea bream stuck on the harpoon. Andy inhaled sharply. Maria seemed to be all curves, her olive-coloured skin offset by a white bikini. She waved cheerfully.

'Hi Andrea. What are you doing over there? Come closer so we can talk.'

Andy picked up his things and laid them out next to Maria's. She came up the beach and bent down to pick up her towel. Andy gulped and tried to focus on his book.

'Here,' Maria said, passing Andy a bottle of suncream. 'Would you do my back, please?'

'Of course,' Andy said, as Maria lay down on her stomach. He'd do her back any time she wanted. He poured some cream on his hands and gently rubbed it in.

'Mmm. You've got good hands,' she said. 'Would you do mine?' Andy said.

'Of course.' She got to work on his back as he lay on his stomach. Please don't stop – that feels so good, Andy thought.

'You have a strong back.'

'It's probably all that walking in the mountains with a heavy pack.'

'Oh yes, I forgot. You're a mountaineer as well as an expert on the Minoan and Eteo-Cretan languages, and Linear A.'

Andy looked sharply at Maria, but she was grinning mischievously. He smiled. They lay in companionable silence for a while.

'Andy.'

'Yes?'

'Tell me about your wife.'

Andy winced and groaned inwardly. That was the last person he wanted to talk about. He stared out to sea for several moments. 'Alison? Alison is a nurse, a theatre sister. She's at the top of her profession, very skilled, very well thought of.'

'Is she attractive?'

'Attractive? Yes, she's a good-looking woman. She looks much younger than she is.

She keeps fit, never out of the gym.'

'And Eilidh is your only child?.'

'Yes.'

'How did you and Alison meet?'

'At the disco in the Students' Union..'

'And?'

What do I say? Andy thought. What do you think happened? 'And one thing led to another.'

'Meaning?'

'We were attracted to each other, we started going out together, we had sex together, and we got married.'

'What happened after that?'

'Well, I had become fascinated with the history of Classical Greece as a student, particularly the Minoans, went on to do my PhD, and became an academic. But Alison isn't interested in ideas or history or social research. She exists in an ultra-pragmatic world of surgery and dressings and stitches and ventilators, everything else is airy-fairy nonsense – and she's very bossy. That said, we seemed to get on all right, we had a pleasant, comfortable relationship. If it wasn't terribly passionate, it was trouble-free. Or so I thought.'

'What went wrong?'

That's a good question, Andy thought; I wish I knew the answer. 'With the wisdom of hindsight, I think we were living in parallel universes, although perhaps we weren't fully aware of it. Come to think of it, perhaps I didn't want to be aware of it. The only thing we really had in common was Eilidh. Alison eventually realised this, she got fed up, found another man, and left me.'

Andy turned his head away from Maria, rested it on his arms, and flicked a tear away with his finger.

'Did you love your wife?'

'I thought I did. I think I thought that being married automatically meant being in love. But now I know that's not necessarily true.'

'I see. How sad..'

'Yes. Yes, it is.'

'If you really love someone, you know it,' Maria said. 'It's unmistakeable. You can't miss it. It takes over your life.'

Andy nodded as he wiped away another surreptitious tear. He felt as if he was going to break down and inhaled sharply. Maria spotted this and put her hand on his. 'I'm sorry, Andy. I didn't mean to upset you.'

'It's all right.'

Maria squeezed his hand and stood up. 'I must go now to help my father. We have a walking group coming to the taverna this evening.'

She slipped into a skirt and blouse, put her feet into sandals, placed her things in her bag and picked up the spear-gun and the fish. 'I'll see you later.'

As she climbed back up the path, Andy admired her effortless grace.

## Chapter 33

Andy, Eilidh and Maria sat round the kitchen table, with the map of the area spread out in front of them.

'The only direction my grandfather could have gone after he was wounded was south,' Andy said. 'Maybe a bit east or more likely west of south, but south. Here's the Skoutsio ridge he was on with Kostas, Maria's grandfather, when they were ambushed by the Germans.' He tapped the map with a pencil and outlined a triangular shape. 'The cave has got to be somewhere in this area, even although I can't see it through my binoculars. What I propose is that we form a line and search this area systematically, section by section. If the cave is in there, we'll find it.'

'If you're lucky,' Maria said. 'These caves are often well-hidden.'

'If we're lucky,' Andy said. 'Now, Eilidh. I know you're fit, but these are dangerous mountains. The first thing to remember is that it will be very hot. And there is no shade.

We've got to be plastered with suntan cream, and wear a hat, and take plenty of water. The next thing is the terrain. It's shattered limestone, so it's hard to make progress. Two steps forward, one step back kinna thing. You've got to conserve energy up there. But we've also got to keep our eyes open as it would be easy to trip and injure yourself. I'll take my binoculars so we can check out the sections we're going to cover.'

'I'll bring a first aid kit, just in case,' Eilidh said.

'Good thinking,' Andy said. 'What we'll do is drive up to Niato at dawn tomorrow, climb up onto the Skoutsio ridge, and search the first couple of sections before it gets too hot. Agreed?'

'Agreed.'

When they reached the ridge early the next morning, they moved into a position where they could see clearly down to the south, towards Kefala. Andy scanned the area carefully through his binoculars. 'Let's spread out and search this first section as far as that holm-oak tree down there. And remember to look behind you. Okay?'

'Okay.'

With about fifty metres between them, they moved slowly down the mountain, scanning all round them. An hour later, they reached the tree without having spotted anything. Andy moved them on to the next section, and they worked their way back towards the Skoutsio ridge. He didn't see the flash of sunlight reflecting off a pair of binoculars behind them.

Shortly after noon, Andy decided to call it a day as the heat was relentless.

'That's it for today,' he said. 'We'd better quit before we're fried. But there's one thing for sure.'

'What's that, Dad?'

'There's no cave in this area.'

## Chapter 34

Andy decided to take a day off and go for a walk over the mountains to the village of Kallikratis in eastern Sfakia, where the Germans had executed about thirty villagers in 1943. He set off early from Korifi, descended onto the Askyfou plateau, and continued on the dirt road past the small village of Asfendos.

Later, Andy approached the kafeneion in the centre of Kallikratis and sat down outside in the shade. A middle-aged man was also sitting there reading *Haniotika Nea,* the local newspaper, and smoking. The owner of the kafeneion asked Andy what he wanted, and he ordered a Mythos beer. A cold bottle, a glass and a saucer of peanuts was set in front of him, and the owner indicated that it was paid for by the middle-aged man.

'Thank you,' Andy said in Greek as he poured some beer – another example of Cretan filoxenia, the gracious hospitality towards travellers. He raised his glass. 'Se yeia.'

'Se yeia,' the elderly man replied. Then he said in English, 'Are you English?.'

'No, no,' Andy replied. 'I'm Scottish.'

'Ah, Skotia,' the man said. ''The Famous Grouse'.' Andy laughed. 'That's right.'

'Where do you come from in Scotland? Edimvourgo?.'

'No,' Andy said. 'I'm from Glasgow.'

'Yes, Glasgovi. Selltik football club.'

Andy laughed again. 'That's right. Celtic is my club.' He took a sip of his beer. 'Are you from Kallikratis?'

'Yes. I have a mitato in the mountains above the village where I make Graviera cheese.'

Andy drank some beer and said, 'You speak good

English, sir.'

'I learned English at school, and from an English lady who comes here on holiday every summer. She is an anrop, anthop-.'

'Anthropologist?'

'Yes, an anthropologist. She studies the life of the shepherds. My name is Dimitris Mavridakis.'

'I see,' Andy said. 'My name is Andrew Gallagher..'

'But I think you speak good Greek,' Dimitris said.

'I'm a Classics Professor at the University of Glasgow,' Andy said, 'and I've been travelling in Crete for twenty or so years. That's why I speak Greek.'

'And how about the Sfakiani dialect?'

'Ah,' Andy said. 'That's another matter. It's difficult. But I'm trying to learn it..'

'Good, good. And where are you staying? In Hora Sfakion?'

'No,' Andy said. 'I'm staying in Korifi..'

'Oh,' Dimitris said. 'Where about?'

'I'm staying with the Sfakianakis family. The family which has the taverna and pension.'

'I've heard of them,' Dimitris said. 'And why did you choose to go to Korifi, Professor?'

'Well, my grandfather was here during the War,' Andy said, 'and he was based in Korifi training the Andartes. So, I wanted to see where he operated. He was known as Kapetan Yiannis.'

'I see.' Dimitris stood up, folded his newspaper, came over to Andy's table, and held out his hand. 'It has been a pleasure to meet you,' he said. 'If you come back to Kallikratis, you must come and eat with me.'

Andy stood up and shook Dimitris's hand. 'Thank you. And if you're passing through Korifi, please come and see me, and we'll have a drink.'

'I will, I will. Go well, Andrea.'

## Chapter 35

As Andy turned into his lane, he passed a Lexus coupé with CC plates parked at the side of the road. Driving up to the house, he saw a man with a straw hat and a linen jacket sitting in his courtyard reading the English-language newspaper, *The Athens News*. Andy parked his car and got out. The man stood up.

'Professor Gallagher, I presume?' he said, extending his hand.

'I'm Professor Andy Gallagher. Are you Henry Morton Stanley, by any chance?' The man laughed. 'No, no. I'm Jeremy Fotheringay from the British Embassy in Athens.' He handed Andy a business-card.

Andy sat down. 'And what can I do for you, Mr. Fotheringay?'

'Oh, nothing really. We just heard of your presence, and as I was in Crete on Embassy business, I thought I'd pop in and say hello – a courtesy call, so to speak.'

'That's very courteous of you. Can I offer you a cold beer?.'

'Splendid, old boy.'

Andy went into the house and returned with two cans of Mythos and two glasses. The two men popped the cans and poured the beer.

'Cheers,' Fotheringay said. 'Cheers,' Andy replied.

'Yes. I read your book on *A Minoan Language?* Fascinating. Splendid piece of work.'

'Well, that's my job.'

'Indeed. But a convincingly argued, highly original, and very well written monograph nonetheless.'

'Thank you,' Andy said, thinking, this guy flatters to

deceive.

'And what are you up to here, Andy? May I call you Andy, by the way?'

'Of course, that's my name. I'm taking a bit of a break at the moment, but I'm also working on my new book about Minoan culture.'

'Splendid, splendid. I'll look out for that. When is it due to be published?.'

'Oh, not for some time. It's a work in progress. I've a lot more research to do.'

'I see,' Fotheringay said, taking a sip of his beer. Andy noticed he seemed to be studying his waistband. 'But I hear you've got family connections with this area.'

Oh, oh, oh, Andy thought, what's this bloke up to? 'What do you mean, Jeremy?.'

'Well, I hear a relative of yours was with SOE here during the War.'

'And how did you hear that?.'

'From the horse's mouth..'

'The horse's mouth?'

'Yes. P.L.F. The expert on Crete. The distinguished author of *Roumeli* and *Mani*..'

'Ah, Patrick Leigh Fermor. Of course.'

Andy felt his shoulders tense involuntarily. There's something fishy going on, he thought. Neither book was about Crete. But he maintained a carefully neutral expression as he said, 'I know my grandfather was in Layforce in the Battle of Crete, and I know he was on the run in the mountains for a year afterwards. But I didn't know he was with SOE.'

'Yes, P.L.F. said he was a Sergeant attached to a Communist band of Andartes in the Keramies area.'

'Really?'

'Oh yes. Paddy wouldn't make a mistake about a thing like that..'

'Communist Andartes?'

'Yes, ELAS. A bunch of Communists.'

'I know Leigh Fermor says that. And Beevor. But that's inaccurate. Cretan ELAS was composed of Venizelist Liberals in the main.'

'Cover story, old boy. Paddy was here, and he says they were Communists..'

'Well, he would say that, wouldn't he? His political sympathies are no secret.'

Fotheringay took a long sip of beer, looking quizzically at Andy. 'You didn't know your grandfather was with SOE?'

'How could I? All my family knows is that he was posted Missing in Action early in 1945, nothing further was heard from him, so he was presumed dead.'

'And dead men tell no tales,' Fotheringay said. He stood up. 'Well. It's been a pleasure meeting you, Andy. And thanks for the beer. I'll look forward to your new book. You take care now. Crete is a volatile place. Good day to you.'

'Cheerio,' Andy said. As Fotheringay left, he patted Andy's back low down, brushing his hand along his waistband. Watching him stride down the lane towards his car, Andy thought, that man's a spook, old boy. He was frisking me to see if I was carrying a pistol. Someone's checking me out, so someone in Korifi must know why I'm here. But I've only told Manoussos and Maria, and they've been asked not to mention the business with the cave. And they're completely trustworthy. But someone in Korifi knows enough, and is well enough connected, to have me checked out with Leigh Fermor back in Britain. But who could it be? And why are they doing it? Maybe they think I'm a spook. That could be it.

## Chapter 36

Eilidh, a keen runner, had learned about the forthcoming Samaria Gorge Race from the kids in the village. One of the local teenage boys had entered and ridiculed the idea of a foreign girl attempting such an arduous race. Thoroughly nettled, Eilidh decided to enter, and caused a minor sensation as she went for a training run every morning in shorts and a singlet, her hair streaming behind her in a ponytail. The number of young men in the kafeneion seemed to increase when she went running. Hardly surprising, Andy thought, for she's a very attractive young girl, so initially he was worried. But the local young men never wolf-whistled or yelled crude sexist remarks in the way they would do in Glasgow.

That evening, Eilidh was going with some other teenagers to an Eorti, a name-day party, in the nearby village of Imbros.

'Just watch the bevvy,' Andy said. 'The guys will be testing you, and young women don't get bevvied in Crete, okay?'

'Dad, I'm a big girl. Don't worry.'

Andy wandered down to the taverna where a group of the local shepherds were sitting outside enjoying the early evening heat, being served by Maria. They were obsessively curious about him and Eilidh. Although they all knew by now he was the grandson of the legendary Kapetan Yiannis, Sfakiani men simply did not trust foreigners, and up here in Korifi, Haniotes were foreigners even though the town was only an hour's drive away. So, he wasn't surprised when he was called over to join the company of the shepherds, who were drinking Tsichoudia. Yorgos and Stratis were present and pulled up a chair for him.

As they drank, Andy was bombarded with questions about

Scotland. He was asked if whisky was made from onions! Then he was asked if he believed in the Loch Ness Monster. Of course, Andy said, thinking that's some job the Scottish Tourist Board is doing. But then came the question shared by men around the world. Which team did he support? Andy admitted it was Celtic. There was a shepherd called Tassos Mavridakis at the table who for some reason didn't like him. Andy couldn't work out why but thought it might be to do with the fact that he spoke good, idiomatic Greek. He knew that Greeks believed that their language was too difficult for foreigners to master. He also knew the Greeks were wrong.

'We slaughtered Celtic,' Tassos said. 'Who are we?' Andy said. 'Korifi F.C?'

The men laughed; Tassos was not amused. 'AEK,' he said. A big Athens.

'I wouldn't call it a slaughter,' Andy said. 'You won 3 – 2 on aggregate.' Tassos snorted and tossed off his Tsichoudia. Andy beckoned Maria over and called for another round, as it was important to shout your round in a company of Cretan men. In that sense, they were just like Glaswegian men. Maria put a carafe of Tsichoudia and a cucumber on the table, for Greek men never drink without eating something. Andy took out his Puma folding knife, opened it, peeled the cucumber, sprinkled it with salt and chopped it into pieces. He put his open knife on the table and raised his glass.

'Se yeia,' Andy said.

'Se yeia,' the shepherds said.

Tassos picked up Andy's knife and tested the edge with his thumb. 'Hmm. Sharp.

It's a good knife. I'll just keep it.'

He folded the knife shut and put it in his pocket. There was silence round the table. 'Give me my knife back,' Andy said.

Tassos said nothing but stared at Andy and casually loosened his jacket. He carried a pistol in his waistband.

Practically every man in Korifi carried one. Oh no, Andy thought, here we go again, more macho posturing. It's like wee boys in a school playground in Glasgow shouting: 'ma Da will batter your Da'. But wee boys in Glasgow didn't carry pistols. Andy realised that to save face, he had to beat Tassos at his own macho game. He took a very deep breath and as calmly as possible said, 'Give me back my knife, or I'll come over the table and take it back.'

Tassos sneered. 'We know you don't carry a pistol, Andrea. You're a foreigner, you don't count. I could just shoot you and throw your body down a ravine, and nobody would know.'

The men round the table watched the exchange with inscrutable faces. Maria stood holding the tray, watching, as expressionless as the men.

'My daughter Eilidh would know. And she would tell my brothers. And my five brothers would come from Scotland and kill you, and all your sheep, and blow up your house.

You don't mess with my family.'

Tassos studied Andy for several moments, reached into his pocket and threw his knife on the table. 'I've got a better one,' he said, taking out his own knife, and opening it. It was much bigger than Andy's, a French Opinel knife with a wooden handle. Tassos laid it on the table.

'I think we need another round,' Yorgos said. 'Maria!'

Later, as Andy left the taverna, Maria followed him. She looked at him, shook her head in admiration and smiled. 'Ekanes kara, Andrea,' she said. Andy translated in his head: you done good, Andy.

Maria patted him on the shoulder. 'Five brothers, eh?.'

'To tell you the truth, I've no brothers. And one sister.'

Maria doubled up with laughter. 'Bravo, pedi mou.' Bravo, kid! Just as well she can't see the tremor in my knees, Andy thought. I was shitting myself back there.

## Chapter 37

It was early evening, and still. Andy took a bottle of Mythos beer out of the fridge and sat looking out over the plateau with his map, trying to work out where his grandfather's cave could possibly be. He was thinking that if it wasn't in the most likely place, it must be in an unlikely location, when Maria roared up on her motorbike. She jumped off and hung up her helmet.

'Yeia sou, Andrea,' she said. 'Is Eilidh here?'

'No. She's gone to Askyfou with some of the other kids.'

'Oh. I was going to ask her if she would like to come shopping to the village of Vrisses with me. Not to worry.'

'Why don't you sit down and have a drink? What can I get you?.'

'A beer would be good,' Maria said, sitting down.

Andy fetched the beer from the fridge, opened it, and handed it to Maria with a glass.

They sat looking out over the plateau.

'Eilidh is a lovely girl,' Maria said. 'She's very bright, very open, very warm, and mature for her years.'

'Thank you. I happen to agree.'

'And you have a very good relationship with your daughter.'

'Thank you.' My goodness. Another compliment. They drank.

'So, Andrea. You seem to like it here.'

'No, I don't like it, I love it. It's so beautiful. And peaceful.'

'Yes. Even I, who come from here, think it is beautiful.' She took a slug of her beer. 'Do you think you could live here?'

Andy stared at her, surprised at the question. 'I've no land. And no sheep.' Maria laughed.

Andy took a sip of his beer and considered the question more seriously. 'In theory I could, and in some senses, I would love to. But I think it would be difficult living here on my own.'

'That's very true.'

An agrotikon passed slowly on the road below and stopped at the junction with the dirt road up to the house. Maria leaned forward and frowned. The truck moved off. Maria muttered something nasty under her breath.

'What's up?' Andy said.

'That agrotikon belongs to Dimitris Mavridakis from Kallikratis,' Maria said. 'And ...'

'Really?' Andy said. 'I met him last week in the village. He was very friendly.' Maria looked aghast. 'Andrea. My clan and the Mavridakis clan are historic enemies, and ...'

'Do you mean vendettas?' Andy said.

'Yes, but in a muted sense. We avoid each other and tend to stay out of each other's villages. It's too risky otherwise.'

'What's that all about?'

'It's lost in the mists of time. But it's probably originally got to do with sheep-stealing.'

'And Mavridakis?'

'His family were in EOK during the War, and were strong supporters of the British, while my family was in ELAS, and did not trust the British. They are right-wing and we are left-wing. His grandfather died in mysterious circumstances during the War, and his family believe he was killed by ELAS. Nobody knows for sure. But one thing is sure: Dimitris Mavridakis is no friend of my family.'

'I see.'

'He's not a good man. And you should have nothing to do with him, because as a friend of our family, *you* are now a potential enemy.'

'Oh. Oh dear.'

Maria turned and looked straight into Andy's eyes. 'You may be a sophisticated Classics Professor in Scotland, Andrea, and you may know a lot about Eteo-Cretan and Minoan languages, but you know nothing about the culture of these mountains. Be careful. We have a saying up here: 'Αγριά βουνά, άγριοι άνθροποι'.'

"Wild mountains, wild people',' Andy translated. 'Correct. Remember it. Thank you for the drink.'

Maria got up, put on her helmet, started her motorbike, and drove off down the lane.

Well, I'll be damned, Andy thought. Wild people right enough.

## Chapter 38

The next morning, Andy sat outside the taverna with a Greek coffee checking his emails on his phone. Manoussos was out on the plateau tending his sheep, and Andy could hear the clanging of a metal bucket and a swishing noise as Maria cleaned the rooms above. She emptied the bucket down the stairs and began to mop them. Suddenly, she yelled and there was a series of metallic clanks as the bucket tumbled down the stairs, followed by loud groaning. Andy jumped to his feet and raced up the stairs. Maria was sitting on a stair, her face contorted with pain, holding her leg. 'My knee,' she gasped. 'I slipped on the water and fell.' She winced.

'No problem,' Andy said. 'Put your arm round my shoulder.' As Maria did so, he lent down, lifted her up, carried her down the stairs and sat her on a chair.

'Put your leg up on that chair,' he said, 'and let me see.'

He slid Maria's skirt up a few inches so that he could examine the injured knee. Maria promptly pulled it down again.

'Ntropi!' she exclaimed.

Andy knew what she meant. 'Ntropi' was one of these Greek words which was difficult to translate into English, but in this case it meant she was referring to sexual modesty, and the shame incurred for breaching it. He leant back and said in Greek, 'Maria. There isn't a problem with ntropi. I'm a married man with a teenage daughter. I've seen female skin before. And I've seen you in a bikini. Entaxi?' He took a breath and said, 'And furthermore …'

''Furthermore? What does that mean?'

'It means 'and also,' or 'besides which'.' Andy looked Maria in the eye with a mischievous grin and said,

'Furthermore, as the Bible says, I am pure of heart.'

Maria looked at Andy for a second or two and suddenly laughed – followed by another gasp of pain.

'Let me look at that knee.' Maria nodded reluctant assent.

As Andy gently probed her knee with his fingers, Maria winced and gasped. 'There. Just there.'

'You've banged your patella – your kneecap – and I can feel the heat,' Andy said. 'That can be painful. Have you got any bags of frozen vegetables in the freezer?'

'Yes. There's …'

'Don't move.' Andy hurried into the kitchen and found a large cellophane bag full of green beans in the freezer compartment of the big fridge. 'Tickety-boo,' he said to himself, taking out the beans. He went back outside, put the cold bag of beans on Maria's knee, and said, 'Hold it there. I'll be back in a minute.'

He ran up the stairs to his room, grabbed his toilet-bag and took out a packet of Nurofen. He extracted two capsules, went back down into the kitchen, filled a glass with cold water, and handed it and a capsule to Maria. 'Take this and wash it down with water. It's an anti-inflammatory and a painkiller. Take the other one in four hours from now.'

Maria swallowed the capsule and took a drink of water, still holding the cold bag on her kneecap. 'Where did you learn all this?'

'Playing football. I play in a football team in my university – it's called Achilles Athletic – and there's always some kind of sporting injury.'

'My goodness,' Maria said. 'Classicist, Minoan expert, Greek-speaker, mountaineer, paramedic – and footballer!'

Andy grinned. 'Well, I am Scottish.' Maria laughed.

A little later, Manoussos appeared. 'What's all this?' he said, pointing to the bag of beans on Maria's knee.

'I fell and hurt my knee, and Andy has been treating it.'

As Andy watched, the old man said, 'Bah – nonsense!'

– and went into the kitchen. He reappeared with a clean rag and a bottle of Tsichoudia. He soaked the rag with the spirit, removed the bag of beans, threw it on the table, and tied the rag round Maria's knee as Andy watched, astonished. 'It will soon be better,' Manoussos said.

Maria smiled at Andy. 'Aches and pains, coughs and colds, cuts and bruises, knife and bullet wounds – Tsichoudia is the universal medicine in Sfakia.'

'So I see. Unreal!'

That evening, as Andy prepared to go home, Maria limped out of the taverna.

'Thank you for your help, Andrea,' she said. 'I put the bag of cold beans back on my knee when my father isn't looking. It works. You have good hands.'

My goodness, Andy thought, she's paid me another compliment.

## Chapter 39

Andy took a deep breath at the summit of the mountain called Spathi: the Sword. It had been a hard slog up through the shattered rock. He sat down with his back to a boulder, took out his water-bottle, and looked round. At first glance, the White Mountains constituted a trackless stony desert. But Andy knew that in fact, they were criss-crossed by the songlines of the shepherds from the surrounding mountain villages. He also knew it was crossed by the long-distance E4 European footpath. But it was still a rocky wilderness, and you had to be a competent mountain walker to venture into the waterless interior.

Just as Andy bent down to take his sandwiches out of his day bag, there was a crack – thump, a chip of rock flew past his head, and a bullet ricocheted off the boulder with a whine. Jesus! Andy grabbed his bag and bounded into cover just as another bullet hit the boulder. He was paralysed with fear. He couldn't see the shooter but guessed he must be to the south of his position, so with his heart in his mouth, he worked his way north, contouring round a ridge. Suddenly, he found himself up against a dead end, a steep rock face perhaps seventy feet in height. Andy took it in very quickly. It looked like it was climbable. He took a deep breath and launched himself onto the face, climbing down. As he did so, a shower of rocks flew past him, missing him narrowly. Some bastard is trying to kill me, he thought as he swung into a narrow gully. Jamming his back against one side of the gully, and the soles of his boots on the other, he began to chimney his way down as quickly as he could. He remembered when he was practising on the Backstep Chimney route on The Whangie, his father had told him the trick was to maintain as much friction as possible. A large boulder whizzed past him only a couple of feet away. Fuck me! His knees began to tremble uncontrollably, and his heartbeat was thundering in his ears, so he accelerated.

At the foot of the gully, Andy scrambled away as fast as possible, the convex shape of the cliff making another shot impossible. Reaching the cover of a cluster of large boulders, Andy looked up, just in time to see a figure move away from the top of the cliff. He paused for a couple of minutes and took several deep breaths for his whole body was trembling, and he felt as if his knees wouldn't hold him up for long. A few moments later, he jogged towards the main Vrisses to Hora Sfakion road in the distance. He reached the village of Vrisses just in time to catch the bus which went to Hora via Korifi, Askyfou and Imbros. On the way, he decided he would say nothing about this incident to Maria, Manoussos and Eilidh, because he did not want to alarm them, on the one hand, and he did not want to be responsible for starting a vendetta, on the other. And he wished his knees would stop trembling. He had to find that bloody cave and its contents as quickly as possible.

# Part 10

## John Gallagher: Crete, 1944

## Chapter 40

As winter approached, Themia arrived in Panayia with an understrength platoon of ELAS Andartes from Sfakia, and while I was pleased to see her, her presence was giving me a headache. She was making no attempt now to hide the fact that she fancied me. I was flattered as she was a lovely woman, very bonny with it, and I've got to admit I fancied her too. But I was spoken for back in Glasgow. I was promised to Maeve, I'd asked her to marry me, and I couldn't go back on that, especially as she now had our wean. I've been worried sick about that.

My billet was in a small, abandoned farmhouse on the top of a steep hill just to the south of Panayia. It commanded good views of the surrounding countryside. I had made it comfortable, brought in a stock of firewood, stashed some ration-packs, and had plenty of wine and Tsichoudia. Normally, I shared the house with my teenage runner, Vangelis, but I had given the boy the weekend off to visit his family in Armenoi. Outside, the weather was foul, with a swirling wind and heavy rain containing a lot of sleet. The nights were fairly drawing in, I thought, as I put more wood on the fire and lit the oil-lamps. I poured myself a glass of wine, sat down at the table and started to write another letter.

There was a loud knock at the door, and a voice called, 'Kapetan Yianni!' I opened the door to find Themia outside holding up a steaming pot.

'Soupa yia sena,' she said. Soup for you. 'Ella,' I said. Come in.

She came in. Her cap, hair, battledress tunic and trousers were soaking, and water ran down the barrel of her rifle, slung upside-down. I took the pot from her and put it at the side of the fire as the girl shivered and warmed her hands. I rummaged in a drawer and pulled out a dry British Army woollen shirt and pullover, and a pair of khaki denims.

'Ella,' I said, handing her the dry clothes and a towel. It was a good all-purpose Greek word. On this occasion, it meant, 'here you are'. Then I deliberately turned my back on her and began to make some supper. As she stripped off her wet clothes behind me, I chopped up an onion with my Commando dagger and fried it gently over the fire in some olive oil. I then sliced a couple of cloves of garlic, flattened them with the blade, and added it to the onion. Opening a tin of bully-beef, I emptied it into the frying-pan. When it was all bubbling, I added it to the soup. Themia hung her wet clothes on a chair in front of the fire, and sat at the table, smiling as she watched me cook while drying her rifle. That's the mark of a good soldier, I thought. I poured her a glass of wine.

'Se yeia,' I said. I gestured expansively with my arms round the room. 'Taverna Kapetan Yiannis.'

She laughed out loud. 'Se yeia,' she said as I reheated the soup. She watched me for a moment, then with a serious expression said in Greek, 'Kapetan Yiannis. Why are you here? Why are you fighting with ELAS, with us? The British officers don't do any fighting. Only you fight with us.'

Well, bugger me, I thought, that's a good question. 'I'm here because we're allies,' I said. 'But there's more to it than that. I'm with ELAS because you and the other Andartes and me – we're much more than Allies, we're comrades. We all believe it's possible to have a more democratic society after the War. We must believe it's possible. I want to help you achieve this. And I will try – because I'm a comrade too.'

Themia nodded. 'Yes. We want Laokratia. And no King.'

Well, I could drink to that! People's Rule and no King? You bet! I poured myself a glass of wine, and we clinked glasses. 'Laokratia. And no King.'

I added a pinch of salt to the soup, stirred it in and set the pot on the table. I found two bowls, filled them, and we ate. The soup was made from beans and the odd potato, but the bully-beef, onion and garlic gave it some body, and it was hot. Themia ate like there was no tomorrow, and I realised the girl was starving. I knew the diet of the Andartes was poor, so I filled her bowl again. She smiled her thanks, wolfed the soup down and took a gulp of wine.

I picked up the jug of wine and refilled her glass. As I did so, her fingers caressed my hand. I put the jug down. She took my hand in both of hers, very slowly, and held it tightly. She had been looking down at our clasped hands, then slowly raised her head. The reflection of the fire flickered in her eyes, which held an ineffable longing. She opened out my fingers and kissed the palm gently. I took a deep breath, and said, 'Themia. I'm spoken for. I have a fiancée back in Scotland.'

She put a finger on my lips and said, 'She's there. I'm here.'

What to do? I knew I still had deep feelings for Maeve, but I had to admit that I also really wanted Themia. And as she said, she was here, and she knew what she was doing.

Bending down, she took off her boots. Then she stood up facing me, took off the khaki pullover, slowly unbuttoned her British army shirt, and slipped it off. She was wearing nothing underneath. Still looking directly at me, she undid her trousers, wriggled her hips to let them fall, and stepped out of them. The reflection of the flames of the fire danced over her naked body. Oh my God, she was absolutely gorgeous, she was all curves. Still looking straight into my eyes and smiling, she held out her hands. I stood up. She unbuttoned my shirt and slid it off. As I took off my army vest, she knelt, unlaced my boots, and pulled them off. Then she stood up, undid my belt, and let my trousers fall to the floor. I stepped out of them and slid off my underpants. We looked deeply into each other's eyes, then at our lips, and slowly, ever so slowly, kissed. That kiss went on and on until I thought I would lose my breath. I could taste the wine we had been drinking on her lips. Themia broke loose and taking my wrists in her hands, drew me back towards the bed. She lay down on it, smiled, and opened her arms. 'Ella, agapi mou,' she said. ' Come here, my love.'

I lay down beside her. My fingers explored her body, gently tracing the outline of her breasts. Her hand reached out and held me close, stroking my back while her eyes danced yes-yes-yes. As I stroked her gently, her breathing accelerated and suddenly, she grabbed me and slipped me inside her. We lay like that for some time, rocking gently backwards and forwards, the fire crackling behind us. I grew harder and harder until she grasped my buttocks and pulled me into her, wrapping her legs round my back. As I drove into her, she gasped, 'Ne, ne, ne – tora!' I could translate that all right – yes, yes, yes – now! – as she cried out and arched her back, pulling me tightly to her. I collapsed on top of her, and she held me close. We lay still like that for what seemed a long time.

I suddenly realised from the rhythmic shaking of her body that Themia was weeping silently. I raised myself up and kissed her tears away gently. She smiled and said, 'Oh Yianni mou, Yianni mou.' With a sudden surprisingly strong move, she rolled on top of me and began kissing my face. She moved down onto my chest, then my stomach, and I felt myself growing hard again. Reaching down between her legs, she slipped me inside her again. She sat up and rocked backwards and forwards, gripping me with all her strength, and grinding into me. She began to rotate her hips, slowly gaining speed until I thought I would explode. Then leaning backwards, she rode me until I did explode inside her, with a deep shuddering groan. She moved faster and faster until she too came with a cry. She collapsed on top of me, her whole body contracting in a series of violent spasms. She took my face in her hands and studied it, then kissed me again and again and again.

'Oh Yianni,' she said. 'You make me so happy.'

A little later, the cold woke me up. I slid out from underneath her, covered her with hand-woven blankets, and built up the fire. As I climbed back in beside her, she reached out, smiling, with her eyes still shut, and enveloped me in her arms. As I closed my own eyes again, I thought, I've died and gone to heaven.

Shortly after dawn, Themia shook me awake. As she hurriedly tied her bootlaces, she jerked her head to a sudden sound. To the north, from Panayia, there was the rattle of rifle-fire. She grabbed her rifle, kissed me briefly but passionately, and sprinted out of the door.

## Chapter 41

Shortly afterwards, Major Ford dropped in to assess the local situation, as my Andartes were the nearest to the Germans. I briefed him, then asked him what the reaction to his Report had been from SOE HQ in Crete.

'I've heard nothing, Sergeant,' he said, 'and I don't think I'm going to. It's plain to me that Colonel Dunbar's attitude towards ELAS has been coloured completely by that twerp in SOE HQ in Cairo who's in charge of the Cretan desk. The Colonel was already anti-ELAS before he even came to Crete and he's not going to change his mind. The twerp is a fanatical monarchist and fanatically anti-Communist, simple as that.'

I knew he was referring to that officer with the double-barrelled name who had given us the lecture about Greek Resistance politics at the guerrilla warfare school. The one who had slapped me down. I objected, 'But Cretan ELAS isn't …'

'I know. I know. But the Colonel doesn't want to know. SOE in Cairo believes that Greek ELAS – including Crete – is a communist-controlled organisation manipulated by Moscow. Therefore, SOE wants to make sure that it doesn't have any power as the War draws to a conclusion. That way, they believe they will prevent ELAS staging a coup and taking over the Greek state.'

'What a load of keech.'

'Keech, Sergeant?'

'Sorry, sir. Scots word. "Shite".'

'Correct. But the western Allies are afraid of Russia and its postwar intentions, and that's why they're afraid of ELAS.'

'It makes our position with ELAS here dodgy, sir.'

'It does. But we must continue to do the best we can. I'm trying to funnel some arms and ammunition to them on the sly, and you must continue to train them, not least to prevent the Germans from liquidating them – or anyone else, for that matter.

'Och, I'll do that no bother, sir.'

'I know. You're very popular with the Andartes, Sergeant. They trust you, and they seem to trust me. We must work to maintain that trust – but we can't control what happens in Greece after the end of the War.'

'And it's not our business anyway, sir.'

'Exactly. But I fear that London and Washington are going to make it their business whether the Greeks like it or not.'

I said nothing but thought plenty. What a bloody mess. I wondered if it would be smart to get out of Crete before the shit hit the fan. But how on earth could I do that?

## Chapter 42

I leopard-crawled up to the skyline and peered over. German soldiers were skirmishing forward behind a mortar barrage, being fired on by the Andartes on the surrounding hills. Focussing my binoculars, I could see that although the Germans had superior firepower, they were making slow progress towards the village. This was because they were advancing up the road from Mournies so that they could be supported by a couple of half-tracks, but this gave the Andartes the advantage of height. As I watched, several Germans went down.

There was a rattle of stones, and Vangelis slid up beside me. The boy had an MP 40 sub-machine gun, which must have been a trophy from the Battle of Crete, probably taken from a German paratrooper he had killed.

'Vangeli,' I said. 'I want you to work your way up to the forward position of the Andartes. Do not, I repeat, do not, engage the enemy unless your life is in danger. Ask the Andarte commander for a situation report and tell him to conserve ammunition at all costs. Come back and report to me here, okay?'

'Okay, Kapetan.' Vangelis slithered backwards and disappeared. For the next twenty minutes or so, the boy worked his way forward, making excellent use of dead ground and natural cover. A half an hour later, he re-appeared, panting like an overworked sheepdog. I let him get his breath back.

'Themia is in command of the forward platoon,' Vangelis said. 'She says she can hold the Germans for the time being, but she can't attack them and drive them back because of a shortage of ammunition. They've only got about twenty or thirty rounds per man left. And the Germans are supported by two Hanomag armoured cars mounted with heavy machine-guns. Themia reckons they can just about hold out until nightfall when the Germans will withdraw back to Hania. She needs more ammunition urgently.'

'Well done,' I said, patting the teenager on the shoulder. Vangelis glowed with pride. I focused my binoculars and, in the distance, could see the two German half-tracks laying down heavy repressive machine-gun fire. It was going to be touch-and-go keeping them out of the village before nightfall.

At dusk, the Germans retreated without having penetrated the village's defences, and I went back to my house with Vangelis. An hour or so later, Themia arrived. 'The Germans have retreated,' she said, 'but we killed quite a few of them. Colonel Micheloyiannis reckons we can hold the position, but we are desperately short of ammunition. And the wankers from EOK have run away up to the village of Madaró and watch us while we do the fighting. We think they, and the British, want the Germans to destroy us. Is there anything you can do about more ammunition, Yianni?'

'I'll try,' I said. 'But it's now clear to me that SOE isn't going to give ELAS any arms or ammunition.'

Nevertheless, I wrote a short note and gave it to Vangelis. 'There is a British Liaison Officer at Zourva. Find him and give him this note.'

After the boy left, I put together a meal, and then Themia and I went to bed. As I wrapped my arms round her, I realised that she was already sound asleep.

The next morning, Vangelis arrived back and handed me a note as the crackle of gunfire grew closer to Panayia. I opened it and read:

Aleko is at a briefing meeting in Rethimno. I am his 2 i/c. His orders are explicit: We do not repeat <u>do not</u> supply

ELAS 14th Brigade with any arms or ammunition.
Stephanos.
Capt.

'Bastards,' I muttered. I knew that Aleko was the codename of the SOE officer in charge of western Crete, but Stephanos – also a code name – was a new arrival. SOE was now flooding Crete with British Liaison Officers (BLOs) and training NCOs. By now, I had little doubt that it was to ensure that ELAS did not gain any local power when the War ended.

'Who did you see up in Zourva, Vangeli?'

'There was this English Captain called Stephanos, and an English Sergeant-Major,' the boy said. 'Stephanos told the Sergeant-Major that there was a truck with boxes of ammunition south of Panayia which was for EOK. I saw it parked near the track as I returned. But they don't know where EOK is because of all the fighting in the area, so they don't know where to send it.'

'Right, Vangeli. Find Themia and tell her to hang on and say that I'm going to try and bring her more ammunition this afternoon. I'm going to go and get that truck.' I winked, and the boy grinned.

I found a British Army 15-hundredweight truck hidden underneath the trees beside the dirt track which ran roughly east-west along the foothills of the White Mountains but couldn't see any driver or sentry. I approached it, pistol at the ready, and lifted the tarpaulin cover. There were about a dozen metal boxes of .303 ammunition in the back, and a couple of wooden boxes of Mills 36 hand-grenades. I jumped in, started the engine, and drove the lorry towards Panayia. I could hear increased gunfire and see a rising plume of smoke – the Germans must have broken into the village. Parking the truck, I ran forward to see what was going on. There was fierce fighting at the northern edge of the village, and a couple of houses were already ablaze.

I yelled at a young Andarte to find Themia and tell her to come here at once with a couple of men as I had more ammunition for her.

Suddenly, I heard a motorbike approaching. It was a Wehrmacht motorbike and sidecar combination, but the driver was an EOK Andarte with someone in British Army and battledress in the sidecar. The motorbike hit a bump, stalled, and a British officer jumped out of the sidecar, looked round, spotted me, and ran towards me. He was a Captain. The EOK Andarte dodged into the village. The Captain was furious. 'Sergeant, I'm Captain Stephanos,' he yelled, 'and my explicit orders were no ammunition for ELAS.'

Just then, Themia and two Andartes ran up. 'The Germans have broken into the village,' she said in Greek, 'but we're running out of ammunition and will have to retreat, and the Germans will torch it.'

The Captain yelled at me again and I told him to shut the fuck up, as we were involved in a firefight, one we had to win to save the village. I then told Themia that there were boxes of ammunition and hand-grenades in the back of the truck, and to get them up to her Andartes as fast as possible. She jumped up into it and began to pass the boxes out to her comrades. Captain Stephanos was livid.

'Tell that woman to put these boxes back in the lorry, Sergeant,' he yelled. 'Immediately!'

'No Sir,' I replied. 'That is an illegal, immoral, and improper order which I refuse to obey. 'That woman' is our Greek ally, and she and her men are fighting the common enemy – who are the Germans, in case you'd forgotten.'

Stephanos went berserk. 'You're on a charge of wilfully disobeying a legitimate order,' he howled, 'and I'll see you court-martialled for it.' He turned to Themia and yelled, 'Stop! Stop it once.'

Themia ignored him and continued to throw the boxes of ammo out as fast as possible. The Captain fumbled his pistol out of his holster, and I realised he meant to shoot Themia. I whipped out my own pistol and just as I was about to shoot him in the leg, one of her Andartes shoved him roughly aside. He fell forward and my shot hit him in the head, killing him instantly. I saw his EOK Andarte staring at me, his eyes popping out of his head before he sprinted off down a lane and vanished. The enormity of what had just happened made me freeze. But as Themia finished unloading, I pulled myself together and told her to distribute the ammunition, give her Andartes two or three grenades each, make a frontal attack on the Germans using the grenades, drive them out of the village, and try to disable the half-tracks.

As the two Andartes doubled back for the last ammunition boxes, Themia smiled and patted my cheek. 'S'agapo, Yianni mou,' she said, and sprinted away. Jesus, what a time to tell me she loves me. A minute later, a whistle blew a piercing blast, there was a sudden series of crumps, increased rifle-fire, and war-cries from the north of the village. That was the counter-attack going in. It was successful. The Germans were driven out of the village with heavy losses.

A little later, Themia appeared and hustled me back to the house for I was in a state of complete shock. I had just killed a British Army Captain, a member of the same unit as myself. The fact that it was an accident was beside the point. Nobody in SOE would believe that. I was in a state of complete panic, my heart began to palpitate, I felt nauseous and dizzy, and I had trouble breathing. I was finished. What was I going to do?

## Chapter 43

That was the worst night of my life. I couldn't sleep a wink, for I realised I was in deep shit. Not only had I killed a British Army officer, but an SOE officer at that. An Inquiry and a court-martial were inevitable, and as I had disobeyed an explicit order, there could only be one outcome. And they would never believe it was an accident. If I went on the run in Crete, they would come after me, and SOE had plenty of trained killers who would shoot me without blinking an eyelid. Even if I managed to get back to Scotland undetected, they would come after me there, and there would be a fatal 'accident.' If I managed to hide on Crete, and there was a possibility of that, I would never see Maeve again, and never ever see my son. I was in despair and couldn't think straight. My whole body was trembling, my brain was paralysed, and I was gibbering uncontrollably.

Themia eventually came up with the solution. 'Listen, Yianni mou, I've got an idea,' she said. 'First of all, I'll take care of that EOK Andarte. Don't you worry about that. Then, both the British and the Cretans must think you're dead. We will spread the story that you've been killed in the fighting at Panayia, for this is something people would believe because they know you're involved. Then you must vanish.'

'But ... but how on earth am I going to fake my death?.'

'You'll think of something.'

Then I remembered seeing the grave of a British soldier at the side of the road to Mournies, with a makeshift wooden cross with the date: 24.8.44. He was probably one of the men on the run caught and shot by the Germans.

After dark, Themia and I moved carefully forward north of Panayia. I had an entrenching tool. There was nobody about. The Germans had retired behind their perimeter, and the Andartes to the Keramies villages behind us. We were literally in no-man's-land. As Themia stood guard, I dug up the grave. I came across the body quickly, a couple of feet below the surface. However, it had nearly dried out, and I could see the holes in his shirt where he had been hit by machine-gun fire. I detached the dead man's identity discs and replaced them with my own. I filled in the grave again, tamped the earth down, threw several handfuls of dust over it, and removed the wooden cross. Then we went back to Panayia, and on the way, I broke up the cross and dropped the dead soldier's discs into a drain.

The story was spread that I had last been seen charging a German machine-gun post outside Panayia, lobbing grenades at it. I had not been seen since, so it was presumed that I had been killed in that action. Vangelis hung about in Panayia for a couple of weeks spreading that story, and that I had been buried nearby, and sure enough, Aleko and two British NCOs came looking for me. But the Andartes repeated the story of my death, and after digging up the grave, the British soldiers went away. The EOK Andarte had apparently been killed in action.

To stay alive, I had to vanish, simple as that. But how? Themia again provided the solution. She was desperate to hang onto me, I knew that, and she came up with an ingenious plan.

Her idea was that I should go with her to Korifi and assume the identity of her late husband. The story would be that I had miraculously survived the War on mainland Greece, I had been fighting with ELAS continuously and had been unable to get home to Crete until the end of the War. We would live in Korifi as man and wife, for I could never return to Scotland. And Themia insisted on us getting married for that would legitimate the story – and any children we might have. Although the idea of never being able to return to Glasgow and see Maeve and my son appalled me, I had no option but to agree.

Themia and I were secretly married by a priest sympathetic to ELAS, and the small wedding party was attended by comrades from Themia's unit. Themia was over the moon to acquire a new husband, but for me, it was a bitter-sweet occasion, for although I was very fond of Themia, I was crippled with guilt about having to abandon Maeve and Michael.

What on earth was I going to tell Maeve?

I started working as a shepherd with Themia's first cousin Nikos, also an ex-ELAS Andarte. Some of the villagers knew that I was not Themia's original husband, but most would believe the story. And as Themia had been a respected Andartissa, and as my reputation as Kapetan Yiannis preceded me, they participated in the conspiracy of silence. On the other hand, a few – a very few – villagers objected to the story saying that I was not Themia's missing soldier husband. Themia shut them up by saying: are you calling me a liar? Her wartime reputation ensured their subsequent silence.

# Part 11

**Andy Gallagher: Crete, 2010**

## Chapter 44

Andy stared at his map. If the cave wasn't in the obvious place, then it must be in some place which wasn't obvious. Elementary, my dear Gallagher. But where? He and Eilidh had scoured the area to the south of the Skoutsio ridge to no avail. Where could the wounded John have staggered to? His journal said that despite extensive searching in the postwar years, he had never been able to find the cave again. The only possible remaining place was the valley of Mavri Laki to the south-west of the ridge. But that seems too far for a wounded man to have staggered, Andy thought. Then again, as John was likely to have been in a state of shock, he might not have been aware of his heading. Best search it to be on the safe side. Andy showed Maria the search area on the map and asked her what she thought.

'It's the only possible other place,' she said.

The next morning, Andy, Eilidh and Maria made their way from the Skoutsio summit west-south-west into the Mavri Laki Valley. They all studied the terrain.

'That's rough country,' Eilidh observed. 'I wouldn't want to be lost in there.'

'Me neither,' Andy said.

They spread out and began to search the valley systematically. But by midday, they had found nothing. They sat down, and Andy scanned the remaining area through his binoculars. 'Hey! Look! What's that up there, beside that lone tree? A fencepost?'

'There are no fence posts on that mountain,' Maria replied. 'Right. Let's go up there and find out what it is,' Andy said.

They scrambled up the steep slope. Andy paused, focused his binoculars again, and gasped. 'It's a rifle,' he said. 'Now I remember. John's journal said he lost his rifle in the snow when he was wounded and couldn't find it again. What we're seeing is the butt sticking up in the air. It must have fallen vertically into the snow and got jammed in that position. Can you see it?'

'Yes,' Eilidh said.

'That means that the cave must be somewhere close by,' Andy muttered. He and Eilidh and Maria looked at each other with excitement.

'Give me the binoculars,' Maria said. She focused on the tree, high above them. 'Yes. That tree is a juniper, which can grow at height. And frequently the caves in the mountains are camouflaged by trees or bushes. Our cave's got to be nearby. Obviously, your grandfather wandered off to the west after he was wounded and probably found the cave by sheer accident.'

'Right,' Andy said.

'Cool,' Eilidh declared. 'What do we do now?'

'What we do now is nothing,' Andy replied. 'Keep looking at me. Look at me!

We're not going up to that tree because I've got a feeling we're being watched. Don't look round! We'll go back down the mountain looking as if we have found nothing of importance.'

Back down at the house, Eilidh said, 'I don't get it, Dad. Why are you into all this evasion?.'

'I've got a feeling that we're being watched by this Mavridakis dude,' Andy replied. 'Why do you think that?'

'His family are hereditary enemies of Maria's, he's curious as to why I'm searching in the mountains, so we've got to find the cave, get into it, find what is buried there, and get out again without him knowing. We'll go back early tomorrow morning and get that rifle. And then do a detailed search of the area round the tree.'

Eilidh's face creased in a frown. 'Maria is worried about this whole deal, Dad. I can't quite work out what the problem is, but she seems to be genuinely afraid of something. She seems to think we might be getting ourselves into some kind of trouble.'

'I know. And I think I know what it might be. I read in John's journal that he executed a traitor amongst the Andartes during the War. He got a fair trial, but John found they butchered him with their knives, so he shot him dead to put him out of his misery and dumped his body in a ravine.'

'Oh my God.'

'Quite. It seems possible that he might have been a Mavridakis from the village of Kallikratis, and I met a guy called Mavridakis from there. Maria says he's no good.'

'Are he and the executed man related?'

'I think the man who was executed may have been the grandfather of the man in Kallikratis. Maria says there is an old feud between their two clans.'

There was the familiar roar of a motorbike from outside. It stopped, and Maria came in, taking off her helmet.

'Yeia sas,' she said. 'You two look very serious. What's going on?'

'Well,' Andy said. 'We're worried because you're worried. But we're not sure what it is precisely that you're worried about.'

Maria sat down. 'Remember that agrotikon which stopped briefly at the foot of the road below the other day?'

'Yes. You said it belonged to Dimitris Mavridakis, who was no good.' Maria nodded. 'Yes.'

'Well, there's something I haven't told you,' Andy said. 'My grandfather's journal says that he executed a traitor during the War. Do you know his name?'

Maria gasped. 'Yes. Phillipos Mavridakis from Kallikratis. He was Dimitris's grandfather. The family suspected that he had been killed by ELAS but never knew how or why. This must never get out. And you must leave as soon as possible. Because Dimitris Mavridakis is following you.'

Andy and Eilidh looked at each other in consternation. 'How do you know that?' Eilidh said.

'When I was up on Niato the other day, I saw Dimitris through my binoculars watching you on the Skoutsio ridge through his binoculars. He wants to know why you are here, and what it is you are looking for. And if he finds out that it was your grandfather who killed his grandfather, he will kill you. That is the law of the blood-feud in Crete.'

'Jesus,' Eilidh said. 'That is really, really heavy.'

A leaden silence hung in the room.

'It is,' Andy said. 'It's heavy enough for someone to have taken a pot-shot at me the other day. Several, in fact.'

'Oh my God,' Eilidh said.

'You were shot at?' Maria said simultaneously. 'Yes.'

'Then you must leave Crete immediately.'

'No bloody way,' Andy said. 'I'm not leaving until I find that cave and what my grandfather buried in it. I want to know what the Hell is going on here.'

'I agree,' Eilidh said. 'We must finish the job.'

Maria shook her head with admiration. 'Crazy Scottish people,' she said. 'That's us,' Andy said happily. 'Trozos.' Nuts.

'Wait. I've an idea, 'Eilidh said. 'If this Mavridakis dude is tailing Dad, then he can't be tailing me. Or Maria.'

'So?' Andy said.

'So why don't we send Mavridakis on a wild goose chase? Dad goes somewhere that has nothing to do with the cave, Mavridakis follows him, while we search the area where that rifle is, and find the cave.'

'I'm not at all happy about that,' Andy said. 'This search is getting too dangerous, and I think it's time you went home.'

'No,' Eilidh said, bristling. 'I'm not in danger. It's you that's in danger. And if you're in danger, I'm staying with you. We're family. You're my Dad. And we must make one last effort to find whatever it is. That's the deal.'

'Thank you, Eilidh. I appreciate that. Right. Can you make some suggestions as to how we might do this, Maria?'

'Yes, that's easy,' Maria said, laying out the map of the White Mountains on the table. 'Dimitris Mavridakis already knows that you are interested in the Skoutsio area. So, I suggest you go up to Niato, park your car, and head down the path towards Kali Lakkoi. But when you reach the ruined house at Trikoukia, here' – she tapped the map – 'turn left on the new path and make your way back to the Tavri plateau. You can't miss it because you will see the Greek Alpine Club mountain hut. But Mavridakis has the advantage because he is fit and knows the area, whereas you don't. You must move fast so that he doesn't see you turn off and carries on towards Kali Lakkoi. That will give us time to search the area of the rifle in Mavri Laki.'

'Oh, you don't have to worry about Dad,' Eilidh said. 'He may be a dinosaur, but he's a very fit dinosaur. He runs half-marathons and is good in the mountains. So, he'll have no problem.'

'My goodness,' Maria said, grinning. 'Distinguished Professor, ancient Cretan language expert, mountaineer, footballer, paramedic, and athlete – my hero!'

Andy and Eilidh burst out laughing.

## Chapter 45

The plan Andy, Maria and Eilidh eventually devised was simple, but hopefully effective. Maria and Eilidh were going to head up to Niato before dawn on the motorbike, climb into Mavri Laki at first light, and head straight for the cave with a headlamp and a large trowel in a day bag. Andy was going to head south out of Niato on the footpath to Kali Lakkoi, followed by Mavridakis, but a little way down, he was going to double back to the Tavri plateau on a minor path. They would all rendezvous back at the house where hopefully Eilidh and Maria would have obtained whatever was buried in the cave.

Eilidh and Maria climbed up to the rifle, which was embedded between two rocks with its muzzle stuck in the earth. Maria pulled it out of the ground. 'It's a good souvenir,' she said. 'We'll clean it up and put it on the wall of the taverna.'

The two women climbed up to the juniper tree, and when they got there, the narrow entrance to the cave was just visible above them. But you would have walked right past it below if you didn't know it was there. Eilidh took off her day bag and opened it. She put on a Petzl headlamp and picked up the trowel.

'Here goes,' she said. 'Keep a good lookout.'

Maria nodded as the girl slithered into the cave. Once inside, Eilidh stood up. The cave was dry, and perhaps fifteen feet in diameter, with rock walls which converged ten feet above her head. The floor was uneven and formed mainly of pebbles.

Eilidh tilted her head so that the headlamp beam covered the floor, but she could see no obvious signs of disturbance.

Squatting, she started digging in the centre of the floor with the trowel. Within a minute, there was a metallic clink. Scraping carefully, she unearthed an aluminium tube nearly one centimetre in diameter. She pulled it out; it was quite heavy. *Oh my God*, she thought. *What is it?*

'I've found something,' she called out to Maria. 'It's a metal tube, quite heavy.'

She continued digging and within a few more minutes, had unearthed another nine tubes. Eilidh carefully banged the pebbles down with the flat of her trowel and stamped on her handiwork. She threw the trowel out of the cave, passed the ten tubes out to Maria, wriggled out, turned her headlamp off, and dusted herself down. 'All clear?'

'All clear,' Maria said.

Andy jogged off down the kalderimi going south from Niato towards Kalo Lakkoi. The minor path to Tavri he was looking for could not be far away, and sure enough, within a few minutes, he found it.

Half an hour later, Mavridakis realised that Andy was not on the path in front of him. He swore, turned on his heel and hurried back to Niato, just in time to see Maria and Eilidh on the motorbike vanish on the other side of the plateau. It looked like they had come from the direction of Mavri Laki, so he set off uphill. Once in the feature, Mavridakis spotted the trowel lying under the juniper tree. He found the entrance to the cave within seconds, and with difficulty, crawled in. He could tell from the colouring of the pebbles that they had been dug up. But what had they dug up?

That evening, Andy, Maria and Eilidh sat around the table looking at the ten aluminium tubes.

'You found them, Eilidh,' Andy said, 'so you open them.'

Eilidh lifted one of the tubes and unscrewed the cap gingerly. She tilted the tube, and a rain of coins spilled onto the table with a ringing sound.

'Oh my God!' Eilidh said. 'It *is* treasure.'

Andy and Maria looked at each other in astonishment. 'Jesus,' he said, 'you're telling me.'

Andy picked up one of the coins and examined it. 'It's a sovereign. Ah! I know what must have happened. During the War, the Brits dropped more than a million gold sovereigns into Greece to pay the Andartes in the Resistance. This lot must be from one of the drops to pay the Cretan Andartes. And my grandfather must have been in charge of disbursing them. He must have buried them when he knew he was going to have to stay on in Crete after the War.'

'What does 'disbursing' mean?' Maria said.

'Paying them out,' Andy said. 'I remember reading that it was something like one sovereign per month to a married Andarte with a family. Anyway, let's count them and see how many we have.'

It transpired that each tube contained one hundred coins; one thousand gold sovereigns in total. Andy sorted through the pile.

'The majority show the head of Queen Victoria as an older woman, but there are also some showing her as a younger woman,' he said. 'See?'

He showed Eilidh and Maria examples of the two different coins. Maria counted them.

'There are nine hundred of the old heads and one hundred of the young heads..'

'How much are they worth?' Eilidh asked.

'Get onto your laptop and find out,' Andy said.

Eilidh got to work. A few minutes later, she said, 'The old heads are fetching about £230 each, and the young heads about £240.'

'So, we're looking at about £230,00 here,' Andy said, struggling for breath. 'A small fortune.'

'Wow!' Eilidh gasped. 'A quarter of a million pounds. Awesome. Talk about treasure!'

'What are you going to do with them?' Maria said. 'Good question,' Andy said.

'Presumably they're the property of the British government,' Maria said.

'Are you going to give them back?'

Andy hesitated for a moment, staring at the pile of coins. 'No, I don't think so,' he said. 'If the British government and the British Army were biassed enough to refuse to arm and equip ELAS, the biggest and best Resistance movement in Crete, because it was left-wing, they don't deserve their sovereigns back.' He looked at Maria and Eilidh, and grinned.

'Finders-keepers,' he said, 'losers-greeters.'

Maria's brow wrinkled, showing her lack of comprehension.

'It's a saying,' Eilidh explained. 'It means we found them, so we keep them. And 'greeting' is Scots for 'crying'.'

'Yes,' Andy said. 'My grandfather wanted Dad to have them, so we'll take them back home and Michael can decide what to do with them.'

'I think that's a very good idea,' Maria said. 'If you tried to sell them here, there would be trouble immediately. If you took them to a bank, they would want to know where you got them. If you told them that you found them on Greek soil, you can be sure they would confiscate them as the property of the Greek state. Or – or someone would kill you for them.'

There was absolute silence for a moment. 'You're kidding?' Eilidh said tentatively. 'No, I'm not,' Maria said. 'During the War on the mainland, ELAS buried a lot of them secretly, and some have never been recovered. There are still caches out there. People have been murdered in the search for them. And many villagers in Crete believe that the British Army buried its gold during the retreat over the mountains after the Battle of Crete.'

'That's daft,' Andy said. 'The British Army didn't pay its men in gold during the Second World War. Or the First World War, for that matter.'

'You try telling that to the locals,' Maria said. 'The fact of the matter is that there were so many gold sovereigns in Greece at the end of the War, and inflation was so high, that these coins became the de facto currency for a while. Every family in Greece has a few sovereigns. We have some.'

'Awesome,' Eilidh said.

'Maria's right,' Andy said. 'We've got to find a way of getting these sovereigns back to Scotland. We can't risk taking them on a plane because they could be discovered in security. But we should sleep on that. Right now, I think we deserve a celebratory drink!'

## Chapter 46

A couple of days later, Andy went over to Anopolis with Manoussos in his agrotikon to meet the old man's first cousin, Nikitas, and celebrate his name-day. He was keen to do this as he had never been to the village, which was spread-out on a big saucer-shaped plateau like Korifi. There was the usual feast of pilaffi with lashings of wine, and Andy heard even more stories of his grandfather, Kapetan Yiannis. Since the War, these stories had been embroidered in the telling to the extent that it seemed as if Sergeant John Gallagher had defeated the Germans in Crete single-handed. The celebrations went on well into the night, so Andy was slow to rise the next morning. Manoussos was driving back to Korifi, but Andy decided to walk back on the path which went down to the deserted village of Kali Lakkoi and on to Niato. He didn't know this area, and the walk would help clear his head.

Sometime later, as he passed the spring at Skafidakia, he saw unseasonal clouds closing in, and he could smell rain, so he accelerated, for in late summer in Crete, rain was most unusual. But just as he passed Kefala, there was a deafening rumble of thunder and a cloudburst. Apart from his shepherd's crook, all Andy had were the clothes he stood up in, a fleece, and a packet of food in his day bag which Nikitas's wife had given him. Andy stopped, put on his fleece, and hurried on towards Kali Lakkoi. It was pouring down now and by the time he reached the village, he was soaked to the skin and the light was fading fast. He remembered Maria had told him that a shepherd occasionally stayed there for some days at a time in high summer, and so there was a cottage which was open to all, with a supply of essentials. He recognised it by the crocheted curtains in the windows and knocked at the door. There was no answer, so he tried the door; it was open. Andy entered.

A sparsely furnished room contained a table and a couple of chairs, a kanabes with a pile of hand-woven blankets on it, and a tzaki, a stone-built fireplace with a stack of firewood and kindling beside it. There was an ancient Tilley-lamp, several boxes of matches, a carafe of Tsichoudia and several glasses on the table. Andy pumped the lamp up and soon had it going. Just as well, he thought, for it was almost dark. He then lit the fire, which proved easy as the kindling was bone-dry. In no time at all, he had a cheerful blaze going in the tzaki.

Andy stripped off all his soaking clothes and draped them over the back of a couple of chairs in front of the fire. Putting a blanket over his shoulders, he opened the packet of food to find a couple of paximadia, the double-baked Cretan rusks, two hard-boiled eggs, a large slice of Graviera cheese, and a paper spill of rock-salt. He poured himself a glass of Tsichoudia and ate while sitting in a chair in front of the fire. A meal fit for a Kapetan, Andy thought, as the raki warmed his stomach, and the rain poured down outside.

Andy then made up a bed on the kanabes with the blankets, banked up the fire, had another glass of Tsichoudia, lay down and was soon asleep. A couple of times during the night, he woke, put more logs on the fire, adjusted his clothes which were by now nearly dry and went back to sleep.

He woke with a start. It had stopped raining, the sun was just up, and the fire was still glowing. Then he heard a faint clink of rock outside as careful footsteps approached the cottage. Remembering what Maria had said about Dimitris Mavridakis following him, Andy rolled off the kanabes, grabbed his shepherd's crook, and flattened himself against the wall beside the door. The footsteps stopped outside the door, and it creaked open. Andy tightened his grip on his crook. A hooded figure stepped into the room and Andy swung his crook back. The figure started and spun round to face him. It was Maria, with a sakouli on her back. Andy stopped his crook in mid-swing and Maria jumped back with a cry of fear.

'Panayeia mou, Andrea,' Maria gasped. 'What on earth are you doing?'

Andy lowered his crook. 'I ... I didn't know who it was. I thought it might have been ...'

Trembling, Maria shook the sakouli off her back. 'My father told me you had decided to walk back from Anopolis. When the cloudburst occurred, I knew you would be soaking wet, so I went to the house and got a dry shirt and trousers for you. I knew you would look for shelter here because I had told you about it, so I got up at dawn and drove here with the dry clothes.'

Her eyes moved down slowly over Andy's body, paused for a moment at his groin, then came back up again. To his horror, he realised he was bollock naked.

Maria took an involuntary step back and froze. He realised she was terrified. He prised the sakouli from her fingers, put it on the floor, and pushed the door shut. As he stretched out his hand to flick the hood of her anorak off her head, she flinched. He took her hands in his, and said, 'It's all right, Maria.'

But Maria's eyes were still wide with fear. Andy drew her gently to him. Her body became taut with resistance, her eyes locked on his. He let go her hands, and his own went round her back and pressed her to him in a gentle hug. They both seemed to be holding their breaths, paralysed by the moment. He kissed her, lips just touching. She sighed. It unlocked them. He kissed her again, this time for real. She kissed him back, her hands seizing the back of his neck. She kissed him again, her mouth racing all over his face. She pulled off her anorak, unbuttoned her blouse and removed it. Bending down, she took off her boots, then stood up, undid her belt, and slipped off her trousers. She unfastened her bra and threw it aside. Andy slid the back of his hands down over her breasts, his fingernails grazing her nipples. She moaned once as she slid off her panties.

Andy stared at her body, its shape silhouetted against the fire. He hadn't seen a naked woman's body apart from Alison's for twenty years, and Maria's seemed to be all voluptuous curves. He took her hand, led her to the kanabes, and laid her on her back. Lying down beside her, he began to stroke her gently. When he caressed her breasts, and slid his other hand between her legs, Maria moaned again and pulled him to her. With a quick move, he straddled her, slipped himself inside her, and kissed her all over her face while rocking backwards and forwards. Andy thrust into her faster and faster, deeper and deeper, until she finally came with a cry which echoed round the room. She grabbed him to her, gasping 'Oh, Andrea mou.'

Andy, still hard, kept pushing inside her as deep as he could. She clasped his buttocks and pushed backwards and forwards until he came with a shuddering groan. She smiled up at him. 'That sounded good,' she said. 'Was it?.'

'Oh yes,' Andy said. 'Just a wee bit.'

Maria laughed out loud. 'Is that all?' she said.

He slid off her, pulled the blankets over their naked bodies, and clasped her to him.

They were quiet for a while. 'Maria,' he said.

Yes?'

'Your husband. How did he die?'

Maria shuddered, and her eyes filled with tears. 'Pavlos was murdered. Shot dead..'

'By whom?'

'We don't know. I wasn't there at the time. I was in Hania. Someone drove up to the house at night-time, called out his name, and when he came to the door, shot him dead.'

'You must have some suspicions.'

'It's better that you don't know about these things. Of course, I have suspicions, but I can prove nothing. So, I say nothing. And I do nothing. But as I told you, my clan has been involved in a vendetta with a clan from Kallikratis for a hundred years. It is supposed to have started with sheep-stealing, but nobody can now remember the precise incident. Then in the inter-war years my family was Venizelist, which …'

'Which means anti-monarchist.'

'Bravo, that's right. But like most Cretans, my grandfather Kostas was in fact a very strong Venizelist liberal …'

'Which means very anti-monarchist.'

'Exactly. He fought with your grandfather and was killed by the Germans at the Niato parachute drop. There are some people in my clan who believe that members of this other monarchist clan betrayed the drop to the enemy, so they killed one of them. And so it goes on.'

'But the War ended more than sixty-five years ago..'

'Not up here. Cretans have long memories.'

Andy couldn't think of anything to say, so he hugged Maria tightly and kissed her.

They then fell asleep in each other's arms, as the fire crackled inside and the sun rose outside.

# Part 12

## John Gallagher: Crete, 1944-45

## Chapter 47

In Crete, we all rejoiced at the news of the liberation of Athens on October 12th, 1944. I was particularly over the moon as it seemed that there was a real chance of realising the primitive type of socialist society EAM/ELAS had created in the wartime White Mountains. The sense of community and social responsibility constructed amongst these peasants was pure amazing. It was a society based on villages normally full of conflict and envy between extended families. It seemed to me that there was now a real chance of establishing a genuinely democratic postwar society in the whole of Greece.

But these hopes were dashed and our joy soon turned to misery when we began to hear the news of the repression and forced disarming of ELAS on the mainland. And the misery turned to despair in December, when the Greek Police fired on a huge EAM demonstration in Syntagma Square in Athens, killing twenty-eight protesters and wounding one hundred and forty-eight. Churchill was so obsessed with paranoia about Communism that he believed EAM/ELAS were about to launch an armed attack to seize power in the Greek state. He ordered the British Army to be deployed, martial law was declared, and the scum of the Security Battalions and Fascist organisations like Grivas's 'X' released from jail and let loose on members of EAM/ELAS.

But this alleged armed attack was nonsense. There was no such plan. The only political slogan in Greece – and in Crete – for the postwar years was 'Laokratia' – 'People's Rule.' But there was no strategy, no elaborate Party manifesto, for this rule, and nobody really knew what it meant anyway – except that it was flatly opposed to the return of the Greek King. It was just a Leftie slogan. And while there was supposed to be a Moscow-inspired Communist conspiracy to seize power, the Russians were conspicuous by their absence from – or even interest in – Greece, apart from a small token military liaison team. In Crete, they were invisible. A white terror was launched on the Left in mainland Greece, hundreds of patriotic wartime ELAS fighters were executed or imprisoned, and the Civil War started. Themia and I were absolutely horrified – and to our dismay, internecine fighting and tit-for-tat assassinations began to occur in Crete.

We discussed the situation at length. Themia argued that our main priority was to continue to camouflage my existence. By now, I was working as a shepherd with Nikos high above Korifi, where we could see anyone approaching, and it would be easy for me to disappear into the high peaks. And in the village, nobody would betray us. Nevertheless, Themia argued that we shouldn't get involved in any political activity which could draw Police attention to the village, and I agreed. She also pointed out that the Greek Communist Party – KKE – was now orchestrating political protest in Crete, but she wasn't a Communist. She didn't trust KKE, and as she said, 'What does Stalin know about milking sheep and making Graviera and Misithra cheese?' She also was emphatic about avoiding any action which could result in a vendetta – and I certainly agreed with that, for the end of the War had seen quite a few old scores being settled. Although we agreed to keep our heads down, the situation was so unstable that we stashed our weapons – two rifles, a Bren gun, ammunition, and a few hand-grenades – in a couple of safe places and hid a couple of pistols in the house.

Apart from political considerations, we were kept busy, for life was hard in those immediate post-war years. For a kick-off, there was a drought in the summer of 1945 which destroyed the grain harvest. Then there was very little meat about. The prewar flocks of sheep and goats had been decimated by the Germans and Italians and could only be rebuilt slowly.

Consequently, in the countryside, we ate what we could produce – which was mainly vegetables and pulses like lentils, kidney beans and chickpeas. Every village house had a kitchen garden, a couple of fields out on the plateau, and some olive trees and vines. Themia grew lettuce, onions and courgettes in the garden, potatoes in her fields, and was self-sufficient in olive oil and wine as her family owned a couple of olive groves and a vineyard. There were also a couple of globe artichoke plants, and pear and fig trees, in her garden.

And we acquired a few chickens. We also foraged for horta and vovlous, wild onions, and the snails which came out after the rain.

There was no mains water-supply in the village, so water was precious. Each house had a sterna, a stone cistern perhaps twenty feet deep, in the yard, and winter rainwater was drained by hoses off the flat concrete roofs into these tanks. A bucket on a rope was used to collect household water, and Themia washed her dishes and pots and pans with a wet sponge to conserve water. Baths were unknown, but I made a shower from an olive-oil tin with holes punctured in the bottom and suspended from a rope round a hook in the kitchen ceiling. I had to stand guard outside when Themia was having a shower, and vice-versa.

She had a good-sized vineyard out on the plateau with Romeiko grapes, and after trampling the grapes to make her wine, she took the skins to a neighbour who had a kazani for distilling Tsichoudia. The kazani looked exactly like an Irish poteen still! So, there was always enough to drink. I could get some meat by hunting mountain hare at night with the male villagers and soon learned their tricks.

We climbed high up into the mountains at nightfall, then

taped a torch under the two barrels of a shotgun with strands of rubber from an old inner tube. We then crept out into the darkness with levelled shotguns and switched the torch on at random intervals. If the beam caught a hare, it froze, and we shot it. It made a very welcome addition to the diet.

## Chapter 48

Politically, things went from bad to worse. There was a General Election in 1946, followed shortly afterwards by a referendum about the return of the monarchy. The KKE boycotted both, which I thought was a major mistake on its part because it meant that the right-wing achieved a landslide victory in the election, and while Crete voted overwhelmingly against the return of the King – 68% against 32% – nationally it was approved. This led to unrest in Crete where former ELAS Andartes believed that they had not only been fighting to rid the island of the Germans, but also for postwar democracy – the famous Laokratia. A law was passed banning the illegal possession of firearms, a law guaranteed to provoke Cretan men who regarded the right to bear arms as their birthright. Consequently, the KKE formed what was called the 'Democratic Army,' composed of wartime ELAS Andartes and their supporters and ordered its members to join up.

Shortly afterwards, a battalion of the Gendarmerie was formed. Themia and I noticed that this was not composed of trained Gendarmes, but of jailbirds and sheep thieves. Quite simply, it was an anti-communist private army. Sporadic armed clashes occurred, and in no time, they became frequent and serious violent encounters. A curfew was imposed in Hania province, and the Gendarmerie set off in relentless pursuit of the guerrillas. The Greek Civil War had broken out in Crete, to our horror. This was not what we had been fighting for during the German Occupation.

While I was working up at Nikos's mitato, a couple of these Communist guerrillas came to see Themia and tried to persuade her to join them because of her combat experience. She refused, saying that she was not prepared to kill fellow-Cretans. The guerrillas then suggested she was a traitor. Themia promptly produced a pistol and told them if she ever saw them again in Korifi, she would shoot them dead. They left in a hurry.

The fighting became increasingly vicious – ambushes, mutual assassinations, and hostage-taking. It was quite appalling. Nevertheless, many of the mountain villagers continued a clandestine support for the guerrillas, taking them food and supplies. I noticed that Nikos frequently disappeared at night from the mitato, and although I never asked any questions, I knew he was taking supplies to the guerrillas in the White Mountains. But on one occasion, he didn't return. A couple of days later, the Gendarmerie drove into Korifi in a jeep with the bullet-ridden body of Nikos strung up in the back for all to see. This was a quite deliberate ploy to show the villagers the fate of anyone who assisted the guerrillas. I had to restrain Themia forcibly from shooting up the jeep. What was even worse was they cut off Nikos's head and displayed it on a spike on the Kladissos Bridge in Hania.

The greatest problem the guerrillas faced was obtaining food, for by now they were forced to exist on the run in the mountains and live in caves. In Hania, the sale of large quantities of food to individuals was forbidden to starve the guerrillas out, and the curfew was tightly enforced. But Themia and I managed to slip out from time to time and take food and water to them. Themia knew every inch of the territory around Korifi and could move silently, like a wild cat. Sometimes we stashed the supplies in a pre-arranged spot.

On one occasion in the middle of the night, I was moving silently with a canister of drinking water to leave it out for the guerrillas, when I felt the cold muzzle of a rifle on the back of my neck. A voice whispered, 'Just leave it there,

Yianni.' I recognised the voice of Yorgos Tzombanakis, one of the Communist guerrillas, but I couldn't see anything for it was pitch black. I put the canister down and as I left, he murmured, 'Thanks, comrade.'

Another problem the guerrillas faced in the mountains was that their clothes and boots became rapidly worn out because of the harsh terrain. So, when they captured government soldiers, which was frequently, they stripped them off their uniforms and boots. We became quite used to seeing barefoot soldiers hobbling into Korifi in their shirttails.

In 1947, an amnesty was offered to the guerrillas and quite a few accepted. But others joined up, including some deserters from the Regular armed forces. My estimate was that there were never more than 300 men and women in the Democratic Army in Crete at any one time. Eastern and central Crete were cleared of guerrillas, and in western Crete, they were concentrated on the Omalos plateau and in the Gorge of Samaria, centuries-old refuges for insurgents. That was the beginning of the end as Gendarmerie Colonel Vardoulakis decided to clear them out once and for all.

He attacked from both the north and south, but the guerrillas wanted to avoid a pitched battle and slipped away into the night. Vardoulakis took their base near the village of Samaria, capturing the livestock on which they depended. On a quite literally dark and stormy night, the guerrillas climbed up out of the Gorge over what were called the 'Rotten Cliffs' and dispersed. But now, they had no safe place to go, so by January 1949, there were only about forty guerrillas, including eight women, left in the mountains. It was all over bar the shouting, and in October 1949, KKE called an end to the hostilities. Even then, a handful of Communist guerrillas fought on. The Cretan struggle was nowhere near as dramatic or bloody as the pitched battles on the mainland, where the Nationalists were routinely using artillery and napalm against the Democratic Army, but on the island, it was bad enough. There wasn't a family which didn't have someone involved on one side or the other, or who experienced a tragic loss of life.

During this local Civil War, Stavros, an uncle of Themia's, appeared in the village, and gave us a grim picture of the situation on the mainland. He had been a soldier in the Cretan 5th Division fighting the Italians in Epirus at the start of the War. When forced to surrender by the Germans, Stavros, along with some other Cretan soldiers, started to walk to the Peloponnesus in the hope of finding a caique – a traditional Greek fishing boat – which would take them home. But on the way, he encountered a band of ELAS Andartes, promptly joined them, and fought with them until the end of the War in a highly successful 'train-busting' regiment on the east coast. He fought on with the Democratic Army on the mainland in the Greek Civil War, was captured, and sent to the island of Makronissos. There, along with other left-wing Andartes, he was brutally tortured during a 're-education' programme designed to make them recant their communist allegiance. But as he told me, he wasn't a Communist, he wasn't a member of KKE. But that didn't matter to the Nationalists, and the torture continued. However, he refused to recant, was eventually released, but walked with a limp until the day he died, for his jailers had broken his leg with a pickaxe handle during a torture session.

Stavros was also stripped of all his civil rights. He wasn't allowed to vote or travel, he was denied employment by both local and central government, and he had to report to the Police weekly. In short, he was a marked man for the rest of his life. But I also observed that many villagers, including Themia, ensured that Stavros and his family did not starve, by throwing anonymous parcels of food into his courtyard in the middle of the night during curfew. In the meantime, the hunt for the remaining few Communist fugitives in the mountains of Crete continued relentlessly.

One day, towards the end of the Civil War, when I was working up in the family mitato, a couple of policemen from Hania appeared in the village. They said they were looking for a foreign resident. The Korifiotes ridiculed them. A foreigner living in Sfakia? Bah! Don't be ridiculous! There were many foreigners – British, Australian, and New Zealanders here during the War, but they all went home. And everybody knows that Sfakiani only marry Sfakiani. There are no foreigners at all living in the county. It looks like someone has been playing a joke on you, and you've been led on a wild goose chase. The policemen were filled with food and drink, and sent back to Hania, empty-handed but happy. My anonymity was safe.

When I came back down to Korifi from Nikos's mitato, Themia told me about the policemen's visit. 'Someone's betrayed us, and I think I know who it might be.' She told me there was a middle-aged woman in the village who was so crazed with grief that it was a distinct possibility. Her husband had been killed fighting with the Cretan Division in Epirus at the beginning of the War, and she had never recovered. Themia went to speak to her. All she told me was that she had threatened the woman with a deadly spell involving a vampire if she spoke out about us. And although it's hard to credit in the twentieth century, locals still believe in the power of such spells. I never learned the components of Themia's threat, but it worked. The woman was silent for the rest of her life, enabling us to live quietly and happily in the village.

It was very sad that we couldn't have any weans. Themia was desperate for a baby, but it just didn't happen. It was too risky to think of going to see a gynaecologist in Hania, so we never learned what the problem was. That was our only regret in a long and happy marriage.

Then in August 1951, a party called EDA (Union of the Democratic Left) was formed, and all underground organisations were to be disbanded. Themia and I suspected that this was a KKE-front organisation, established to pursue the parliamentary road to democracy after the failure of the armed struggle. But even then, there were still thirteen guerrillas, including two women, fighting on in the White Mountains. They were all Communists. By 1959, there were only eight left, and they were ordered to leave by the KKE. But as is well-known, diehard Communists Tzombanakis and Blazakis refused to leave, and were to fight on until they were amnestied in 1975 after twenty-six years in the mountains, incredible as that may seem. It says something about the amazing solidarity of the Cretan people that these two men were kept supplied and not betrayed for over two decades. Themia and I do not want to talk about our modest role in this miracle.

# Part 13

**Andy Gallagher: Crete, 2010**

## Chapter 49

In the sitting-room, Andy poured Eilidh and Maria a glass of wine. As she took a sip, Eilidh frowned. 'If we can't take the sovereigns out on the plane, and we can't cash them here, how are we going to get them out of Crete?'

'I think the only way we could do it is to drive home,' Andy said. 'But we haven't got a car,' Eilidh observed.

'I have,' Maria interjected. 'I have a car.'

'What would you do?' Eilidh asked. 'Would you come with us?'

Maria put her hand round Andy's waist with a smile. 'Oh yes. I would really like to see Scotland.'

Eilidh grinned. 'Awesome. But what would the chances be of getting stopped at a Customs Post and the car searched?'

Andy grimaced. 'There is that chance. But within Europe there are only usually random checks. We would just have to chance it.'

'How would we go?' Maria said. 'What would be our route?'

'Well,' Andy replied, 'for starters we would obviously go from Souda to Piraeus.

Then up to Patras, the ferry to Ancona, and up through Italy, across Switzerland and France to Calais, and then cross over to Dover. I think Dover would be the danger point, for Maria's car has Greek number plates. They might well stop it.' There was silence for a moment or two while this information was digested.

'I have an idea,' Maria said. 'It would be easier if we were in a car with British plates.'

'Of course,' Andy agreed.

'Well,' Maria said, 'sometimes one of the many

British expatriates who live in Apokoronas sells their car second-hand. They have their own website, and we could advertise on that.'

'That's a great idea,' Andy said. 'I'll write an ad..'

'When would we go?' Maria asked.

'As soon as we can buy a car with British plates,' Andy said.

'Wait a minute,' Eilidh snapped. 'I've entered the Samaria Gorge race, and I don't want to miss that. I've been training hard.'

'Oh damn. I forgot about that,' Andy said. 'When is it?.'

'The end of the month.'

'Just over two weeks,' Andy said. 'Well, if we can find a car, we'll go as soon as possible after that.'

'Cool,' Eilidh said. 'That would be an interesting drive, right across Europe.'

'No,' Andy objected, 'no way. You're not going in that car. You're flying home.'

'Wait a minute,' Eilidh said. 'You can't …'

'Oh yes I can,' Andy said. 'This whole trip is dodgy, and I don't want you involved. You take your booked return flight and go home and wait for us there. There are all sorts of dangers on this trip. We might get arrested at a border post, for example.' Eilidh scowled.

'Your father's right, Eilidh,' Maria said. 'It's far safer if you are not involved at all in this trip.'

'Okay, okay,' Eilidh said.

As the day of the race approached, Andy grew more and more nervous, for there had been no reply to his advert. He considered buying a second-hand Greek car realising that the number plates would increase the chances of being stopped at Dover. He decided that if he was forced to adopt this option, he would drive back on his own as he didn't want to risk Maria getting into any trouble with British Customs.

'Oh no, you don't,' Maria said. 'We're a team. I'm not

letting you go on your own. I'm coming with you whether you like it or not.'

'But …'

'But nothing. I'm coming with you.' Maria made a hand-wiping gesture and said in Greek, 'Afto einai.' That's it.

'All right,' Andy said reluctantly.

But a few days before the race, a British woman living in Vamos in Apokoronas phoned Andy. She had a 2010 Ford Mondeo TDCi Zetek for sale. Andy looked up the list price, which was in the region of £5,000, and took it for a test drive on a mountain road. The woman was keen for pounds sterling in cash, so when Andy offered £4,000 with an immediate online bank transfer, she accepted at once.

## Chapter 50

Eilidh continued her training for the Samaria Gorge Race. This started where the dirt road up to the mountain refuge at Kallergi branched off the main road to Xyloskalo, continued to the start of the 'Wooden Steps' down into the Gorge, carried on down the steps, descended into the Gorge, then hooked back up into the mountains well before the deserted village of Samaria, and crested at the Poria saddle. Then it went back down the Kallergi dirt road and finished at Xyloskalo.

'Eilidh, you're crazy!' Maria said. 'It's a brutal race, and the climb up to Poria is a killer. I know because I've walked it.'

'Well, there are brutal mountain races in Scotland too,' Eilidh said. 'Like the Ben Nevis race. That's fourteen kilometres up and down, with an ascent of one thousand, three hundred and forty metres. I've done that.'

'Eisai trozi!' Maria said. You're nuts!

As Eilidh laced up her trail running-shoes, Andy said, 'I'm not happy about you going off running on your own, Eilidh. If you wait a minute, I'll get my kit and come with you.'

'There's no need, Dad, honest,' Eilidh said. 'I'm a big girl and can look after myself.

If there's any trouble, I'll simply outrun it.'

Andy managed a smile, but exchanged an anxious look with Maria, who said, 'Where are you going to run just now?'

'I'm going to run down to Askyfou, across the plateau, carry on past Imbros village, and then down the Imbros Gorge,' Eilidh said. 'That will give me good downhill experience.'

As she warmed up, Maria said, 'Okay. I'll pick you up with the motorbike at the foot of the Gorge. In an hour.'

'Cool,' Eilidh said, slipping her hand through the loop of her Amphipod Minimalist water-bottle. She waved goodbye to Dad and Maria and set off at an easy lope.

As Eilidh ran down towards the Askyfou plateau, she reflected that her Dad was obviously really relaxed here in Crete and showed no signs of the stress he faced in Glasgow. It was also obvious that he was nuts about Maria, even if he didn't know it yet. And he'd be mad not to be anyway, because she's lovely. And Eilidh had a hunch that she fancied him too. That was all good, and Eilidh hoped something would come of it. As for herself, she just loved this place. It was so beautiful, and the people were so cool. She thought it would be awesome if her Dad could find an excuse to spend some more time here doing his research into these bloody Minoans.

Eilidh jogged down over the Askyfou plateau, the air throbbing with heat, and entered the Imbros Gorge. The path was clear and shaded from the sun by the steep walls, the fragrant aroma of wild herbs, particularly sage, oregano and verbena, was everywhere, and she was going well. After about a half an hour, as the Gorge narrowed to a couple of metres, she spotted a man about fifty yards in front of her sitting on a boulder, and immediately felt uneasy. She slowed down and as she approached she saw that he seemed to be carrying something. He stood up abruptly; he was a middle-aged Cretan man carrying an automatic shotgun. She accelerated to run past him, but he jumped out in front of her. He racked the gun and pointed it at her, yelling, 'Stop!' Eilidh skidded to a stop, her heart racing. The man grabbed her arm with unexpected strength and dragged her up a track away from the Gorge. She tried unsuccessfully to break free but managed to drop her water-bottle without him seeing it.

He bundled her into a pickup truck and took off uphill. The man kept glancing sideways at her bare legs. She couldn't stop herself trembling with fear, and she thought she would throw up at any moment.

After about ten minutes he stopped at one of those stone huts which Dad said was called a mitato or something. He pulled her inside and pushed her into a chair beside a table with a bottle and a couple of glasses on it. He had piggy eyes and a pungent B.O. His hot breath stank of alcohol and tobacco.

'Someone in the Sfakianakis family killed my grandfather during the War,' he growled in English. 'Do you know who it was?'

Eilidh gulped, and said, 'I don't know what you're talking about. I know nothing about the War.'

The man snorted. 'What were you doing running in the Imbros Gorge?' he said, glaring at her, his eyes running up and down over her body.

'I'm … I'm training for the Samaria Race,' Eilidh said.

He then produced the trowel, and Oh-Jesus, she realised that she had forgotten to pick it up from outside the cave. She gulped in panic.

'What was your father looking for?' the man said. 'What did you find in that cave?'

Eilidh realised that she was in deep shit. She was petrified, she felt as if she was going to wet herself, but she decided the best plan was to say nothing at all.

'What did you find in that cave?' the man snarled again. Suddenly he slapped her hard across the face. Nobody had ever hit Eilidh in the face in her whole life. She reeled back, her head ringing, but realised she had to do something, for the bastard was taking off his leather belt. As he lent forward and ripped her singlet down over her chest, she grabbed the bottle and hit him over the head with it. The bottle shattered, his scalp spurted blood, he yelled with pain and dropped the gun. As he cradled his head in his hands, she jumped up, pushed his chair over and he crashed to the floor. Eilidh bounded out of the door and took off downhill as fast as she knew how, hurdling boulders, sliding down screes, ripping through bushes, her heart in her mouth and adrenalin surging through her body. She didn't know where she was going but it didn't matter. She just flew down that mountain.

Maria pulled her motorbike up on the stand and glanced at her watch. Twenty-to-twelve. Eilidh should be out by twelve; there was a good path down the Imbros Gorge and the terrain was not difficult.

At noon, Maria started to stroll up the Gorge, expecting to see Eilidh at any minute.

At quarter-past, Maria sat on a boulder and rang Eilidh on her smartphone. No answer. Maria started to walk quickly up the Gorge. At half-past twelve, she called Eilidh again, no answer. Worried, she turned round and jogged back to her motorbike. She tried calling one more time, to no avail. Maria drove back up to Imbros village, parked the bike and started walking down the Gorge. She met a group of German walkers coming up and asked them if they had seen a girl, running down the Gorge. The Germans had seen no one since starting. Maria hurried on. At a narrow point in the Gorge, she saw something glinting in the sunlight, some distance off the path to the left. It was Eilidh's distinctive Amphipod water-bottle. Maria thought quickly. There was no reason for Eilidh to be off the path, which was quite clear. Maria ran back up the Gorge, started her bike and drove back to Korifi at speed, skidding to a halt outside Andy's house and honking the horn. He rushed to the door.

'Eilidh hasn't turned up,' Maria gasped. 'Look. I found her water-bottle a little way off the path. I think Mavridakis might have kidnapped her.'

'Jesus Christ!' Andy said. 'Why would he do that?'

'He would want her to tell him what you were looking

for. Come on, get on.'

Andy jumped on the pillion, and Maria roared off to the taverna. She ran inside and came back out with a .303 rifle which she stowed in the back of her father's agrotikon.

'Let's go,' she said, jumping into the pickup. As she drove off, she handed Andy a Sig Sauer P210 pistol.

'It's loaded,' she said. 'You cock it by pulling the slide back.' Andy did this. 'Now engage the safety-catch on the left-hand side. Good. It's now ready to use.'

If Michael could see me now, Andy thought, driving around with Maria-get-your-gun.

'If Mavridakis has Eilidh,' Maria said, 'he's more likely to take her up to the family mitato than his house in Kallikratis. There are too many witnesses in the village.'

'Right,' Andy said. 'But I should never have let her go off on her own in the first place. What on earth are we going to do?'

'There's a dirt road which goes up to an old unused mitato near his new one. We'll go up there, contour round the mountain, and spy out what's going on at Mavridakis's mitato. There's a pair of binoculars in the glove compartment.'

Maria swung the truck off the road, engaged four-wheel drive and began to bump up a rough, steep dirt track. As they rounded a bend, Andy exclaimed, 'Jesus! Look!'

Above them, Eilidh was bounding down the track at full speed. Maria blasted the horn, Eilidh saw them, waved, and shot right down the mountainside, cutting a bend. Andy got out as Maria did a fast three-point turn. Eilidh arrived and fell into Andy's arms, gasping.

'Are you …?' Andy said. 'I'm okay, I'm okay..'

'Get in, quick.'

'Then he took off his belt,' Eilidh said.

'Oh my God,' Maria said, looking over Eilidh's body. 'Did he …?.'

'No.'

'What happened next?' Andy said.

'He bent towards me and ripped off my singlet, so I hit him with a bottle which was on the table.'

'Panayeia mou!' Maria said. 'You Scottish people are completely crazy. And the women are worse than the men.'

'Nemo me impune lacessit,' Andy said.

'I don't speak Latin,' Maria said.

'Wha daur meddle with me,' Andy said, and then translated it into Greek: 'Kaneis then me kseyela atimoritos.'

Maria shook her head in disbelief as they arrived back in Korifi. In the taverna, they told Manoussos what had happened. He swore at length and had to be restrained from going out immediately to kill Mavridakis. He said, 'The bastard. I'm going to take some precautions.' He got up and went to the telephone.

'What will Mavridakis try and do now?' Andy said.

'It's hard to say,' Maria said. 'He will want revenge. He has been made to look like a fool, his honour has been insulted, and by a mere girl, and a foreign girl at that. But the very fact that it *was* a girl will be something he will want to keep secret, so I don't think he'll be telling the story in Kallikratis. But we cannot afford to let Eilidh go anywhere on her own now, and Andy, you must watch your back.'

Just then, Eilidh jumped to her feet and ran into the toilet. Andy and Maria could hear her vomiting. Andy went in after her and found the girl was shivering and crying uncontrollably. He cleaned her face, lifted her up in his arms, and carried her up to her room, saying, 'It's delayed shock,' over his shoulder to Maria.

'I'll make some tea,' Maria said.

A little later, having drunk a mug of Malotira herbal tea with honey, Eilidh fell into a deep sleep.

'I think it's high time she went home to Scotland,' Andy said to Maria. 'It's been some bloody holiday!'

'I agree,' Maria said.

Later, Yorgos, Stratis and a couple of other village men were deep in conversation with Manoussos. They weren't even bothering to hide their rifles, and one of them was carrying a Kalashnikov. When Maria saw Andy's worried face, she said, 'Don't worry. The village has just been turned into an armed camp. There is no way Mavridakis could enter unseen.'

## Chapter 51

In the taverna, Andy wagged his finger at Eilidh, with Maria watching. 'Under no circumstances are you going on that Race, and that's that,' he said. 'It's far too dangerous. I think what we need to do is get you on the first possible flight home. It's been a hairy time for you here and that's not what I planned. Your mother is going to kill me when she finds out what happened.'

'She's not going to find out, Dad,' Eilidh said. 'I'm certainly not going to tell her, and neither are you. Look, being kidnapped by that horrible man was no joke, and I know I was lucky to escape. It's something I won't forget in a hurry. But I want to do that race, and I'll tell you why. The boys here in the village don't think a girl can do it and I want to prove them wrong. And there's another thing. I want to do that race to prove to myself that I've not been totally defeated by that bastard. It's my way of revenge. He can hurt me emotionally, but he can't defeat me. Do you see what I mean?'

Andy shuffled his feet. 'I do, but still and all, I ...'

'Look, Andy,' Maria said. 'My father and his men are going to guard the route, and it will be impossible for Mavridakis to get near it. My father and uncles know that area like the back of their hands. That's where they operated during the War. Mavridakis has no chance of penetrating it.'

Maria explained that Manoussos had mobilised the Sfakianakis clan and armed men were to be posted at every conceivable point on the route where Mavridakis might try something on. Manoussos himself, along with Yorgos and Stratis, would patrol the Poria saddle, and the Potistiria path up to it from the Gorge, the most dangerous area.

'You see, Dad,' Eilidh said. 'It looks like a plan.'

'All right, all right,' Andy said. 'I'm still not happy with the idea but I can see you're determined. But once the race is over, we get you out of the country as soon as possible. Agreed?'

'Agreed.'

During the race, Andy advised Eilidh to run in the middle of a group until she was well down the dirt road from Kallergi on the last leg where she could accelerate on her own. He and Maria would wait with the motorbike at the Greek Alpine Club chalet at Kallergi and follow her all the way downhill to be on the safe side.

On the eve of the race, Andy, Maria and Eilidh stayed in the Omalos Taverna, while Manoussos and his men vanished into the Gorge and the surrounding mountains. At dawn on the day of the race, Maria and Andy drove to the junction with the dirt road up to Kallergi, parked the motorbike, and found a vantage point from where they could watch both the main road up to Xyloskalo, and the dirt road.

After the last of the runners were well on their way to Xyloskalo, Maria and Andy drove up to Kallergi on the motorbike. Andy marvelled at Maria's skill as she navigated the powerful bike up the steep, rocky road. He wrapped his arms round her body as she rounded yet another alarming hairpin bend close to the vertiginous drop into the Gorge of Samaria, and smiled to himself as she squeezed his arm as if to say, don't worry, you're in safe hands.

Once up at Kallergi, they took their coffee outside and admired the view. To the east were the peaks of the high wilderness of the White Mountains which continued to Korifi and Askyfou. It looked like a trackless stony desert, but there were not only several high-altitude mitata there, manned in the summer by shepherds from Anopolis, but also the long-distance E4 footpath crossed right through it.

Opposite them to the south was the massive crenelated peak of Gingilos, and to the west, the range of mountains which stretched into the province of Selino.

Andy went to the wooden toilet down the road a bit, cunningly cantilevered over a near-vertical drop hundreds of feet into the Gorge. It wouldn't do to have vertigo in here, he thought, as he looked at the sheer drop below the toilet bowl. It brings a whole new meaning to the term long-drop. As he rejoined Maria, a shadow passed over them. Andy looked up and saw a raptor with a wingspan of fully eight or nine feet, and a distinctive lozenge-shaped tail, planing overhead.

'Wow!' Andy said. 'What's that bird?'

'It's a lammergeyer,' Maria said. 'It feeds mainly on bones. It's the biggest bird in Crete.' They watched it spiral on a thermal high up into the sky above the Gorge and eventually vanish behind the peak of Gingilos. Just then, Maria's mobile rang. It was Manoussos to tell her that the first runners were approaching the Poria saddle. From Kallergi, they watched the leaders through binoculars reach the saddle and turn onto the road up to the Refuge. They picked up Eilidh in the first batch, running easily.

'I'll wait here until Eilidh passes,' Andy said, jumping up onto a boulder to watch. 'Okay,' Maria said, starting the bike. She paused at the side of the dirt road as the first runners streamed towards them. Eilidh was in the first twenty, going well, and they yelled encouragement as she ran past. She grinned and gave them the thumbs up.

'I'll let them get past,' Maria said over her shoulder. But a second group of runners appeared, and Maria let them get well clear before she engaged gear and moved out onto the road. Eilidh accelerated, and just as Andy jumped down off the boulder, there was a crack – thump, and a bullet whistled over his head. Mavridakis appeared over the lip of the road working the bolt of a rifle. He must have been hiding over the drop, Andy thought, as he froze with terror. What happened next remained engraved on his mind for the rest of his life.

Maria looked over her shoulder as she heard the shot. As she saw Mavridakis raising his rifle, a ferocious scowl crossed her face. She slewed the bike round amid a spray of gravel and gunned it straight at him, hunched down over the handlebars. He whipped his rifle up and fired at her. The shot zipped over her head. She accelerated and Mavridakis dived out of the way, dropping his rifle. Maria braked and spun the bike round through 180 degrees. Mavridakis grabbed his rifle and in his haste to cock it, jammed the bolt. I've got to do something, Andy thought, or Maria's had it. He grabbed a rock and threw it at Mavridakis, who ducked. As Mavridakis cleared the bolt and aimed at Maria again, she drove the bike at speed straight at him, the engine roaring. He flew into space in one direction, his rifle going in another. Maria and the motorbike sailed airborne over the Gorge, in slow motion, it seemed to Andy. Oh my God, he thought, oh no, no, no, as he glimpsed Mavridakis's body spiral down into the Gorge followed by an echoing, spine-chilling scream. There was a thud from the dirt road below him and the motorbike reappeared, wobbling wildly. It slid off the road and careered down the hillside with Maria fighting to correct it.

Just as she went into a broadside skid towards the sheer drop, she twisted the throttle, the bike surged uphill and landed back on the road with a resounding thump. For a nanosecond, Andy thought that he had passed out. He staggered down towards Maria, feeling decidedly light-headed.

'Are you all right?' she yelled over her shoulder.

'I'm fine. No problem.' No problem except that I'm shitting myself. Andy glanced back over his shoulder and saw that Maria had jumped a Z-bend and landed in the same direction the bike was originally headed, only about twenty feet lower, directly beside the drop into the Gorge. Nobody had witnessed this incident. Thank God for small mercies, Andy thought, as he climbed onto the bike.

'Good riddance to bad rubbish,' Maria said.

At the end of the race, and before they joined Eilidh, Andy and Maria agreed not to tell the girl of Mavridakis's attempt on them, nor his fate. Eilidh had experienced quite enough trauma for one school holiday. But Maria suggested that they leave the village as soon as possible, and anyway, Eilidh's flight home was in a couple of days' time.

'Mavridakis has a brother and several cousins,' Maria said. 'They know that a man of his experience in the mountains would not slip and fall to his death in a place like that. He had no good reason to be there in the first place, so they will deduce he was up to something, and that something was us. If they find that out, they might come after us. So, we'll go to our house in Hania tomorrow, just in case.'

'Oh,' Andy said. 'I didn't know you had a house in town.'

'Oh yes. Many villagers do. The old village houses can be very cold in winter. Our house in Hania is in Splantzia, the old Turkish neighbourhood, but we've modernised it.

You'll like it.'

They joined Eilidh, who was over the moon with her official time of two hours, forty-seven minutes. It was an excellent time for a seventeen-year-old girl, a result of which she should be very proud.

Back in the taverna in Korifi, Maria opened a bottle of Cretan bubbly to celebrate Eilidh's success, while Manoussos took a phone-call.

'You're not going to believe this,' Manoussos said, sitting down beside them, and accepting a glass. 'Dimitris Mavridakis fell off the mountain below Kallergi and he's dead.'

Andy and Maria exchanged a glance.

'He must have slipped,' Maria said with a deadpan face.

'Malaka,' Manoussos said. Wanker. He shook his lapel with his thumb and forefinger in what Andy knew was one of the supreme unspoken Greek insults.

Maria turned to face Eilidh. 'Here's to our new Scottish-Cretan athlete.

Congratulations! Se yeia!" "Se yeia!"

## Chapter 52

The next morning, Andy packed carefully, stowing the cylinders containing the sovereigns at the bottom of his suitcase and covering them with clothes. He had bought a small new suitcase in which he stowed all his grandfather's papers, journal, Commando dagger, and the manuscript book. He told Maria to bring some warm clothes and a good raincoat as even in August, the Scottish weather could be unpredictable. Then he, Maria and Eilidh loaded their suitcases into the boot of the Mondeo, said goodbye to Manoussos, and drove down to Hania.

Maria's house was in a narrow street in Splantzia, too narrow for cars, so they parked under the old Venetian city wall and trundled their suitcases to the house. Maria opened the door to an open-plan, T-shaped flat on the ground floor with a bed under a barrel-vaulted space in the cross of the 'T.'

'This is your room, Eilidh,' Maria said. 'The toilet and shower are opposite..'

'Cool,' Eilidh said. 'It's awesome.'

'We're up here,' Maria said, climbing the stairs, followed by Andy lugging his suitcase. She opened the door to a bedroom full of light, with a large double-bed, a chest-of-drawers, a dressing-table with women's lotions and potions, and a rack full of blouses and dresses.

'This is us,' Maria said. 'Do you like it?'

'It's lovely,' Andy said, dumping his suitcase. 'But ….'

'But what?' Maria said, frowning.

'Well, Eilidh's just downstairs, you know, and, and I'm, em, I'm embarrassed.'

Maria laughed and took Andy's hand. 'There's no need to be embarrassed,' she said. 'Her bed is on the other side of the house. And anyway, Eilidh knows about us.'

Before Andy could say anything more, Maria kissed him with attitude.

A little later, they went out to eat in a small taverna in Daskaloyiannis Street which was owned by a cousin of Maria's, and which she swore was excellent. She insisted they have fish to celebrate Eilidh's successful completion of the demanding Samaria race. It was served with a delicious garlicky aioli, and Eilidh wanted to know the recipe. Maria had a word with her young cousin Alekos, and Eilidh disappeared into the kitchen with him. Judging by the peals of laughter, they were having a good lesson. Maria smiled at Andy.

'I think they're having a good time,' she said.

'Well, it's great to be young,' Andy said.

Maria reached over the table and took Andy's hand. 'You're not old, Andy.

You're a good-looking man. And you are fit and healthy. Any sensible woman would want you.'

Andy felt himself blush. 'I hope you are sensible.' Maria smiled. 'I can be – when I want to be.'

Eilidh arrived back at the table, excited, licking her fingers, and waving a sheet of notepaper.

'It's not that difficult,' she said, 'and Alekos has shown me how to do it. He's cool.'

Later, when Maria told Alekos that Eilidh had run the Gorge of Samaria race the previous day, the young man was astounded. He placed another half-litre of white wine on the table and refused all payment. It was a happy trio which wended its way back to the house.

In the bedroom, Maria kicked off her shoes and peeled off her dress. 'I am feeling very, very sensible tonight,' she said, with a wicked grin.

There was a passionate urgency about Maria's lovemaking

which was almost desperate. It was as if this was the last chance she was going to have in her whole life. But it was electrifying, and Andy gasped as Maria collapsed on top of him. After her husband's death, it seemed as if she was asserting her vitality urgently. A little later, as he drifted off to sleep, with Maria's arms and legs wrapped round him, Andy thought he had never felt better in his life. He felt utterly relaxed, safe and happy in the arms of this gorgeous woman. He was an extraordinarily lucky man.

The next morning, at the entrance to Security at Hania Airport, Maria hugged Eilidh and said, 'We'll see you in a week's time in Glasgow.'

'Cool,' Eilidh said.

Andy hugged his daughter. 'Now don't pick a fight with lover-boy when you get back home. Your mother is entitled to her life, okay?'

'Okay, Dad,' Eilidh said.

'We'll be in contact every day after school on WhatsApp to let you know where we are, and how it's going,' Andy said. 'We leave on the ferry tomorrow evening, and we should be back in Glasgow in five or six days.'

'Cool. Kalo taxidi, Papa,' Eilidh said, kissing her father.
'Hey, check the Greek,' Andy said.

'I've a good teacher,' Eilidh said. 'You look after her..'

'I will. You can be sure of that.'

Andy and Maria watched as Eilidh disappeared into security, waving goodbye cheerfully. Maria took Andy's hand. 'Are you feeling sensible?' she said.

'Just a wee bit,' Andy said with a grin.

## Chapter 53

As he strolled round the harbour in Hania, Andy kept an eye open, just in case, but he couldn't detect anyone following him. He marvelled at the maritime power of Venice when Crete was part of the Empire. The harbour was still lined with the 16th century Venetian Arsenales, the handsome barrel-vaulted shipyards built over a period of three centuries. They were open at the side facing the sea so that galleys could be hauled out of the water for repair or launched. The Grand Arsenal had been restored recently and was now an impressive building hosting exhibitions and other events.

Andy sat on a bench at the harbour side, and gazed at the collection of fishing boats, pleasure craft and Greek Coastguard launches. Maria had gone shopping to the municipal covered market. Andy was falling hopelessly in love with her. It wasn't just that she was beautiful, which she was. It wasn't just that she had a stunning figure, which she had. And it wasn't just that she was highly intelligent, which she also was. Maria had something else.

She had depth, she had gravity, she was a serious person despite her excellent sense of wit. In short, she had a lot of class. She was a woman whom you had to take seriously. And this worried Andy. He felt for her in her palpable grief about the death of her husband and knew that it would be unthinkable to cause her any more pain. And he wasn't very self-confident regarding relationships with women anyway. As Eilidh had pointed out, he couldn't be all that smart emotionally as he hadn't spotted the growing crisis in his marriage at all. Did he have what it would take to care for a woman who was suffering from profound grief? He wasn't at all sure that he had.

He stood up and started walking towards the lighthouse at the end of the mole, again glancing behind him. He was pleased that Eilidh and Maria got on so well. But that posed another problem. Eilidh had another year of high school to go, and Andy felt that he had to be in Glasgow for his daughter. And there was also the issue of his job at the university.

What was he going to do about that? Although he was growing increasingly disenchanted with academia, he still had to earn a living. And it didn't seem fair to ask Maria to abandon Korifi suddenly and come to live in a foreign city, where she might feel out of her depth, especially given the combativeness of Glaswegian culture. Could he live in Korifi? Much as he loved the village and the area, he would always be a foreigner, and there was no getting away from the fact that he was a city boy, not a country boy – and if the truth be told, he loved Glasgow and its continuous cultural cabaret. What was it Bertolt Brecht said again in that poem? So many questions.

Andy was so wrapped up in his reverie that he started when a couple of German tourists asked him to take their photograph beside the lighthouse. He framed the shot carefully to take in the Alcanea Hotel across the harbour. After the tourists had thanked him profusely, Andy started to walk back along the mole towards Maria's house in Splantzia in the Old Town. Splantzia? Another Venetian word, he thought, a corruption of 'piazza.'

As he turned into Daskaloyiannis Street, Andy reflected that his introspection wasn't getting him anywhere. The only outcome was that he was getting more and more confused. I know what I'll do, he thought. I'll ask Eilidh for her advice. That girl's got good intuition for a teenager, and it's obvious that she and Maria get on a like a house on fire. Turning into Pezanou, Maria's street, she appeared, laden with bags of shopping. When she saw him, she smiled with pleasure. His heart leapt.

Andy watched as Maria battered the small fish known as Atherina in flour, semolina, cumin, sweet paprika, and salt and pepper and fried them in olive oil. She served them on the roof terrace with slices of lemon, a Greek salad, fresh bread, and Malvasia white wine. There's another thing, he thought, she's a terrific cook.

After lunch, they went to bed for a siesta and made love for what seemed like a long time. Maria rested her head on Andy's shoulder, and said, 'I really like your body. It's strong. Do you like mine?'

'No, I don't like your body, I love it. I can't get enough of you..'

'That's good.'

Andy was just dozing off when Maria said in a serious tone, 'Andy. Are we having a relationship?'

'Oh yes. I think you could say that..'

'But is it a committed relationship?'

Andy propped himself up on his elbow and looked down at Maria. 'Committed? I think so, but I'm not sure, to tell you the truth. I'm a bit confused by the suddenness of it all.'

'But you just said you couldn't get enough of me.'

'I did. But that's passion. You're a very desirable woman, Maria. You're gorgeous..'

'Couldn't we have a committed *and* a passionate relationship?'

'I'd like to think so. But the thought is a bit scary. I don't know if I'm capable of that kind of commitment.'

'I think you are. I think you are fundamentally a very honest and principled man. I wouldn't be in bed with you if you weren't.'

'Oh. I would like to think you're right, my love.'

'I am right. Oh! Oh! I feel something stirring. Could it be passion?'

## Chapter 54

Alert to the possibility of being tracked by someone from the Mavridakis clan, Andy booked a first-class cabin on the Souda-Piraeus ferry. On board, he and Maria scoured the ship several times looking for a potential enemy, but they couldn't discern one. Andy was horrified to find that Maria had brought a pistol and pointed out that this was a recipe for disaster in Scotland where illegal possession could mean five years in prison.

'There's nobody after us on this ship,' he said. 'And nobody knows we've gone. Britain is not Crete. People with guns are not tolerated in Britain, Maria. Get rid of the pistol.'

Leaving Piraeus, Andy drove north-west along the Gulf of Corinth towards Patras where they were booked on the ferry to Ancona in Italy. It was a lovely day, the sun glittered off the water, and there was no hurry. He glanced at Maria, who was unusually silent, and wore a slight frown on her face. He wondered if she was in a huff about the pistol. He put his hand on her thigh. 'You're very quiet. What are you thinking?'

Maria put her hand on his, turned her head and smiled at him. 'I'm thinking about you, Andrea mou.'

'Oh dear. Are you still angry with me?'

'No, not at all. In fact, I was thinking how lucky I am to have met you..'

'Oh. That's encouraging.'

'Yes. You're kind, you're intelligent, you're a thoughtful lover, and you are always cheerful.'

'But?'

'But sometimes you are naïve, emotionally and politically naïve..'

'So, there's no hope for me?'

'I wouldn't say that. I can work on that naivety..'

'When you're feeling sensible?'

Maria squeezed Andy's hand and grinned. 'I can be very sensible..'

'When you want to be.'

'Yes, when I want to be. With you, I often feel sensible. More than often.'

'Anything else in your character assessment?'

'Yes. You can be impulsive.' Maria looked out of the window for a moment. 'But your impulses are often good.'

'Sounds even more promising.' They drove on in silence for a while. 'Andy.'

'Yes?'

'Do we, could we, have a future? Together, I mean.'

He took his time in replying. 'There is nothing I would like better. It would give me a great deal of pleasure to make you happy. That would be my mission in life. But it is an idea which also worries me.'

'Why?'

'Well, after the mess with Alison, I think I became disillusioned about relationships, a bit cynical. Or at least, confused.'

'That's understandable. But I'm not Alison and I would work very hard to convince you that I'm trustworthy.'

'I see.'

'But what would we do? Where would we live?'

'At the moment, I don't know. But I can tell you this. I love Crete in general, and Korifi in particular. I'm beginning to think that I could possibly live there, even although I'm a city boy. Especially if it was with you.'

Maria stared at him. 'Are you being serious?.'

'Absolutely.'

'I would like that very much. Sometimes you have very good impulses. Tell me, what are you going to do back in

Glasgow?'

'You know the answer to that. We're going to change the sovereigns.'

'No. I meant after that. Will you go straight back to work in the university?'

'I've been thinking about that. But I'm not sure, to tell you the truth. I've been too busy recently.'

'Yes. We have been rather busy.'

'But it has made me realise several important things..'

'Such as?'

'Such as the fact that my life has been very unbalanced in recent years. I have been spending far too much time on my academic research. It has become far too obsessive. I hate to say it, but Alison was right.'

Maria nodded. 'So?'

'So, I must find a way of spending more quality time on myself. And Eilidh.' Andy looked at Maria and put his hand on her shoulder. 'And you.'

She laughed. 'A very good impulse, Professor. How do you propose to do that?'

'I haven't got a plan. Yet. But I will have. I really enjoyed my time in Korifi. It was so, erm, so relaxing. And peaceful. And I would also like to find a way of spending a lot more time with you. If you would like that.'

Maria studied Andy's face for a moment. Then she leaned forward and kissed him lightly on the cheek. 'There is nothing I would like better in the whole world. But I must confess to a problem.'

'What's that?'

'While I am strongly attracted to you, I also feel guilty about betraying my late husband. I sometimes feel as if I shouldn't really be experiencing this attraction at all. I loved Pavlos, and I don't know if I could love twice. Do you see what I mean?'

Andy stared into the distance. 'I do. I can understand

you feeling that way. The only thing I can say is that I'm prepared to accept your confused feeling. You wouldn't be human if you didn't feel some guilt, for you said yourself that your relationship was based on love. So obviously there will be some confusion. We just must accept it and talk our way through it honestly. I'm prepared to do that.'

'Thank you. I think you are a good man.'

'I hope so. I really hope so. But I too have a problem..'

'What's that?'

'I thought I loved Alison. But I now know I didn't. If I didn't really love my wife, then I have a lot to learn about love. I have to learn how to love you..'

'I'll tell you what.'

'What?'

'I'll help you.'

Andy laughed out loud. 'Now that sounds like a plan!'

Maria dropped her pistol overboard from the Patras-Ancona ferry that night, watched by Andy. In the morning, on disembarking, they double-checked again but were relieved to find no trace of anyone following them.

# Part 14

## Andy Gallagher: Dover & Glasgow, 2010

## Chapter 55

At Dover, Andy drove the car carefully down the ramp of the ferry and as he went up the approach to Customs, a woman officer waved him over to an inspection area.

'Shit!' Andy said. 'It looks like we're going to be inspected.' As he got out of the car, Maria murmured, 'Keep calm.'

'Good evening, sir,' the unsmiling Customs officer said. 'Who are you, where are you coming from, and where are you going?'

'I'm Professor Andrew Gallagher from the University of Glasgow, I'm coming from Crete, and I'm going home to Glasgow.'

'Passport, please.' Andy handed it over.

'And yours, Madam.' Maria did the same. The Customs officer looked through her passport.

'You're Greek?.'

'I am.'

'And the purpose of your visit to Britain?.'

'A holiday. In Scotland.'

'And is this your car, sir?.'

'It is.'

'May I see your logbook and your insurance certificate?'

'Of course.' Andy took the folder with the car's documentation out of the glove compartment and handed it to the officer who examined the papers carefully.

'This document states that the insurance policy is made out to a Mrs. Smythe of London.'

'Ah yes,' Andy said. 'I bought the car recently from Mrs. Smythe in Crete and haven't been able to change the name on the policy yet.'

'Then you're not insured to drive this vehicle, sir.' There was nothing Andy could say, so he nodded assent.

'Your address in Glasgow?' Andy told her.

'Just wait here a moment, please.' The Customs officer went into an office and Andy could see her speaking on her mobile phone. She re-appeared with a male officer, and their manner was distinctly chilly.

'Please take your luggage out of the car and put it on the ground here,' said the male officer.

Andy gritted his teeth and did so. 'And your hand luggage too,' the officer said. Maria put her handbag and the bag containing their sandwiches and water-bottle beside the suitcases.

'Now open the suitcases,' said the woman officer, whom Andy had already silently designated as a Nurse Ratched. He unlocked the suitcases. As the two Customs officers went through them, Andy could sense Maria stiffening beside him. The female moved the towels to reveal the aluminium tubes. She lifted one out and examined it.

'What's this?' she said.

'Only gold sovereigns,' Andy said, with a cheeky grin.

'Gold …?' the officer said, exchanging an astonished look with her colleague. She fingered the remaining tubes. 'All of them?'

'All of them,' Andy said.

The Customs officer unscrewed the lid of the tube, took out a sovereign, and examined it. 'To whom do they belong?'

'They belong to my father,' Andy said. 'They were bequeathed to him by his late father, my grandfather, who lived in Crete since the end of the War. I was in Crete settling his estate.'

'Can you prove that?'

'No,' Andy said. 'Wait a minute. Yes. Yes, I can. My grandfather's widow sent my father a letter saying he had left him personal belongings in a box in his house in Crete.'

'Where is this letter?'

'In my father's possession in Glasgow.'

The male officer cut in. 'Are you aware that you must declare any cash in excess of ten thousand pounds you are bringing into the country?'

'No,' Andy said. 'No. I wasn't aware of that.'

'How did your grandfather come into possession of so many sovereigns?' the male officer said.

'I have no idea,' Andy lied.

The two officers exchanged a knowing look.

'Wait here.' They disappeared into the office with the tubes, and Andy could see a mini conference was taking place. Andy patted Maria's shoulder and winked. She smiled nervously.

After several nerve-racking minutes, the two officers reappeared with a senior officer, who said, 'We are impounding these sovereigns until proof of ownership can be established. One of our officers will visit your father in Glasgow to have sight of the letter you described. Then a decision will be made about their provenance. And you may be liable to a five thousand pound fine for importing more than ten thousand pounds worth of coins.'

'Right,' Andy said. 'My father's name is Michael Gallagher, and his address is 47 Stromness Street, Glasgow G11. But I would like a receipt for these sovereigns, which are legally in my possession. We wouldn't want any of them to go astray.'

The senior officer glared at Andy. 'We'll have to count them first..'

'There are one thousand,' Andy said.

'Wait here. You can put your luggage back in the car.'

The Customs officers returned to the office and Andy could see them counting the coins. A little later, the woman officer came out and handed Andy an official receipt for one thousand gold sovereigns.

'You can go now,' she said. 'Thank you,' Andy said.

## Chapter 56

Back in his sitting-room in Glasgow, Andy introduced Maria to Michael. Andy watched as they chatted, Maria's hand on his father's arm. Whatever she was saying, she seemed to make Michael laugh a lot. They were getting on like old pals, and his father seemed to shed years in front of his eyes.

A few days later, an official letter from H. M. Customs & Excise arrived for Andy. He read it, and summoned Michel, Eilidh and Maria.

'Here's the situation,' Andy said. 'Following the visit of the local Customs officer to Dad, and his reading of Themia's letter, they are returning the sovereigns to us on payment of a five thousand pounds fine for not declaring them. They think they were in the box of Kapetan Yiannis's papers, and I'm certainly not going to contradict them. But as the value of the sovereigns far outweighs the fine, I propose we just pay it. I'll fly to London and collect them. Now, Dad. Morally, they belong to you. So, it's your choice. What would you like to do with them?'

Michael paused for a moment. 'Well,' he said, 'I agree with Andy. The British Government doesn't deserve them back because of its ridiculous discrimination against ELAS during the War because they were Lefties. So as a boring old Leftie myself, I propose we keep them. For starters, I think each of you deserves a one hundred sovereigns reward for all your hard work searching for and finding them. And I think I deserve one hundred sovereigns for my beer money. I also think we should put aside another hundred sovereigns as an emergency fund – like to pay for a certain wedding and eventually a certain funeral. That leaves five hundred sovereigns. And we need about twenty-one to pay the fine.

So that leaves, erm, …'

'About four thousand, nine hundred and eighty,' Eilidh said.

'Correct,' Michael said. 'Top of the class for mental arithmetic, Eilidh. Now I've been reading in *The Guardian* that Greece is in the middle of an economic crisis, and the standard of living of Greek people has taken a nose-dive because of Germany and the EU waging war on its economy. So, I propose that we give the remainder to the people of – what's the name of that village again?'

'Korifi,' Andy said.

'Korifi,' Michael said. 'But I think we want to do that in a kinna clever anonymous way so that we don't cause trouble. We don't want the authorities asking questions about where this money came from, know what I mean? Can you think of a plan, Maria?'

'Yes, I can,' Maria said. 'I think we should sell the sovereigns and donate the income anonymously to the parish priest. He's a good man, completely trustworthy, and could be relied upon to channel the money to the poorest families in the area without asking awkward questions. We should specify that the money is not for the church but for the parishioners. So, the assistance comes from God, as it were. And as God is obviously Greek, most likely from Crete, and probably from Sfakia, nobody is going to ask questions.'

'Aye,' Michael said. 'That sounds like a plan right enough. All those in favour raise their hand.' Three hands shot into the air. Michael slowly raised his. 'Done and dusted.'

'God moves in mysterious ways, his wonders to perform,' Andy said in a solemn tone. They all laughed. 'Right,' he said. 'When I go to London to collect the sovereigns, I'll sell them to a bullion company down there. I'll book a flight tomorrow.'

A couple of days later, Andy spoke with Eilidh on the phone

from London. 'Sorted,' he said. 'No problem. The London Precious Metals Company has agreed to buy all the Old Head sovereigns at £233.61 each and the Young Heads at £238.28. That's £234,077. Then it will take another twenty-four hours or so to assess them, and all things being equal, the money will be paid into my account immediately afterwards by bank transfer.'

'Cool or what?' Eilidh said. 'Didn't you have to explain where you got them?'

'No, rather to my surprise. We had a quite a long chat, and I said they were a legacy from my late Crete-based grandfather. All I then had to do was show my passport and a couple of utility bills with my address on them.'

'Awesome,' Eilidh said.

## Chapter 57

Andy sat facing Diane, his Head of School, in her office in the University; he had requested the meeting.

'Well, Andy,' she said. 'I must say you surprise me. You're back to your old self, only more so. The trip to Crete must have been a success.'

'A monumentally great success. It couldn't have been better, in fact.'

'I'm pleased to hear it.'

'But I have a proposal for you.'

'Go ahead.'

'I would like to apply for early retirement.'

'Oh. Hmm. That's rather sudden. I'll have to think about that. But what about your career?'

'To tell you the truth, I'm not too worried about my career. I've spent the last twenty years working on my career, and now I want to spend some time on me. I feel I haven't paid enough attention to my personal life and happiness, and that's what caused Alison to leave me. If retired, I could pursue my research interests at my own pace.'

'Don't you think that's a bit drastic? I mean if anyone is going to crack Linear A, it's you. It would be a tragedy to abandon that line of research.'

'I wouldn't abandon it. I would just pursue it at a more leisurely pace.'

'I see. You sound very confident about that decision.'

'I am. I'm finished with full-time academia. I've had enough of bureaucratic pricks like Professor Ramsay telling me what to do. And I've had more than enough of the university turning itself into a business enterprise. I'm an academic, not a businessman.'

Diane chuckled. 'I know what you mean. Right, Andy, leave it with me and I'll see what I can do. One question.'

'Yes?'

'Would you be interested in an Honorary Professorship? It would give you access to an office and the library, and so on.'

'Absolutely.'

'Well, Andy, you may be a nutter, but you're a very talented nutter, and your contribution to the life of this School has been outstanding. I will recommend that you receive early retirement, retain your pension, and receive a lump sum commensurate with your years of service. I will also recommend that you receive an Honorary Professorship within the School. Leave it with me.'

Andy phoned Eilidh to say he was on his way home; she had agreed to make the dinner. 'It's a Thai fish curry,' she said. 'I decided to do a curry because Maria knows nothing about curries.'

'Great. I'll bring some white wine.'

At dinner, Andy explained the situation to Eilidh and Maria. 'It's really worked out well. Diane, my boss, has agreed to recommend me for early retirement. If I get it, and she's a smart operator, then it means I would receive my academic pension and a lump sum of ...'

'A lump sum?' Maria said.

'A one-off amount of cash in my hand. But even better, she has agreed to nominate me for an honorary professorship in the School of Classical and Byzantine Studies. That means I can retain my office, membership of the university library, and access to all the usual support services. That's useful. So, during the school term, I can work on my book on early Cretan languages when I want to, and at Easter and summer, we can come to Korifi where I can edit my grandfather's journal, and his manuscript book, for publication.'

'And help Maria in the taverna,' Eilidh said.

'And help Maria in the taverna. What with my pension, if it comes off, the income from the sovereigns, and my share of the former marital home, we would be financially independent. We could do what we want, when we want, where we want.'

'That's fantastic,' Eilidh said. 'It would mean we could go back to Korifi whenever we wanted.'

'That's right. And the owner of this house has agreed to sell it to me without putting it on the market, as she is going to live in Spain.'

'You're kidding,' Eilidh said. 'How did you manage that?.'

'I made her an offer she couldn't refuse.'

'It looks like we have the best of both worlds,' Maria said.

'It does,' Andy said. 'Glasgow and Korifi – a good combination.'

'What next?' Eilidh said.

'Once the details of my academic pension rights are sorted out, and Alison and I have sold the house, and I have finalised the purchase of this one, Maria and I will go back to Korifi. And you can come out during the October week holiday. After that, we'll see.'

Andy put a pint of Guinness in front of Michael in the Lismore Bar and sat down beside him with his pint of IPA.

'What did the Doc say?' Andy said.

'He said that if I didn't overdo it, I'm good for another hundred years.' Andy groaned. 'Aw no!'

Michael laughed. 'No. He said the two stents would keep me going for a while, but I've got to take it easy.'

'That's good. You're looking much better, you know.'

'Aye, I feel better an' aw.' Michael took a pull at his pint. 'I finished reading my father's journal last night, by the way. What a story.'

'It is.'

'He was some guy. I would really have liked to have met him. I feel proud to have had a father like that, a brave man who stood up for the truth, for his political principles. And I can see now why he couldn't come home. But it's a pity that he didn't send a letter to my mother explaining what had happened, though.'

'Like he said, he thought that it would be too painful for her. Better that she thought he was dead and gone.'

'Aye. That's right.' Michael took another slug of beer. 'I want you to do something for me, son.'

'What's that, Dad?'

'I want you to write a book about my father. His story deserves to be told, know what I mean?'

'I do. And I agree. It would be a pleasure.'

Michael took another sip of beer. 'What are you going to do with Maria, by the way?

She's a great lassie, you know. Are you going to make an honest woman out of her?'

Andy grinned. 'The thought had crossed my mind. I don't rule out getting married in due course – if she would have me. She …'

'She would.'

'How do you know that, Dad?'

'I asked her. Because you can't leave a classy woman like that hanging about..'

'You fly old fucker.'

Michael laughed. 'That's me, son, as wide as the Clyde.'

It was Andy's turn to laugh. 'Well, you can come to Crete and dance at our wedding.'

'I'll do that. The pair of you look happy together, do you know that? You seem like a good couple to me. And she's a lovely lassie.'

'She is. I've never felt happier in my life, Dad. And that's a fact.'

## Chapter 58

Andy stared at the email message on his laptop with disbelief. It read:

*Dear Andy,*
*After due reflection, I have realised that I was being far too hasty in asking you for a divorce. Although I can never share your interest in Minoans and Linear A, I believe we have more in common that we have differences, Eilidh for starters. And domestically, you are easy to be with.. So I wonder if you would be prepared to meet and discuss the possibility of a reconciliation? I should tell you that for my part, I would be prepared to consider going to a marriage counsellor. Let me know what you think. I am sure you will realise that it has cost me a lot to send you this message.*
*Best wishes,*
*Alison.*

Andy felt utterly confused, for Alison was offering him the very thing she had taken away. He didn't know what to think about her proposal, but he was sure of one thing. He wasn't in love with her. He picked up the phone and made a couple of discreet calls. He learned that Jason had dumped Alison when his wife found out about the affair and made her husband an offer he couldn't refuse. And Alison had panicked. Hence the email. But it was too late. He was now in love with Maria. What's it Dad says? No way, José. He wrote her a message.

*Dear Alison,*
*Thank you for your message, which took me by surprise. But I'm afraid I can't possibly consider a reconciliation as I*

*have realised that I am not in love with you. Consequently, to think of restarting our relationship would be a big mistake. However, if you retain some residual goodwill towards me, can I suggest we agree an amicable divorce? This would benefit both of us, as well as Eilidh. And we can work out some kind of practical agreement about what to do with the house.*

*Best,*
*Andy.*

## Chapter 59

Andy had put up some new bookshelves, and hung several paintings and photographs, so the sitting-room in Garrioch Drive looked much neater. And as Eilidh had brought some flowers, it also looked more homely. Andy poured two glasses of wine and gave one to his daughter.

'Eilidh. I'd like to ask your advice about something.'

'Cool. Although I think I know what it might be.'

'Oh, really? Well, it's like this. I'm, erm, I'm really keen on Maria, but erm …'

'But what?'

Andy took a sip of his wine as he tried to marshal his thoughts. 'But there are problems. Maria is still grieving for her husband, who was murdered, as you know. She was deeply in love with him and sometimes feels guilty about having a scene with me. I don't know if I can handle all that. I'm worried that I'm going to create even more grief for her.

Do you see what I mean?'

'I do. I know all about it because Maria has told me.' Andy's jaw dropped. 'Really?'

'Yes, really. Maria and I talk a lot.' Eilidh took another sip of her wine. 'I can understand her feelings of guilt about her husband. But you're both aware of these problems and you've already discussed them. That's cool. I think that what you've got going between you so far, is like, strong enough to face up to them. What you've got to do is develop a sensitivity to Maria's emotions, Dad, which means opening up your own. Emotions, I mean. Forget the bloody Minoans. Maria is far more important. You've got to work on your own emotional make-up so that you're like, tuned into what she's feeling. And she's going to have conflicting emotions, and she's going to have periods of confusion. But I do think you two have got a lot going for you already. And as I say, Maria really likes you. I think you must be honest with each other, all the time, and share your feelings, even if they are confused.'

Eilidh paused and looked directly at her father. 'It's called love, Dad.'

'I see,' Andy said, thinking, where does the girl get so much wisdom? 'What do I do next?'

'Stick to your plan. Spend as much time with her as possible. Be good to her. Listen to her. The next step will come naturally. Go for it, auld yin. You can do it!' Andy laughed. 'Okay. Thanks. I will.'

# Part 15

**Andy Gallagher: Crete, 2010**

## Chapter 60

A month later, Andy drove Michael and Eilidh slowly up the mountain road to Korifi, explaining the layout of the land and the route of the retreating British Army during the Battle of Crete to his father. From time to time, he stopped to make a point. He parked the car on the hard shoulder above Korifi so that Michael could get out and see the spectacular view out over the plateau.

'This is the village of Korifi, John's base in 1944,' Andy said, 'and where he lived after the War with Themia.'

'Oh my God, I can see why,' Michael said. 'It's magic. It's … it's out of this world.

Pure dead sensational.'

Andy parked his car outside the taverna, and Michael and Eilidh got out. Maria came out and Andy could see that she was agitated. She sat Michael and Eilidh down in the courtyard, beckoned Andy into the kitchen, and grabbed his hand.

'Andy,' she said. 'Andy.' She gasped. 'What is it?'

'Andy. I'm pregnant.'

It was Andy's turn to gasp. 'Pregnant? When did you learn?.'

'Yesterday. From a self-testing kit.'

'That's wonderful news. I'm so happy for you. For me. For us. But … but you must have wanted this.'

'I did. I realised that I am in fact in love with you. It's real.'

'What are we going to do? Where are we going to live?'

'I don't know. But I do know we're going to have that baby.'

'We certainly will!' Andy kissed her. 'We must tell Dad

and Eilidh.'

They went out into the courtyard, hand in hand. Andy said, 'Maria's got some news for you.'

They sat down, and Maria said, 'I'm pregnant. I'm going to have a baby. Andy's baby.'

Eilidh laughed out loud and hugged Maria. 'Oh my God! I'm going to have a baby brother or sister. Awesome.'

Michael grinned as he kissed Maria. 'And I'm going to be a grandfather. Some family, eh?'

'I know,' Andy said. 'Pure dead brilliant. It's the happiest day of my life.'

## Chapter 61

A littler later, they all drove to the Korifi cemetery. It was a warm and still day, with a cloudless sky and the autumn sunlight reflecting off the white tombstones. The muted melodic tinkle of sheep's bells sounded in the background. They got out, Andy opened the gate, and ushered his father in.

'This is where John is buried,' Andy said. He pointed. 'Over there.' Eilidh went to take her grandfather's arm, but Andy held her back, smiling and shaking his head. Eilidh got it immediately.

Michael wandered round the cemetery for several moments peering at the gravestones. Suddenly, he stopped dead as he saw his father's photo. He put on his spectacles and leant forward, reading the inscription on his father's gravestone.

'What does that Greek say, son?'

"Kapetan John Sfakianakis. Hero of the Resistance'.'

Michael stared at the inscription for several seconds, then reached into his inside jacket pocket, took out a single red rose, and placed it on the grave. He sat down on an adjoining tombstone and burst into tears, wiping his eyes with a handkerchief. Eilidh sat down beside him, hugging her grandfather.

Several moments later, Michael said, 'That's my Dad. Kapetan Yiannis. He was some fucking guy.'

Andy laughed. 'He certainly was.'

Maria took Michael's hand. 'Telos kala, ola kala,' she said with a smile. 'All's well that ends well,' Andy translated. 'Now. I've got an idea.'

'What's that, son?' Michael said.

'I think we should go back to the taverna and have a celebration of the remarkable life of my grandfather, John Gallagher. Also known as Kapetan Yiannis.'

'Tickety-boo,' Michael said.

## THE END

## Endnote

Although it is based on real events, this is a work of fiction. There is no village called Korifi in Sfakia – or anywhere else in Crete, to my knowledge. But the topography in the area surrounding Korifi does exist and can be checked out on a good map of the area, such as the Anavasi Topo 25 1:25,000 scale map of the Levka Ori/White Mountains. It is an area I know intimately.

By the same token, there is no School of Classical & Byzantine Studies at the University of Glasgow, an institution I also know intimately because I worked there, as Senior Research Fellow in the (then) Department of Sociology & Anthropology, until early retirement.

# Greek Lexicon

Agrotikon: the universal pickup truck of Crete, frequently Japanese.
Aloni: the communal circular threshing ground possessed by each Cretan village.
Amesos: right away, immediately.
Andartes: guerrillas, partisans.
Andartissa: a female guerrilla or partisan.
Barba: the affectionate Greek term for an older man.
Bobota: a bread made from corn.
Entaxi: okay.
Horta: edible wild greens in the chicory family, full of antioxidants, boiled and widely eaten in Crete with olive oil and lemon juice. Two of the most common varieties in Crete are Stamnagathi and Vlita.
Kafeneion: a café, a coffee-shop.
Kalderimi: a cobbled bridlepath in the mountains, often of ingenious construction.
Katsouna: the Cretan shepherd's crook.
Malotira: (Sideritis Syriaca.) a wild flowering plant common in the White Mountains from which a restorative tea is made.
Mantinades: the traditional rhyming couplets of Crete. Locals demonstrate great skill in improvising them and competing in a form which would now be called rapping.
Mitato: a high–altitude sheiling for corralling and milking sheep, and cheese-making, constructed from unmortared slabs of laminar limestone. In the White Mountains, traditional mitata were igloo shaped.

Panayeiamou: literally, My Virgin! (as in the Virgin Mary): equivalent of 'Good Lord!'
Paximadia: the double-baked Cretan rusks.
Philotimo: literally, 'a friend of honour,' but more complex than that, to include notions of conscientiously honouring one's responsibilities and duties, and not allowing one's honour, dignity, and pride to be tarnished.
Proedros: a village headman, mayor or provost.
Se Yeia: Your Health! Cheers! A common drinking toast.
Singlino: the traditional smoked pork of Crete, smoked over green sage bushes.
Tsichoudia: Cretan raki distilled from the skins of grapes trampled to make wine.
Tzaki: a stone-built fireplace.
Trozos: Cretan dialect for 'nuts,' mad, off your head.
Yiannis: John.

# Glossary

*EAM:* Ethnikón Apeleftherotikón Métopon: National Liberation Front. The left–wing, and biggest, wartime Greek Resistance movement.

*ELAS*: Ethnikós Laïkós Apeleftherotikós Strátos: National Popular Liberation Army: the armed wing of EAM.

*KKE:* Kommounistikó Kómma Elládas: the Greek Communist Party.

# Select Bibliography

There are numerous books on the Battle of Crete and the subsequent Occupation and Resistance. Key English-language references include:

Antony Beevor (1991): *Crete: The Battle and Resistance,* John Murray.
While Beevor is good on the military aspects of the Battle of Crete, his account of the Resistance is unreliable as he reproduces only the official SOE account of events. It is also significant that he does not include any of the numerous Greek language books on the Cretan Resistance in his bibliography.

I. Stewart (1991): *The Struggle for Crete 20 May – 1 June 1941: A Story of Lost Opportunity*, Oxford University Press.
A comprehensive account by someone who was there.

N. A. Kokonas (1991): *The Cretan Resistance 1941–1945,* Foreword by Patrick Leigh Fermor and Others, Rethymnon, Crete: Kokonas.
The 'official' SOE Report, which suffers from the same deficiencies as Beevor.

Tony Simpson (1981): *Operation Mercury: The Battle for Crete, 1941*, Hodder & Stoughton.
The New Zealand perspective.

Xan Fielding (1954): *Hide and Seek: The Story of a Wartime Agent, Secker & Warburg*.
The story of an SOE agent with the Cretan Resistance, one who was unashamedly anti–ELAS.

Patrick Leigh Fermor (2015): *Abducting a General: The Kreipe Operation and SOE in Crete, John Murray.*
The kidnapping of German General Kreipe by someone even more relentlessly anti–ELAS than Fielding.

George Psychoundakis (1978): *The Cretan Runner, John Murray.*
An entertaining and unusual Cretan perspective, albeit again one supporting the British point–of–view.

Seán Damer & Ian Frazer (2006): *On the Run: ANZAC Escape and Evasion in Enemy– Occupied Crete*, New Zealand, Auckland: Penguin Books.
A detailed account of the aftermath of the Battle of Crete from the point–of–view of the thousand and more (mainly) Australian and New Zealand soldiers who declined to surrender.

Seán Damer & Ian Frazer (2018): *'SOE in Wartime Crete: An Instrument of Control,' Journal of Modern Greek Studies*, Vol. 36, No. 1.
A detailed and well–researched critique of the official SOE account of the Cretan Resistance.

Colin Janes (2013): *The Eagles of Crete: An Untold Story of Civil War,* Colin Janes.
The harrowing story of the hostilities in Crete after the Second World War ended, a Civil War which never occurred according to the 'official' histories.

Colin Janes (2017): *The Guerrillas of Crete,* Colin Janes. The amazing true story of the handful of Communist guerrillas who fought on for years in Crete after the official end of the Greek Civil War.

Mark Mazower (1993): *Inside Hitler's Greece: The Experience of Occupation 1941–1944*, Yale University Press.

Although not about Crete as such, a brilliant account of the realities of Occupation, and the political complexities of the Greek Resistance.

# Acknowledgements

I would like to thank Irini Kavouras, the Honorary Greek Consul in Glasgow, and my former Greek teacher, for supplying the biblical Greek for the New Testament quotation and checking some other Greek words and phrases.

My old friend Christina Vrettou of Hania in Crete helped me with details of the Samaria Gorge Race, which she herself has completed.

My late partner, Sieglinde Manouras of Münster, who lived in the Cretan mountain village of Anoyia for eight years, supplied me with the Greek for *Nemo Me Impune Lacessit,* and kept an eagle eye on my Greek grammar.

My good friend Professor Tony Fallick advised me on certain academic procedures. Nicholas Ward from The Pure Gold Company in London gave me a very full briefing on the contemporary situation regarding selling gold sovereigns. Mae Boyd kept me informed about counselling practice. Mike Shand yet again supplied me with the very professional maps.

My colleague and friend, Dr. Ian Frazer of Dunedin, New Zealand, read an earlier version of the whole manuscript and gave me encouraging feedback, as did Ian Wilson, Betty Morgan, Donald Harding, Fija Callaghan and Rosie Watts.

Two fellow–writers and Cretan residents, Alex Dunlevy and Elena Lopez, also read earlier drafts of the whole manuscript – Elena several times – and supplied me with a raft of useful comments.

Gill Barnes gave me good advice on certain sensitive issues. Rosie Fiore supplied me with a useful professional edit through the good offices of the Jericho Writers workshop as did J. David Simons, writer and editor, acting for the Blue

Pencil Agency.

The inimitable Emma Darwin gave me an inspiring final crit, as did my exceptionally thorough Ringwood Editorial Committee – Isobel Freeman, Katie McGowan, and Luiza Stoenescu.

I am grateful to them all.

## About the Author

Dr. Seán Damer is a sociologist by training and a writer by inclination. He took up creative writing seriously on receiving early retirement from his academic post, and completed a Master's degree in Creative Writing in the same year as he received his bus pass!

He has been travelling regularly in Crete since 1975, usually on foot, and led mountain walking holidays on the island during the university summer vacations from 1980 to 1985. From 1985 to 1987, he lived in a remote mountain village in Sfakia while studying the local shepherding community.

It was during this period that he explored the White Mountains in detail. And in 2014/2015, he lived in a village in Apokoronas studying the British expat community which had grown up there very quickly since 2001. He is a Greek speaker.

Seán has published academic articles on Crete and co-authored a Penguin Book on the aftermath of the Battle of Crete (see bibliography), and broadcast talks on Crete on BBC Radio.

He commutes between Glasgow and the town of Hania in Crete, where he has a writing bolthole.

# Also By this Author

www.ringwoodpublishing.com
mail@ringwoodpublishing.com

### *Those Tyrannising Landlords*
Seán Damer

In 1912, after yet another rent hike, the O'Donnell family leaves rural Ireland for Glasgow's sooty tenements and shipyards. Peggy, their only daughter, struggles alongside her family to find work as Irish Catholic immigrants

Thrown into a world far from their traditions, the O'Donnells face tension between old and new ways. Peggy finds allies in two feminist sisters and their socialist brother, Archie, who support her dream of becoming a teacher. As Glasgow erupts with trade unions, political unrest, and the fight for women's rights, the family must navigate socialism, atheism, and feminism to survive in a rapidly changing city.

ISBN: 978-1-901514-60-5
£9.99